THE *Stars* ABOVE NORTHUMBERLAND

OTHER BOOKS AND AUDIO BOOKS BY ANITA STANSFIELD:

First Love and Forever
First Love, Second Chances
Now and Forever
By Love and Grace
A Promise of Forever
When Forever Comes
For Love Alone
The Three Gifts of Christmas
Towers of Brierley
Where the Heart Leads
When Hearts Meet
Someone to Hold
Reflections: A Collection of Personal Essays
Gables of Legacy, Six Volumes
A Timeless Waltz
A Time to Dance
Dancing in the Light
A Dance to Remember
The Barrington Family Saga, Four Volumes
Emma: Woman of Faith
The Jayson Wolfe Story, Five Volumes
The Dickens Inn Series, Five Volumes
Shadows of Brierley Series, Four Volumes
Passage on the Titanic
The Wishing Garden
The Garden Path
Legally and Lawfully Yours
Now and Always Yours
Heir of Brownlee Manor
The Color of Love
Lily of the Manor
Love and Loss at Whitmore Manor

THE *Stars* ABOVE NORTHUMBERLAND

A REGENCY ROMANCE

ANITA STANSFIELD

Covenant Communications, Inc.

Cover image: © Lee Avison / Trevillion Images. *Night sky over the forest* © Misha Kaminsky; courtesy of istock.com

Published by Covenant Communications, Inc.
American Fork, Utah

Printed in the United States of America
First Printing: February 2018

24 23 22 21 20 19 18 10 9 8 7 6 5 4 3 2 1

ISBN: 978-1-52440-497-0

Chapter One
Escape

London—1814

The color black screamed hypocrisy to Meri. She stared at her hideous dress in the long mirror while the maid took her time fastening the buttons down Meri's back. Black was meant to represent grief and mourning; Meri felt neither. But she knew well the social façade that was required of her, and she'd learned to be a very good actress in the years she'd been married to Lord Sturgess. Behaving correctly—both in private and public—had become vital to her survival. And now her husband was dead, and she had to continue behaving correctly. If *anyone* in this household—or among her peers for that matter—got even a whiff of suspicion about her true feelings toward the deceased Lord Sturgess, she would surely be subjected to an entirely new brand of misery.

Meri pulled black lace gloves onto her hands while the maid pinned a black veil into her tightly bound hair that was more brown than blonde, with a reddish hue that was so slight it rarely showed other than in full sunlight. She shared no conversation with the maid while they both endured this ritual; Meri had never liked having someone help her with every meticulous detail of her appearance, but her husband had insisted on it. There were five different maids who traded shifts to assist her for different things at different times of the day, and not one of them had ever spoken a kind or conversational word to her. They each merely went about their duty to assist her, speaking only if absolutely necessary—such as offering her a choice of which brooch she might want pinned to her bodice. Given the inhospitable coldness that seemed to have been ingrained in the maids who served Meri, she had never known any of their names. In fact, every person in the entire household seemed to have been born and raised with the same kind of glacial unfriendliness, as if it had been a requirement for employment here. But her husband and his family were much the same way—unless they were choosing to be otherwise for the sake of manipulation, deceit, or public appearance. It stood to reason that they would have hired people around whom they would feel comfortable. Meri had *never* felt comfortable here. She'd lived in this house for seven years, and she'd not known one moment's comfort.

"Thank you," Meri said as the maid held out a white handkerchief. The maid then carefully lowered the black veil over Meri's face and stepped back. Meri glanced at herself again in the mirror, seeing a distorted reflection through the fine lace of the veil. Except for the white handkerchief in her hand, she looked like a formless mass of blackness. She sighed and considered the fact that she felt much the same on the inside. *A formless mass of blackness.*

On her way down the stairs, Meri was glad that her children were not required to attend the funeral—even though it meant leaving them in the care of one of the nameless nannies who kept the children safe and cared for, but who certainly offered no affection or kindness. Still, Meri preferred having Elaine and Crispin—ages six and four respectively—play in the nursery rather than exposing them to lengthy and sultry funeral proceedings, during which they would have to remain perfectly still. She knew well enough from attending church every Sunday that even the tiniest peep from one of the children would attract glares of disapproval and anger from many supposedly Christian churchgoers who obviously believed that children were only meant to be seen and not heard.

Even though one of the nannies always accompanied the children whenever they went out into the public venue, and it was mostly considered inappropriate for Meri to be responsible for their behavior, she still felt an unseemly urge to say something horribly rude to people who glared at her children for simply behaving like children. Elaine and Crispin were every bit as imprisoned as Meri, and she hated it. At least she didn't have to worry about whether they behaved throughout the course of the funeral. She could focus instead on appearing to be consumed with grief over her husband's death. The veil was a blessing; it hid her face enough that no one could tell whether she'd been shedding any tears. And occasionally Meri could reach beneath the veil and dab at her eyes with the handkerchief, just for the sake of appearing to behave correctly. She practiced the gesture while alone in the carriage on the way to the church, and thought about how glorious it would be when this was all over and she could curl up all alone in her bed and allow sleep to offer a reprieve from this madness that had become her life.

When the carriage came to a halt, Lady Grace Meriwether Redding Sturgess stepped down with the help of the footman and walked into the church. She was aware of people regarding her with deference as she made her way to the family pew where she sat with her elderly mother-in-law—a woman whose coldness and cruelty had plagued Meri since the day she'd arrived as a new bride to live under the same roof. Also seated on the bench was the deceased Lord Sturgess's older sister, Patsy, who lived a great distance away with her husband and children; Meri had only met Patsy on the occasion of her wedding to Patsy's brother, and since then she'd not once interacted with her beyond exchanging barely polite greetings since her recent arrival. Patsy's husband and children had not come with her to attend the funeral.

The only other person sitting in the family pew was Lord Sturgess's younger brother, Rowan, who had also lived under the same roof during these last seven years. He was unmarried and well-known for his excessive drinking and frequent bouts of trouble—which were most often related to his despicable and unrestrained gambling habits. For this very reason, he had been allotted only a limited allowance, which was scrutinized by the family's solicitor. Meri barely knew Rowan; the only times he'd been remotely kind to her had been when he was drunk. And it had been in his drunken rambling that she'd become keenly aware of his resentment toward his older brother, since he had inherited their father's vast fortune in its entirety while Rowan was limited to what he called his *measly allowance.* Meri knew that whatever money he had access to would either be lost to his drinking or gambling, and despite her own husband's many weaknesses and deplorable behaviors, he was very conscientious about protecting the family name and the family fortune.

Now that Rowan's older brother had died so unexpectedly, Meri knew that Rowan was angry because *she* had inherited the vast Sturgess fortune—or rather, her son Crispin was in line to inherit everything. As Crispin's mother, Meri would be a steward over all the assets. As decreed in the wills of both her husband and father-in-law, Rowan would continue to receive the allowance he'd been getting for years—which was more than enough to allow him to live comfortably if he would only use it more wisely.

Meri took her seat and blocked out the silent insinuations and accusations that seemed to pour out of her family members by marriage. They hated her and she knew it, but by the same token, she held no fondness for any of them. She'd always tried very hard to behave—and think—like a Christian woman. But she couldn't deny that her years of being a part of the Sturgess family had tested her charitable attributes to their limits—and beyond. She'd said many things she'd regretted in the heat of difficult encounters, but she knew that being forgiven by these people was not at all possible. She'd let go of hoping for such a thing, and instead prayed every day to be able to forgive these people for all the damage they had done to her life—and the lives of her children. She also prayed to forgive herself for being naive and gullible enough to have been lured into this unholy marriage to begin with.

The funeral service was long and tedious; Lord Sturgess was praised repeatedly for being a fine man and an honorable and exemplary pillar of the community. Meri felt nauseous as she recalled her husband's utterly wretched treatment of her throughout their years of marriage. At social events, he would speak to her as if she were royalty, giving others in the community the impression that he was the ideal, doting husband. But in the presence of his family and the household staff, he had talked down to her and had never allowed her to freely express an opinion or thought without making her feel humiliated or degraded. And in the privacy of their own bedroom, he had treated her worse than he treated his dogs—and he frequently kicked his dogs if they got in his way or got on his nerves.

Meri considered the bruises on her body that would take time to heal; bruises that he'd always made certain would never be seen by others. If he'd ever impulsively hit her face, she wasn't allowed outside of her bedroom until the bruises had healed. Sitting on the hard bench now made her more keenly aware of how the bruises pained her. But beneath her lace veil and her carefully feigned grief, Meri's spirit was basking in relief. She never had to encounter her evil husband again. The bruises would heal, and she had no reason to fear that before they did they would be replaced by more bruises. She listened with only half an ear to the vicar's tedious droning while she rehearsed once again in her mind the plans she'd been formulating. The funeral would soon be over, tonight she would sleep for the last time in that terrible room, and tomorrow she would use every resource available to her as Lady Sturgess to escape this prison. She doubted that her scarred spirit could ever heal from what she'd endured, but she would do whatever it took to give her children a better life, and with any luck they would never even remember this one.

* * *

"Leaving?" Meri's mother-in-law bellowed from where she was eating her breakfast at the other end of the long dining table. Meri was glad that Patsy had already left to return to her own home and that Rowan was absent—likely due to a hangover. "Where on *earth* could you go that would afford you the comforts you have right here?" the elder Mrs. Sturgess questioned. "There is *nowhere* you could enjoy such luxuries as this house affords!"

Meri was surprised yet again at how the mentality of this family was all about the lavish decor of the house and the ridiculously expensive artifacts her mother-in-law loved to collect. It was as if she—and every other person under the spell of this place—had become completely unaware of how cold and unfeeling they were as human beings. But Meri had no intention of initiating an argument; she had a plan and she intended to stick to it—even if she had to be somewhat misleading.

"This has all been very difficult for each of us," Meri declared, sounding very much the grieving widow. "Although, I must confess that . . . everywhere I turn in this house I see memories of him, and I'm finding it quite unbearable." Meri fought not to snigger or even smile as she uttered these words. The statement was completely true, but not for the reasons her words implied. Now that she'd gained some momentum, she forged ahead. "I think it would be prudent for me and the children to have some time away to contend with our . . . grief."

"But where would you go?" the older woman countered, as if she couldn't imagine that a world existed at all beyond the one in which she lived, immersed in her own miserable outlook and meanness.

"My aunt has written to me since I sent word of the passing of Lord Sturgess. She has invited me to bring the children and spend some time there, perhaps until I am able to overcome the impact of my husband's death."

"This would be your aunt, Lady Rosewell?" the crotchety Mrs. Sturgess asked, as if allowing the name to pass over her tongue was distasteful at best. "The wife of Sir Angus Rosewell? They that took you in following the demise of your parents?" Her tone implied that the untimely death of members of Meri's family had been nothing but a dreadful inconvenience—and a slur upon Meri's reputation. And this woman's reference to Meri's aunt and uncle held an implication that these people were of lesser value than the rest of humanity, and it was somehow deplorable for Meri to even want to *revert* to living among them after she'd been given the privilege of being elevated to the status of membership in the Sturgess family. Many conversations over the years had acquainted Meri with this snobbish attitude, and her mother-in-law's present disdainful facial expression and the inflections in her voice left nothing to the imagination.

But Meri held her ground and simply stated, "Yes, that is to whom I refer. They've invited us to come and stay, and I confess I've missed them very much. It is my hope that returning to the home in which I was raised from a young age will assist in my recovery from this shocking turn of events."

The older woman made a huffy noise that Meri knew well; it was a wordless implication of disgust and disdain—which Meri had learned to ignore. She focused on eating her breakfast, implying that if her mother-in-law had something to say, she needed to use words to say it. She was able to eat peacefully for a few minutes before this woman Meri detested said in the whiny voice of a spoiled child, "Well, I don't suppose anyone can stop you from going. You're a grown woman—with a fortune at your disposal. . . ."

The woman's voice seethed with resentment, which Meri also ignored; she knew well enough that no one here would have their luxurious lifestyle modified even slightly because of the actual money Meri had inherited. And truthfully, she had no intention of Crispin ever taking on this estate in any way; she was glad to leave it behind and it could crumble to the ground for all she cared. Meri would cease to collect the monthly allowance she'd been given, simply because she wanted no contact with these people, nor any such transactions. If they knew the full details of her plan, perhaps they might actually have cause to rejoice. And in fact, they might all be able to enjoy their lifestyle more freely without the late Lord Sturgess hovering over his family and servants with his disagreeable disposition. "I suppose you must go if that's what you feel you should do."

"I'll be leaving with the children this afternoon," Meri declared.

"As soon as that?" the old woman countered as if Meri had announced her intention to now live a life of sin.

"The maids are already packing our things," Meri stated.

"Already?" her husband's mother echoed, her voice becoming even more childish and whiny. "You'll be taking at least one of the nannies with you, of course. And a maid for you." She stated this as if it were obvious, rather than asking Meri or seeking her opinion. Meri noted there was no regretful comment from the old lady over being parted from her grandchildren, which wasn't a surprise; this woman had hardly given them an occasional nod.

"No," Meri stated, still calling on her well-memorized answers to this woman's predictable reactions. "I will be able to manage for myself and the children just fine." Before the old lady could offer any further protest over the matter, Meri added, "There are ample servants in my aunt's household, and my cousins will surely dote on the children." Meri stood, her gesture implying an end to the conversation. Seeing her mother-in-law's dismayed expression, she wondered if this cold and mean-spirited woman might actually miss her or the children. She had done nothing but complain about their presence in the house; therefore, it was easy to assume that she would be glad for the peace and quiet—and the opportunity to regain control of her own home. But her expression betrayed distress. Meri felt somewhat sorry for her, but not enough to be even slightly tempted to stay. This woman was toxic; this house was toxic. And Meri had to get out of here and take her children with her if they had any hope of ever finding peace and happiness.

* * *

Meri went upstairs to find her children playing, their expressions sullen, which she credited mostly to the hovering nanny, who wore a continual scowl. She dismissed the nanny and sat down on the rug with the children, pulling both Crispin and Elaine close to her sides. Even though she knew that every mother believed her own children to be the most beautiful, she truly believed that her son and daughter had especially attractive features, and they were both kind and tender in spirit—traits their father had not necessarily found admirable. But to Meri, it meant everything. She wanted her children to grow up to be good people, and she was grateful that up to this point, they seemed to have innately pleasant and positive dispositions.

Meri pressed a kiss into Crispin's reddish-brown curls and turned to kiss Elaine's head as well. Their hair color was almost identical, and they had both inherited their father's curly hair. Beyond that and thankfully, Meri could see no other obvious likeness of his in their features. To her, they simply looked like Crispin and Elaine, and she would gladly go through all the suffering again if only to have these remarkable children—a fact that was easier to acknowledge now that she knew their father would no longer be a part of their lives.

"We are going on an adventure," she declared to the children with a bright voice that caught their attention. "Now that your papa is no longer here, we are going to take many of our things and ride in a carriage to go and stay with my aunt and uncle and cousins. They live in a place called Northumberland, in a beautiful house near the sea. At night when you lay in your bed, if you listen carefully, you can hear the waves rolling in and out."

"Is it a magical place?" Crispin asked.

Meri laughed softly. "It's a very real place, but there are things about it that feel magical. I went to live with my aunt and uncle and cousins when I was just a few years older than you are, Elaine, and they took very good care of me. They've written and invited us to come, and I think it would be a very good idea. What do you think?"

Crispin nodded with enthusiasm, and Elaine asked excitedly, "When can we leave?"

"That's the wonderful part," Meri said, glad for her status as lady of the house, which had made it easy to ask the servants to arrange everything they needed. "The maids have already packed most of what we need, and the girls in the kitchen have packed hampers of food so that we will have plenty to eat as we travel. The horses will be harnessed to the carriage very soon. So, let's look around our rooms and see if there's anything the maids have missed that we want to take with us, and then we can go."

The children ran to their rooms enthusiastically, which Meri hoped was evidence of their own desire to get out of this house and away from the people who lived here. Meri quickly examined the contents of the children's trunks that had already been packed, which held all their best clothes and personal items—but not a single toy. Meri dug out a large portmanteau that she'd kept in the bottom of Crispin's wardrobe with this very purpose in mind. Had her husband not conveniently died, she had been hoping to get away for a lengthy visit to Northumberland anyway. She told the children to go and find all their favorite toys and put them into the portmanteau while she hurried to finish packing her own things. She left Elaine in charge of Crispin and knew they would stay together while she went to her room to check her own neatly packed belongings.

A quick examination of her wardrobe and bureau drawers revealed little else that she had any desire to take with her. In a valise that she would carry personally, she put some handkerchiefs, her favorite perfume, and the book from the bedside table that she was currently reading. Given the enormous library here in the house, no one would ever miss it—and it was one of her favorites. She also emptied into her valise the entire contents of her jewelry box. Lord Sturgess had been well-known for spoiling her with expensive jewelry. Each time he gave her a lavish necklace or bracelet, he behaved as if it represented all the love and adoration a good husband should have given his wife, as if the quality gemstones laid in gold filigree somehow made up for his blatant abuse. She had no qualms about taking them with her now; she'd earned them.

Meri also reached far beneath the bureau to grasp hold of a biscuit tin she had kept hidden there for years. One of the privileges of being married to Lord Sturgess was the generous allowance he had given her each month with the expectation that she would spend it on niceties for herself and the children. She had spent just enough for him to see evidence that his money was being used, but she had been much more frugal than he'd ever imagined, and she had put the surplus into this hidden tin, knowing right from the honeymoon that eventually, one way or another, she would need to escape the prison into which she had married.

Meri looked inside the tin and sighed with some relief. She didn't need to count it; she knew how much was there. Between this money and the vast treasure of jewelry, she never needed to come back here again.

She didn't care if she ever received another farthing of her inheritance. And she didn't care who took over the estate or what they did with it. In time, it would probably become obvious to Rowan that she wasn't coming back and he would be only too glad to finally be in charge. And with any luck, he wouldn't gamble everything away, and everyone here would retain their employment. She knew well enough that there were overseers and solicitors aplenty in place to see that everything here ran like clockwork, and it would be up to them to protect the estate from Rowan's mischief. Her advice never would have been heeded, and her presence was not likely to be missed. She was escaping at last, and she had no intention of ever coming back.

* * *

Following a long day's carriage ride, Meri and her children were left at a fine inn with all their luggage, and the carriage belonging to the Sturgess family—along with the driver and footman—returned without her. Meri felt a huge leap toward freedom, even though they still had a great distance to travel. But for the moment, they had everything they needed, and the tethers that bound them to a life of bondage were now broken.

The children loved the spacious and comfortable room at the inn. There was ample space to play and move around to dispel all the wiggles that had been accumulating during many hours in the carriage. Servants brought them hot water for bathing, along with a delicious late supper. After the children were bathed, fed, and sleeping, Meri sat near the window and looked up at the stars, knowing that two days from now she and her children would be safely in Northumberland, and all would be well. She allowed herself only a few minutes of regret, of wondering how her life might have been these last seven years if she'd heeded her aunt's advice and not married Lord Sturgess. But Meri glanced at the beautiful faces of her sleeping children and she could not hold onto any regret. All she had suffered had been worth it, if only for their existence.

But she also knew that if she'd allowed them to grow up within reach of their father's cruelty, their spirits could have been irrevocably damaged. She'd been praying for years for a means to get them away from the baleful environment of the Sturgess home, even if she'd had no idea how it might come to pass. Her husband's untimely death had been a miracle to her, even if it had been perceived as a tragedy by everyone else who knew him. But there was not a single person who knew what he was *really* like. She had become acutely aware years ago that only a spouse could know the most accurate truth about a person's character. Therefore, she had been completely alone in her silent hatred of Lord Sturgess.

Initially she had felt some degree of guilt for acknowledging that she truly did hate him, until a long night of prayer and tears had led her to believe that God would never condone a man treating his wife so deplorably, and surely God understood her fear, her torment, and her broken heart. And surely God would be patient in her journey toward healing and forgiveness. In truth, only God knew the whole truth, and He was therefore her dearest friend and closest confidant. And in her deepest self she believed that God understood and had compassion for the dark secret she was teaching herself to not even think about. Every day she thought about it less, and since no one else knew the truth, she had no reason to believe it could not be left behind, along with every other deplorable detail of the life she was escaping. Meri felt confident that she and her children would be watched over and cared for, simply because she'd prayed about every facet of her plan to escape, and she'd been blessed with an overwhelming sense of calm that had kept her continually buffered with a wonderfully strange peace through every step she'd taken since she'd realized her husband was dead and she had been set free.

* * *

The following day it rained continually, which made travel slower and more challenging. Meri was grateful for the hearty breakfast they'd eaten at the inn before setting out, and she was also grateful for the warm blankets provided by the carriage driver, which kept Meri and her children cozy despite the distinct chill of this heavy spring downpour. Meri was also very appreciative of the kindness of the two men manning the hired carriage. They did their best to see that Meri and the children were comfortable and cared for at each stop, where they would make their way through the rain into an inn or pub that accommodated travelers with a warm, inviting place to freshen up and get something to eat while fresh horses were harnessed to the carriage before they set out on the next stretch of their journey.

That night, Meri and the children again stayed at an inn. It was warm and adequate, but lacked the coziness they'd enjoyed the previous evening. The following morning the rain had stopped, although the sky remained overcast and gray. They were off again right after breakfast, with the same two men committed to delivering them safely to their final destination. During their stops, these men were often chatty and kind, teasing the children and making them laugh. They both spoke of the beauty of Northumberland and how much they enjoyed any opportunity to take passengers there.

On this third and final day of travel, the children became increasingly restless, which left Meri desperately longing to arrive and frequently looking at the watch that hung on a chain around her neck. The hours dragged, and it began to feel as if they would never be free of the confines of this carriage. And then, through the carriage window, Meri caught a glimpse of the sea, and her heart quickened with excitement, as if she'd just seen a very dear friend for the first time in years.

"Look," she said to Crispin and Elaine, and their attention was drawn to the direction she pointed out the window.

"It goes on forever and ever!" Crispin declared upon his first view ever of the ocean.

"It certainly appears that way, doesn't it," Meri said, noting how both Elaine and Crispin had become silently enthralled with the vast expanse of the ocean in the distance, and the sound of the waves rushing onto the shore. The children had also become very still, and Meri felt some relief in the distraction. She also knew their destination was now less than an hour away. The road wound farther away from the coast for a while, which left the children disappointed in not being able to see the ocean, but Meri assured them they would be able to see it—and even hear it—from the windows of their new bedrooms.

When the carriage finally came to a halt in front of the large and beautiful home of her aunt and uncle, Meri felt as if a huge weight had melted off her shoulders. They were here at last! They were safe and they would be cared for! Surely all would be well. She wasn't certain how her cousins would feel about her arrival, given that she'd had almost no communication with them in years, although more than one of them would likely dote on the children. Her uncle would be eccentric at best and grumbling at worst. But her aunt would be nothing but thrilled to see Meri and the children, and she would be eager to give them all the love and security they so desperately needed.

The drivers helped Meri down from the carriage, and she took a moment to look up at the house. In contrast to the cold and colorless house she'd lived in for the past seven years, Rosewell Abbey had a softness to its architecture and a delicacy in the beautiful grounds and gardens that surrounded it. Meri helped the children out of the carriage while the drivers unloaded all their luggage near the main entrance. Meri once again thanked the good men who had seen them safely here, knowing she had paid their fee in advance—along with a generous bonus. She was glad to be able to reward them for their efforts, especially when they had gone out of their way many times to make the journey as comfortable as possible for her and her children.

When the last of the luggage was on the ground, Meri silently counted the trunks and bags to make certain all was there. When no one came out to greet them, she was beginning to wonder if she would need to knock at the huge door. She had expected that the ruckus of the carriage being unloaded and the children running wild would have gotten the attention of at least one of the servants. At the same moment the carriage pulled away, the front door flew open and Meri's Aunt Annabel rushed outside and gathered Meri into her arms as if she'd been a lost prodigal, finally come home.

Annabel was a tiny woman; a full head shorter than Meri and slight in build. But Meri knew well enough that her size was no indication of her inner strength. She had a way of always making Meri feel completely loved and accepted without question. For this and many other reasons, Meri had always looked up to her. There was so much she wanted to talk to her aunt about, but at the same time she wasn't certain she wanted to talk about anything that had happened—ever. For the moment, she just relished the feel of her aunt's embrace.

"Oh, my dear!" Annabel said, following a very long, very tight embrace. "I can't believe you're finally here!" She took Meri's face into her hands as if to survey her expression carefully. While they exchanged a long, searching gaze, Meri noted that Annabel's dark hair was becoming more streaked with gray, and the subtle lines of age were showing more prominently in her face, and yet her beauty was still readily evident; perhaps even more so as her wisdom and love seemed a more literal part of her countenance.

Annabel furrowed her brow, deepening the lines already there while she closely scrutinized Meri, as if she could see right through her. "Your eyes betray how difficult these years have been, my darling—even if I didn't already know from your letters."

Meri resisted the urge to cry, even though she felt moisture gather in her eyes. She had written careful letters to Annabel, knowing her aunt would guard them with great care. But her letters had confessed only a portion of the truth. There was much her aunt didn't know; much that she never wanted anyone to know. It was in the past now. She'd come home, and she was ready to make a new start. Her only objective now was to raise her children in a peaceful environment, and she was grateful to have that available to her—thanks to her precious Aunt Annabel.

"Thank you for letting us come," Meri said, holding to her aunt's arms. "I don't know what else we would have done."

"You would have figured something out, I'm certain," Annabel said with a confidence that Meri didn't necessarily share. "But your coming back is a great blessing to me. I've missed you dreadfully. And I've worried. And . . ." Her attention was drawn to the children who were running in circles as if to literally unwind after being so wound up through the long journey. "Having children under our roof again will be the greatest joy I could imagine!"

"I do hope so," Meri said lightly. She called more loudly, "Crispin. Elaine. Come and meet Auntie Annabel." To her aunt she said, "I've told them all about you. They couldn't wait to get here."

The children came running and stopped to survey Annabel. "You're much prettier than our grandmama," Elaine declared, which made Annabel chuckle. Crispin said nothing, but apparently approved of Annabel by the way he threw his arms around his great aunt's legs with some semblance of a hug.

Annabel laughed and squatted down to hug the child properly. "It's so good to finally meet you, Little Mister Crispin," she said. "Your mother has written me many letters, telling me how very handsome you are. And indeed, she was right! And I hear you are a very good boy!"

Crispin nodded with enthusiasm. "Is the sea very far away?" the child asked.

"Not far at all," Annabel said. "Can you not hear the waves?" They stopped to listen and Crispin nodded. "It's nearly supper time and it will be getting dark soon, but tomorrow we will walk down to the beach and you can see it for yourselves."

Both children were obviously excited over this, and Annabel turned her attention to Elaine, who spoke to her mother's aunt as if they were equals. This apparently delighted Annabel, who said to Meri, "She's every bit as clever and beautiful as you've told me."

While their greetings were taking place, servants had begun carrying the luggage into the house. They had apparently been hired since Meri had lived here, because she didn't recognize them. But the thought of having their bags and trunks in their new rooms, where they could be completely unpacked, filled Meri with delighted anticipation. She knew there were maids here who would help put their belongings away, and help see to their needs. And she also knew they would be much friendlier than the staff she'd gladly left behind. Meri felt no need to be waited on, and she preferred to care for her own children as much as possible—which was much more than she'd been allowed to do under the strict regulations of their father. But it was nice to have some help from the servants—especially after such a tiring journey. It was only her valise that Meri held on to. She'd hardly let go of it throughout their travels, since it contained the means for them to get by—hopefully until long after her children were raised. And she had no intention of allowing *anyone* in the house to know of its contents. She would find a safe place to hide the jewelry and the money once they'd had a chance to get settled in.

Annabel offered a hand to each of the children, and the three of them led the way into the house.

"Everyone's in the parlor," Annabel announced, "as they usually are. Let's say hello and then you can freshen up."

"Of course," Meri said, taking a deep breath to prepare herself to face the rest of the family. She didn't at all dislike her uncle or cousins, but it was Annabel she felt close to and dearly loved. Overall, she felt a kind of indifference toward Annabel's husband and children—not because she didn't love them, because she certainly did—very much. But during all the years she'd been a part of this family, she'd never felt any remarkable closeness to any of them. Still, for all their varied eccentricities, they were usually pleasant to be around.

Annabel moved into the wide-open doorway of the parlor, still holding the children's hands as she announced, "Look everyone! They've finally arrived!"

Meri took in the scene of her uncle and cousins and smiled, feeling almost as if she were looking at a familiar painting that evoked pleasant memories. It was as if she'd walked out of here seven years ago and left them all chatting over tea and cakes, and now she'd walked back in and they were exactly where she'd left them, with absolutely nothing changed. Of course, the idea was absurd since they'd all attended her wedding. Still, just standing there and observing them this way made her feel as if she'd truly come home

Chapter Two
DISPLACED

FOR A MOMENT, MERI WAS able to take in the comfortable view of her family in the parlor, and she absorbed the familiarity and its sense of safety. Uncle Angus was reading a newspaper, and she knew he had no intention of even looking in her direction until he'd finished whatever currently held his interest. Angus had never had much hair on his head, but since Meri had last seen him it had almost completely disappeared. What little hair there was had turned completely gray and was therefore barely visible. He was a big man, tall and broad-shouldered and carrying many extra pounds like a comfortable overcoat. His size was a stark contrast to that of his wife, especially with the added weight he had gained. Angus and Annabel had five daughters who had all been born over a span of less than ten years. Meri's age was somewhere in the middle of her five cousins, but not one of them had ever married.

To outsiders, Meri's cousins were a strange little gaggle of eccentricity and perhaps even oddity. The five girls were all keenly aware that Angus had desperately wanted a son, and that he absolutely resented the fact that he'd only been given daughters. Meri had heard him grumble a great deal about being in a *houseful of women,* and *having no heir,* and especially being annoyed by all the *silly giggling and prattle* he had to endure. Meri had always found it mostly amusing; she loved her uncle dearly. It wasn't until she had reached adulthood that she'd realized his regular degrading comments had impacted his daughters negatively. She would go so far as to say that his attitudes had a great deal to do with the lack of confidence and other challenges her cousins dealt with that had left them all spinsters. Meri recalled many times the way that Annabel had gently corrected her husband's derogatory comments; she had done so for years, until it had become evident that Angus would always argue with her, and such arguments taking place in front of the girls—even though their mother was defending them—only seemed to make matters worse. Annabel had stopped trying to correct her husband and had taken to more private conversations with her daughters in which she expressed love and respect for their father, but also explained to them that his attitude was not appropriate and they should not heed his negative comments. But it seemed that despite all Annabel's efforts, the girls had all been impacted too severely to ever leave home, and now Angus would have to endure all that *silly giggling and prattling* for the rest of his life.

Despite all the overt evidence of imperfections in Meri's family, she loved them all dearly. They had taken her in following her parents' deaths, and she had always felt loved and safe. And she was so glad to be home.

Angus continued to read the newspaper as expected, but all five of Meri's cousins looked up at the sound of their mother's announcement, and there was a sudden chorus of laughter and excitement as they all scrambled to their feet and rushed toward Meri and her children. Crispin and Elaine both clutched onto Meri's skirt and eased back at the overwhelming sight of five women of various shapes and sizes all hurtling toward them.

"It's all right," Meri whispered before she shared loving embraces and tender greetings with each of her cousins. They each in turn bent down to greet the children and commented on how adorable they were, but the children remained silent and continued holding tightly to their mother's skirts.

"This is all very strange to them," Meri explained. She laughed softly and added, "I don't know if they've ever encountered anyone in the whole of their lives who has been so kind and forthright."

"Truly?" Annabel said, astonished.

"Truly," Meri said, comforted by her aunt's validation. "But we can talk about that some other time," she added, hoping she never had to talk about it at all.

At everyone's insistence, Meri sat on a sofa to share tea with the family, and the children sat on either side of her, still taking in this new experience with shyness and skepticism. As Annabel and her daughters all sat down and made themselves comfortable, Angus finally looked over his newspaper at Meri and smiled. "It really is you!" he said with genuine enthusiasm, although he made no effort to get out of his chair to greet her. Meri could see then that with the weight he'd put on, it likely wasn't easy for him to get in and out of the huge chair in which he sat. Angus and the chair seemed to have grown very accustomed to each other.

"It really is," Meri said.

"And these are your little ones," Angus said, smiling at them both, which only encouraged them to duck a little farther behind Meri's arms.

"Yes," Meri said. "I'm certain they'll warm up to you with time."

"Indeed," Angus said. "I'm so glad you've come back to us, my dear, although the circumstances are . . ." he shook his head and took on a grim expression, ". . . just dreadful."

"Indeed," was all Meri said. She'd never given anyone any indication that her life away from here had not been ideal—except for the letters she'd written to Annabel. But she knew her aunt would have kept them in confidence. At this point she didn't know if she would ever tell Angus or her cousins the truth; she doubted that it would ever be possible for them to understand. But that was all right. She had a confidant in her aunt, and she was nothing but grateful to be here and to know that she would be able to settle in with her children and call it home for as long as needed, perhaps indefinitely. She had enough money to be able to manage on her own, but it was the safety of this home and the security of family that she longed for, and she knew it was important for her children to be able to experience such safety and security—something they had never known in their short lives.

The children eased away from Meri enough to be able to enjoy the dainty sandwiches and delicious little cakes they were offered. Once they started eating, it was evident they were hungry, which seemed to be a delight to everyone in the room. None had had much exposure to children, which made Elaine and Crispin somewhat of a novelty. But if that encouraged these people to dote on the children and make them feel at home, Meri could only be pleased.

Meri was glad that everyone seemed to want to avoid discussing her husband's recent passing, although she suspected the subject would come up at some future time, likely when the children weren't present. For the moment, Meri encouraged each of her cousins to tell her what they'd been doing so they could get caught up. The five girls were named in birth order: Faith, Hope, Charity, Joy, and Comfort. It had been Meri's mother's and her sister Annabel's idea to give their daughters names that represented favorable qualities, which might help them aspire to exemplify their names. Meri's first name was Grace, but she had chosen at a young age to go by her middle name—Meriwether—which had been her grandmother's name; shortening it to Meri had suited her well and she preferred it above being called anything else. Meri had been the only girl born to her parents, and her brother had perished from the same illness that had taken her parents, which had left her an only child and an orphan. But she had been taken in by her pleasant gaggle of cousins, and despite their eccentricities, they each *did* exemplify their names—for the most part, at least. Their names connected them as sisters far more than their appearance. Each of them had obvious physical characteristics from both of their parents, and yet no two of them looked enough alike to be known as sisters upon first impressions.

Faith was almost as tall as her father with dark, straight hair and angular features that exaggerated her thin frame. She wore eyeglasses, which suited her well, but she still had to hold books very close to her face when she read—and she read a great deal.

Hope was dramatically shorter than her older sister with a round face and more rounded figure. Her hair was also dark, but it was thick and wavy. She also loved to read, and she and Faith had very similar tastes in literature.

Charity had dark blonde hair with a build and features that were so average she could be described as downright plain. The stark way she always wore her hair pulled back tightly in a bun didn't help, but she insisted on not wanting to fuss with her hair any more than just getting it out of the way. Her choice of wardrobe also enhanced her plainness. Her sisters all enjoyed fixing each other's hair and trying new styles; they also enjoyed new clothes and trying different fashions—which their father allowed if they remained within a certain budget. But Charity was content to stick to the same vapid hairstyle and nondescript wardrobe. Even when she got something new to wear out of necessity, she chose dresses that were long out of fashion and terribly drab. Still, she was kind and generous.

Joy's hair was light blonde. She was average height, but had a propensity toward carrying extra weight, much like her father. She was the most outgoing of the sisters, and Meri noticed how she—more than the others—kept trying to get the attention of the children, playing some silly form of silent peekaboo with them. It seemed to be working, since Crispin and Elaine kept looking at Joy while they ate their cakes and sandwiches, and Elaine was starting to smile and relax. Crispin was remaining more cautious, but he was still taken with Joy's antics.

Comfort, the youngest of the sisters, had medium brown hair, which she loved to have put into lavish styles, and she had a love for fashionable clothing and jewelry more than any of the others. The irony was that Comfort was by far the heaviest member of the family. Even given the extra pounds that Uncle Angus had put on since Meri had last seen him, Comfort was still heavier. Sitting on a sofa between Faith and Charity, Comfort looked as if she were three times the size of her sisters. Meri had always known Comfort to be chubbier than the others—a word her sisters had used—but now Meri felt decidedly concerned. She knew it couldn't be healthy, and she wondered about the reasons why Comfort felt the need to eat so much that it had become an obvious problem. Still, she held no judgment toward Comfort or anyone else in the room. She loved them for who they were, with all their problems and imperfections, and she knew that they loved her the same. And love was what they needed most; love was what Meri and her children had been deprived of all these years.

Meri quickly realized that nothing had changed in this household—except for the passing of years and the gaining of pounds by some members of the family. The sisters rarely attended any social events, and their only outings were into town so they could shop, but apparently that too had become a rare occurrence. They all enjoyed reading to varying degrees, and they liked to talk about what they'd been reading. Their differing preferences in what they read only made for more stimulating conversation, and it was one of the few pastimes they enjoyed. They also enjoyed playing card games. But it was evident they rarely even went out of the house. They were all pale for lack of exposing themselves to sunlight, and Meri wondered how the beautiful gardens and grounds of this house could be so unappreciated. Not to mention their proximity to the sea. It seemed that only Annabel took advantage of these privileges, which was one of many things she and Meri had in common, and Meri looked forward to a walk in the gardens with her aunt.

When Meri saw signs of her children becoming especially restless and fidgety, she knew they needed a break and some time on their own.

"It's so lovely seeing all of you," Meri said, "and we'll have plenty of time together, but I think we all need some time to rest and—"

"Oh, of course," Annabel said, coming to her feet. "All of your things have been taken up to your rooms." Meri stood as well, and the children did the same, once again clinging to her skirt. "You'll find your old room just as you left it." Annabel smiled and took hold of Meri's shoulders. "And the room next to it has been prepared for the children. We can make adjustments later if they're needed. We just want you to be comfortable."

"I'm certain it will all be just right," Meri said, confident that Annabel knew her well.

"I'm so glad to have you back, my dear," Annabel said and kissed Meri's cheek. "Dinner is at seven as usual, and the children are welcome to join us in the dining room."

"Thank you," Meri said, knowing it wasn't necessarily customary for children to dine with adults among those of this social class. Not once had she shared a meal at the table with her children; her husband and his family simply wouldn't have it. She appreciated Annabel's insight more than she could say. Even if or when the time came when others might help look out for the children, right now they were in a strange place and would not likely want to be away from their mother at all. "We will see you at dinner, then." Meri nodded toward her uncle who winked at her, and her cousins who all waved, wearing pleasant expressions that assured her they were all glad to have her back. The ironies concerning her need to return—and the fact that Lord Sturgess had not allowed her to come back to visit even once since she'd married him—were settling in more by the minute.

Meri went up the stairs, holding the hands of her children, and then down a long hallway, around a corner, up a few steps, and down another shorter hallway before she entered the room where she had lived since the age of nine when Angus and Annabel had taken her in. The children looked around curiously and asked a few questions, which was good considering they'd not uttered a sound beyond their initial greetings since they'd arrived. Meri took them through an open adjoining door to the next room and was delighted to see that their arrival had obviously been anticipated. She recalled this room having been one of many guest rooms in the huge manor, but an extra bed had been added to the enormous room. The bedding on one bed was obviously feminine, and the other very masculine. There were also a few toys left in the window seat that quickly caught the children's eye. Crispin rushed toward the collection of tiny horses and toy soldiers, and Elaine scooped up two beautiful dolls and hugged them as if they were her dearest friends.

While Meri unpacked the children's things and put them into the wardrobe and the bureau drawers, she talked to them about some of her memories here; even though she'd done so before, now that they were here, she figured the stories might have more meaning. They tested out their beds and even jumped on them a little and giggled before they each sat in the window seat and looked out. Elaine asked some simple questions about Meri's cousins, expressing her typical curiosity. Crispin just said, "I like them. They're nice. And I like their cakes and sandwiches."

"Well, they didn't *make* them," Meri said with a little laugh. "They came from the kitchen. But I shall take you to the kitchen later or perhaps tomorrow, and you can meet Mrs. Biddle. She's been the cook here for many years, and I used to help her in the kitchen sometimes just so I could get extra tastes of all the wonderful things she makes. She has some helpers, but she's the one who is very talented at making food taste good."

"It tastes better here than it did at our old house," Elaine said, and Meri resisted the urge to verbalize her thought that the atmosphere here could make everything taste better. Meri couldn't dispute that Mrs. Biddle had far more culinary skill than the kitchen staff in the house she'd just left—none of whose names Meri had ever been allowed to know. It was as if they had all meant to be invisible, unacknowledged, and unappreciated; the very idea still irked Meri, but she pushed the thought away, along with every other stray thought that took her back in time. Dark, haunting thoughts tried to push themselves forward; therefore, it was best to not even think about them. She couldn't even imagine what might happen to her or the children if anyone knew the *truth*. She only wanted to look forward, and getting settled into these rooms with her children left her feeling more safe and secure than she'd felt since she'd been married.

Somehow Meri convinced the children to lie down and try to take a nap. She knew they were tired from traveling; she certainly was.

Miraculously, once they crawled beneath the covers of their new beds, they fell asleep within minutes, which allowed Meri to take a nap herself. As she tried to relax, old habits of fearfulness made her heart quicken, and she had to rehearse over and over in her mind that there was no longer anything to be afraid of. She was finally able to breathe normally and her heart calmed down to a steady rhythm. The next thing she knew, Elaine was crawling into the bed with her, having awakened and come through the open door between the two rooms to find her. A few minutes later, Crispin joined them, but he was not as prone to snuggle with his mother as was Elaine. Once he began jumping on the bed, Meri gave up on any attempt to rest further and got up to start unpacking her things. She put the valise with all her valuables in the bottom of the wardrobe, determined to find a better hiding place when the children weren't around.

It felt good to see her belongings fill the drawers and the wardrobe. Fond memories of her youth felt more tangible than they had in a long time, and she never wanted to leave here again. She still couldn't understand what had possessed her to marry Cyrus Sturgess. Perhaps if she could figure out *why* she'd made that decision, she could come to terms with all that had followed.

Dinner with the family went well, although the children once again became mute. More than one of Meri's cousins commented on how well behaved they were, but Meri warned, "Once they warm up to you and feel at home, you will see that they both have a great deal of energy."

"Which is exactly how they should be," Annabel said.

After dinner, they all went to the parlor—just as they had always done for many years—to have coffee and visit. Faith and Hope took turns playing the piano, something that held no interest for the other sisters. The children were fascinated, since they'd never experienced the wonders of the beautiful sounds a piano could make. There had been a piano in the house where they'd lived, but no one had ever played it, and the children hadn't been allowed to touch it.

When the children began to show signs of boredom, Meri was about to excuse herself and take them upstairs, but Elaine whispered something in Meri's ear that made her smile. At Elaine's request, Meri said to Annabel, "I told Elaine about your doll collection, Auntie. She's asking if she might see it."

"Well, of course!" Annabel said, practically jumping to her feet. "Come along, little princess." Annabel held out a hand toward Elaine who took it without hesitation. Apparently, she'd been around these people long enough to realize she could trust them. Elaine tossed a smile over her shoulder toward Meri as Annabel guided her out of the room.

Crispin looked after them as they left, apparently feeling left out. Meri was pleasantly surprised with how quickly her uncle picked up on the child's mood. "Ho there, young man," Angus said to Crispin, groaning as he heaved his weight out of the deep chair, "I dare say I've got something in my den that you might like. Shall we go and have a look?"

Crispin looked somewhat skeptically at the older man's outstretched hand before he looked at Meri, as if waiting for approval and assurance. "It's all right," Meri said. "I promise he's a very nice man. And I'll be right here."

Crispin nodded and took Angus's hand, which made Meri's uncle smile. She watched them leave the room, recalling how Angus was a collector of many things. His den—as he liked to call it—was a room filled with glass cases containing spoons, thimbles, coins, an interesting variety of rocks, and an even greater variety of seashells. He also had a collection of toy soldiers that he'd kept in fine condition since his own childhood, and there were several little porcelain birds that were painted in a variety of beautiful colors. She suspected that Crispin could be entertained for quite some time.

Meri settled in to enjoy some conversation with her cousins, but as they began to ask her specific questions about her marriage, her life as Lady Sturgess, and the death of her husband, she found it increasingly difficult to either deflect the questions or skirt around them to keep from lying. She believed she was handling the well-intended interrogations fairly well until Joy asked, "Are you all right, darling?"

Her question brought the anxiety in Meri's mood to the attention of the others. "Forgive us for badgering you with questions," Comfort added.

"It's just that we've not seen you for so long," Charity said.

"There's no need for concern," Meri said but couldn't force much of a smile. "But . . . it's not been so long since my husband's death, and . . ."

"Oh, of course!" Faith said with obvious compassion. "We mustn't be so insensitive. You must miss him dreadfully." Meri didn't comment, not wanting to lie to them, any more than she wanted to admit to her relief over his death. She was glad when Faith added, "And you must miss your home."

Meri felt comfortable being more honest about *that.* "Actually," she drawled, "I never truly felt at home there. The servants were all so . . . *stuffy.* It was as if it was a requirement for them to be cold and distant in order to maintain deference."

"Truly?" Joy asked. "Even the nanny?"

"Oh, there was more than one nanny, and they were *all* disagreeable. I hated leaving the children in their care and avoided it as much as possible, but there were rules about the children not dining with the adults, and rules about not interacting with the staff on any personal level."

All five cousins made noises of astonishment. Faith said, "Then I certainly understand that without your husband there, you wouldn't want to stay."

"Well, I hope you'll stay with us forever," Comfort said and took a bite of the extra serving of cake she'd brought with her from the dinner table.

"I'm very grateful to be here," Meri said, and she meant it, but as she observed her cousins deliberately changing the subject to spare her any further discomfort, she felt suddenly displaced. Little had changed here at Rosewell Abbey, but Meri had changed. She felt as if she'd aged twenty years in seven, and she had been subjected to a life that had stripped away every bit of her naiveté. The charming innocence she observed in her cousins was now completely absent in her. These gentle, kind women could never imagine and would never believe that human beings could be capable of the cruelty Meri to which had been exposed. And she never wanted to tell them. She preferred that they continue to believe she'd had a loving marriage and a good life. Still, it was becoming increasingly evident that it would take time for her to learn to fit in again with her family, when she had changed so much. And she was a mother now—something her cousins had never experienced, and likely never would. But she knew that she was loved here, and with time, her children would surely come to feel so at home that they would forget they'd ever lived any other life. Oh, how she hoped they would forget! And how she longed to be able to forget as well.

* * *

That night, Meri slept better than she had in a very long time. In fact, she believed now that she'd likely never had a truly good night's sleep in all the time she'd been married to Lord Sturgess. A young maid named Alice—who had come to check on Meri the night before—knocked at Meri's door to see if she or the children needed anything before breakfast. Meri liked Alice, whose hair was very blonde and her lips very pink. She might have looked like a porcelain doll except that her features were rather homely. Yet Alice's genuine kindness shone through brilliantly.

"I believe we have everything we need," Meri said, "but thank you. I'll ring if I need anything," she added, knowing there was a bell rope that would alert someone downstairs if she required assistance.

"Very good," Alice said with an accent that indicated she had likely received little or no education. "How is the children? If I might ask?"

"They're still sleeping," Meri said with a smile, realizing that Alice was thrilled to have children in the house, even though she was trying not to show it. Knowing the children needed to become comfortable with all the people they would encounter in the house, she impulsively added, "Perhaps later you could help me watch them. Playtime can be exhausting at times."

"Oh, could I?" Alice asked.

"If it doesn't interfere with your other duties," Meri said, "we'd be delighted to have your company."

"Oh, Lady Rosewell told me to just look out for you and the children for now, and to make certain you has what you needs."

"Then we will look forward to playtime after breakfast," Meri said, and Alice grinned before she hurried away.

Meri nudged the children awake and helped them get dressed so they wouldn't miss breakfast with the family. She looked forward to this most casual meal of the day and all the lively chatter that would be present—a stark contrast to the harsh silence that had been the norm in her former life.

Meri entered the breakfast room with the children, and just like the previous day when they'd arrived, she came upon a sight that was like a painting with sound and motion. Everything was just as she'd remembered. There were covered dishes of food laid out on the sideboard. Angus had a folded newspaper on the table beside his plate so that he could read while he ate. The cousins were all chattering about trivial things while Annabel drank tea from the green floral china that Meri remembered so fondly.

"Oh, there you are," Comfort said, being the first to see them.

"Come," Annabel said. "Make yourselves at home."

"Thank you," Meri said and moved to the sideboard. Before she could even begin to start dishing up food for the children, Faith and Hope each appeared at her sides, speaking kindly to the children and offering to help them. The children didn't speak but they nodded, and her cousins proceeded to ask them what they wanted to eat while lifting the lids of the serving dishes to show them what was underneath. Crispin ended up with a great many sausages and a scone with jam. Elaine wanted a little bit of everything. Meri followed Elaine's lead and sat down to enjoy a meal that tasted like home. She was pleased to see how her cousins were all doting on the children and pitching in to help them with whatever they might need. It was evident the children were warming up when Elaine began conversing with these women who were like sisters to Meri. Hearing Elaine's voice brought a warm smile from Annabel, and even Angus looked up from his paper to smile. A few minutes later Crispin also spoke, but only to ask for another scone.

Meri observed her children looking relaxed and comfortable; listening to the typical conversations going on around her, she still felt displaced. She felt so utterly and completely changed, and only Annabel had any idea of the difficulties of these past years. But even her aunt didn't know the full extent of how bad things had been. Meri told herself to be patient and allow time to make her feel more at home. Surely the more time that passed, the more she would be able to distance herself from her despicable life with Lord Sturgess.

After breakfast, Meri took the children to the playroom. It too looked much the same as it had when she'd left—even though it had been long before then that she'd stopped coming here to play with her cousins. The children were excited but initially hesitant, as if they feared they might get into some trouble if they moved or touched anything without permission.

"It's all right," Meri said and opened a large tin filled with building blocks, which she dumped out on the carpet and with which she began to build a tower. The children joined her and a few minutes later Alice appeared, introduced herself with a smile to the children, and began to play with them as if she were a child herself. Meri gradually moved to a small sofa nearby to mostly observe, and she decided that she loved Alice already. This young woman was enthusiastically back and forth between building a fortress with blocks, changing clothes on more than one doll, arranging furniture in an enormous dollhouse, and putting together a puzzle of large wooden pieces on the carpet. Within minutes the children were talking to her and they were clearly having fun, but it still seemed that Alice was getting the better deal by the way she often laughed.

They had been there for more than an hour when Annabel entered the room with a tray of biscuits and cool punch. But her declaration that she'd brought a snack didn't motivate the children to abandon their play. Annabel sat beside Meri and squeezed her hand.

"They appear to be having a good time," Annabel said.

"Yes," Meri said and laughed softly, "especially Alice. I really like her."

"I thought you might," Annabel added with a self-satisfied sigh. "She came here looking for work because her family is so large they simply couldn't afford to feed all the children. She's the second oldest in a family of eleven, and she took care of her younger siblings a great deal. She loves children and was utterly delighted when I told the servants you were coming here to live—and you were bringing Elaine and Crispin. If it's all right with you, we will put Alice in charge of the children—only under your supervision, of course."

"That would be lovely," Meri said. She loved the very idea of Alice spending a great deal of time with her children. She had a knack for playing with them that Meri lacked. But Meri especially liked the fact that Alice's care and interaction with the children would be under Meri's supervision. It was nice, after all this time, to feel as if she had a say in her children's lives and how they spent their time.

"How are you doing, my love?" Annabel asked quietly.

Meri turned to look at her aunt and managed a smile. "I'm doing much better than I have in a very long time."

"Good," Annabel said firmly and put an arm around Meri's shoulders. "I'm so glad to have you back where I can take care of you."

"I love you, Auntie," Meri said, resting her head on Annabel's shoulder.

"And I love you, my darling," Annabel said, then they all broke out in laughter as something Alice had said to the children must have been terribly funny. Meri had no idea what it was, but her children were laughing so hard that they literally rolled onto the carpet. Meri and Annabel just laughed because the others were laughing. But, oh how good it felt to laugh!

* * *

After lunch, Meri walked with the children down to the sea. They had to descend a bit of a steep decline, but Meri was completely familiar with the path and was able to help the children navigate it without difficulty. Once they were on the beach, the children just stood in awe, watching the waves roll in and out. They'd never been to a beach before, and had never seen the ocean prior to the glimpse they'd gotten from the carriage window when they arrived.

Meri sat on the ground to remove her shoes and stockings, and the children followed her example. They all laughed as she guided them toward the edge of the water, and the waves lapped up around their ankles. The children inched bravely closer to the water's edge and their laughter grew. Meri gave up on any hope of their clothes not getting wet. But what did wet clothes matter in light of having so much fun? Even the hem of her own skirt got wet despite her trying to hold it high enough to avoid the waves.

By the time they returned to the house and changed into dry clothes, they were all tired, and once again Meri took a nap while the children did the same. Oh, how she relished having the huge bed all to herself, and feeling completely safe there!

Within a week, Meri saw her children blossom in ways she'd never imagined. They loved Mrs. Biddle in the kitchen, who fawned over them and always gave them a treat when they came to visit; therefore, Crispin and Elaine insisted on going to visit at least once a day. Since nearly every servant they encountered took a liking to the children, Elaine talked to Alice about her idea to include the children in sharing tea with the servants. Each afternoon when the servants gathered for their tea, Alice and the children joined them. And sometimes Meri joined them for a short while before having tea with her family, which was a time when they typically enjoyed each other's company and she felt it was important to be present. However, tea with the servants was livelier. How could the children not love all the attention when these people were not only kind, but treated them as if they were actually important?

The children also loved going out to see the horses, and the stablemaster, Mr. Bayliss, quickly got them busy helping to brush the horses—even though they had to stand on a crate to reach. And he also taught them how to give each horse a piece of apple by holding it on the horses' lips with their hands, which always made the children giggle.

Crispin and Elaine also became acquainted with the gardener, Mr. Pattison. They loved the way he told them the names of the flowers that were in bloom now that spring was easing into summer, and they also loved being able to get their hands dirty as they helped Mr. Pattison pull some weeds that were easy to remove because they were so small. Mr. Pattison would never let a weed become very large in *his* garden.

Meri and the children all went to church with the family on Sunday. They had always gone to church in the past, and the children knew how to remain quiet during the sermon. But they were clearly surprised when, following the service, many people—and the vicar himself—acknowledged them personally and declared how good it was to meet them. In the past, the children had surely felt invisible with the way the adults had mostly ignored them. It was also nice for Meri to be able to sit with the children in church instead of having them sit in a different pew with one of the nannies.

As a pattern settled into place during that first week, the children behaved as if they'd been pronounced royalty. Their personalities came forward exuberantly, and it was evident they would thrive living here at Rosewell Abbey. Of course, as a mother, Meri couldn't be more thrilled or relieved or happy—except for the part deep inside of her that was filled with sorrow over what this meant regarding how Crispin and Elaine had been living before. If she thought about the stifling environment and fearful tactics to which the children had become accustomed, she felt nothing less than horrified. If she thought about it too long she literally started to shake and become nauseous. So, she focused on her joy and hope at seeing a bright future unfolding for her children and tried not to think about the past.

For herself, Meri found it immensely more difficult not to think about how it could have been if Lord Sturgess had not died. She still felt displaced, but everything was going well and she knew she just needed to concentrate on how very blessed she was to be able to have a safe place to come home to where she could raise her children.

Chapter Three

Childhood Friends

A month after returning to Northumberland, Meri found satisfaction in how well the children were doing, and she even felt a little better herself. According to their new routine, she shared breakfast with the children in a sitting room they had taken over. The children had both declared that they enjoyed eating breakfast there since they could do so in their pajamas if they chose, and then they could take their time getting cleaned up and dressed instead of having to hurry to do so in order to go downstairs and have breakfast with the family. In contrast, they had both been firm about sharing *lunch* with the family, since they enjoyed the company. They continued to have tea with the servants, and they shared dinner upstairs with Alice so that Meri could have one meal a day with the adults where they could share conversation more freely and not worry about saying anything that might be confusing to the children.

Meri spent most of her time with the children, enjoying the fact that she could do so without being monitored by anyone who might disapprove of her ideas about parenting. Alice was often with the children or nearby in case she was needed, and the children had quickly grown to love her. Meri loved her as well, and she appreciated the comfortable rapport they shared, which made it easy for them both to be flexible in their time with the children and just enjoy these summer days.

When the weather was cooperative, Elaine and Crispin spent time helping Mr. Pattison in the gardens, and they absolutely loved to go to the beach. Sometimes Alice accompanied them, and they all had a lovely time. Occasionally they had a picnic, and the children had taken to collecting shells, which they kept in a special drawer in their room. The children also loved to hear Faith and Hope play the piano, although Meri realized they did so very rarely and had to be talked into it. Their playing the piano on the day Meri had arrived with the children had apparently been a special occasion.

Crispin and Elaine also liked to go to the stables and help Mr. Bayliss brush the horses and give them apple pieces as a reward for their good behavior. And they had to go to the kitchen at least once a day so that Mrs. Biddle and the rest of the staff there could dote on the children and spoil them with some kind of special snack. Meri often thought of how life had been for her children before coming here, and she believed that some spoiling was good for them. She didn't let them get away with misbehaving or being impolite or ungrateful—nor did anyone else in the house—but she believed it was good for them to feel like they were important and that they mattered to the people with whom they shared their home.

After nap time each day, Crispin and Elaine loved sharing tea with Alice and the rest of the staff. Meri found it amusing that her children had declared to her that she was meant to go and have tea with the family, and it had become somewhat of a joke that the servants were all conspiring with Elaine and Crispin, sharing great secrets in her absence. Meri had been told by Alice that they had all begun a game of pretend with the children, telling each other made-up stories about once having been pirates or great warriors or enjoying travels around the world. The children were telling grand tales of their own, which grew more outlandish and ridiculous with each passing day. Meri loved the way the servants were encouraging the children to use their imaginations, and she thought it was good for them to be gaining their independence in this way by declaring that they didn't always need their mother around.

Meri couldn't deny that while she loved her children dearly and she wanted to be actively involved in their lives, she was grateful to not have to be responsible for them all day every day. She'd been given far too little access to them in her previous home, but now that she'd settled into this new way of life, she often felt utterly exhausted. When she shared this with Annabel, her aunt suggested that bearing great emotional difficulty all alone could wear a person down, and Meri had likely had years of sheer exhaustion from which she needed to recover. Meri appreciated her aunt's insight and understanding, and was glad to be able to rest when she felt the need, always knowing that the house was full of people—both family and servants—who loved to watch over the children and keep them entertained.

Following breakfast on a particularly sunny day, Meri left Elaine and Crispin in Alice's care and headed to the solarium, where she was hoping she had left the novel she'd been reading. She hadn't been able to find it in her room, and the last time she recalled reading from it had been in her favorite room of the house. The solarium was a room enclosed almost entirely by glass, situated on the north side of the house so that it would never become too hot in the warmer months of the year. It was furnished with comfortable chairs and a couple of small tables, perfect for relaxing, reading, enjoying tea, and soaking in the sun on cloudless days such as this. But Meri also enjoyed the solarium on rainy days—of which there were many in Northumberland. She loved to watch the rain drizzle over the glass ceiling and walls. And no matter the weather, she always enjoyed the remarkable view of the gardens and the wooded hills beyond them.

As Meri made her way to the solarium, she considered once again how odd she found it that no one else in the family particularly liked the room, and it was rarely used at all. Sometimes she wished that her aunt or cousins—or even her uncle—might join her here for tea. But she'd come to appreciate that she could always find them in the parlor where they spent most of their days, and she could enjoy their noisy conversations about politics, the books they were reading, and the local gossip. However, when Meri wanted to be alone and read, the solarium offered the perfect respite.

Meri walked through the large open doorway onto the stone floor of the sun-filled room, already scanning the chairs and tables for the book for which she was looking. She was completely unprepared to see the outstretched legs of a man coming from beneath a newspaper that was being held in a way that blocked his face and chest completely. She'd not heard anyone mention a potential guest, and she felt puzzled as she considered why a *guest* would be here alone, rather than visiting with the family.

Deciding she would prefer to just leave and avoid any conversation with this man who was lounging in her favorite room, she spied her book on a table and wondered how she might grab it and leave without drawing any attention to herself. She knew she'd already made enough noise to make her presence known when the corner of the newspaper flipped down and she was taken aback to see hair so dark that it was nearly black and green eyes that took her in with the same curiosity that she felt. She gasped softly as those eyes sparked distant memories, and she realized that she knew this man—or at least she had known him years ago. He abruptly lowered the newspaper and Meri could see his entire face, the bottom half of which was covered with a beard. She couldn't remember the last time she'd seen a man with a beard, given that it wasn't presently considered fashionable. His hair was combed back off his face and hung in curly waves to the bottom of his neck, and his brows were as thick and as dark as his beard. But there was no denying the familiarity of his eyes.

In one agile movement, this man set the newspaper aside and stood, giving Meri a better view of how smartly he was dressed. His shirt was brilliantly white, and his brocade waistcoat was mostly blue, interwoven with black and gold threads. His breeches and boots were as black as his hair. For a moment, she felt drab in comparison, wearing a simple day dress of green and cream that was old and comfortable. But something in his eyes made her feel anything but drab. Then he smiled, and even through the beard her recognition of him became clearer.

"Meri?" he said. "Is that you?"

"It is," she replied, and he laughed with perfect delight, as if coming upon her made him happier than anything else could have.

"Meri!" He laughed again, this time carrying her name on its wave into the open air, filling the room. He stepped forward and took hold of her shoulders as he kissed her cheek, and his beard tickled her face. He immediately let go and stepped back, retaining propriety, but his smile didn't diminish. He was genuinely glad to see her, and she couldn't deny that she was glad to see him.

"Elliott," she said and held out a hand; he took it, squeezed it, kissed it, and wouldn't let it go. "I can't believe it. How many years has it been? What are you doing here?"

"It's been nearly eight years, I believe," he said, reminding her that the last time she'd seen him had been at a social event when her engagement to Lord Sturgess had been announced. "And as for what I'm doing here, I could ask you the same."

"I asked first," she said, and he guided her to a small sofa where they sat side by side and he turned to look directly at her, keeping hold of her hand.

Meri noticed the way Elliott looked down, and he shifted slightly in his seat. He didn't *want* to tell her what he was doing here. But his hesitance didn't cause her any suspicion; instead, she felt concerned. The years since she'd last seen Elliott had been difficult for her, and she sensed they had been difficult for him as well.

Elliott was as much a cousin to the Rosewell family as Meri—even though Meri and Elliott were not related by blood. Meri was Annabel's niece—her sister's daughter. And Elliott was Angus's nephew—his brother's son. Elliott had come to stay with his Uncle Angus a great deal throughout his youth—along with his siblings. Hence, Meri knew him well. Or she had many years ago. He'd always been decidedly precocious and also somewhat mischievous. But he'd always been very kind to Meri—a trait that had not necessarily been shared by his older siblings, a brother and two sisters who had been mostly snooty and obnoxious—at least as far as Meri had known them. Meri had never been comfortable around Elliott's siblings, but then, Elliott hadn't been either. When they had all been children, Elliott always came with his brother and sisters to visit, but as they'd gotten older, Elliott had come on his own for extended stays—since he liked his uncle's family, and his siblings had preferred to go elsewhere or just remain at home.

Meri had many pleasant memories of the times she'd shared with Elliott during their growing years. She had enjoyed his lengthy visits to Rosewell Abbey; in many ways, he was like a brother to her. Given that her own brother had died very young, Elliott had filled a hole in her life in that way. Despite how much she loved her female cousins, and she felt completely comfortable with them, she recalled many long and deep conversations with Elliott that had been memorable and stimulating. And she couldn't deny how good it was to see him now.

"Well," she said in a light tone that she hoped would make him feel at ease, "I'm waiting. What brings you here now?"

He lifted his eyes to look at her directly again and said with a smile, "Let's not talk about me. I'd much rather talk about you and what brings *you* here now."

"It's a long story," she said, "and perhaps boring." She wondered if telling him a little about her present circumstances would help him feel more comfortable about opening up to her as he once had.

"Tell me the short version," he urged, "and you can fill in the boring details later." She hesitated, wondering where to start, and he asked, "Is your husband here with you?"

His question felt slightly shocking to Meri. The mere reference to her *husband* brought back a barrage of memories she was trying to forget. But of course, Elliott would ask; he'd known of her marriage even though he hadn't been at the wedding. She was mostly surprised that her aunt and uncle hadn't yet told him about her situation.

Meri took a deep breath and said, "My husband is dead, Elliott."

His head moved abruptly as if he'd been physically struck. "Dead? Truly?" She nodded. "I'm so sorry, Meri." He squeezed the hand he was still holding. "May I ask what happened?"

Meri looked down, not wanting to talk about it, but realizing that except for Annabel, there was no one else with whom she truly felt comfortable enough to talk about the horrible means by which her husband had died.

"Lord Sturgess died when—"

"Lord Sturgess?" he interrupted, completely thwarting her momentum. "You call your husband by his title?"

"That's what he preferred," Meri said, not wanting to talk about *anything* related to her former marriage.

"I see," Elliott said in a tone that indicated he didn't. "Forgive me. Go on." He motioned with his free hand.

"He died from an accidental shooting," Meri stated.

"That's terrible!" Elliott said and clearly meant it. "What happened?"

"No one knows for sure," Meri said, still not looking at him. "The police declared after a thorough investigation that with the angle of the . . . bullet . . . and other evidence . . . that it had not been intentional; meaning he did not . . ."

"Intend to kill himself," Elliott said in a brusque voice that made Meri look at him. The statement was obviously connected to a sensitive nerve for *him*, but she didn't know how to ask when they were already immersed in a difficult topic.

"That's right," she said, again looking away. She took a long, deep breath in order to fill her lungs as she realized her breathing had become shallow and she felt mildly lightheaded.

"I'm so sorry for your loss, Meri," Elliott said with sincere compassion; he obviously believed that she had loved her husband and she was grieving. He had no reason to believe otherwise, and for the time being she preferred to not have him know the truth—even though she was not dressed in black as was the tradition for a widow; she had chosen for many reasons to wear black only when going out in public. Meri and Elliott had once been close, and everything presently seemed to be the same. She had no reason to believe she couldn't trust him, but more than anything she just didn't want to talk about it.

Focusing on the present, she hurried to finish the short version of her situation. "Truthfully, I never really liked my husband's home, and I certainly didn't get along with his mother or brother who still live there. After he died, the memories were just too much. So, I came home. I have no intention of ever going back."

Elliott didn't comment and Meri found the courage to look up, curious over what his expression might betray about his response to her confession. For a moment, she feared that he was not the man she'd once known, and that he might be appalled or disgusted by the feelings to which she'd just admitted. Perhaps she should have been more cautious in being so open with him when they'd not even spoken for so many years. Although, as she mentally reviewed what she'd said, she knew she hadn't revealed even a tiny portion of her true feelings. Perhaps she was afraid he might somehow be able to read her mind, or at least sense that there was much more to the story that she had no desire to share. She was relieved to see compassion in his expression, and no sign of disgust or judgment. She saw his eyes searching hers, as if he *could* sense that there was much more she hadn't told him, and perhaps he might find there the reasons she was holding back.

Elliott finally said, "Again, I'm so sorry for your loss, Meri. But I am very glad to see you. And I'm so glad that you had a place to come home to."

"I'm very glad of that myself," she admitted, glad to no longer be talking about her husband's death.

"We are both very blessed in that regard," he said, which prompted her to turn the conversation around.

"Now it's your turn," she said. "Why are *you* here?"

He didn't seem pleased with having to answer the question, but she knew that he would. He looked toward the view of the gardens and sighed so deeply that his shoulders went slowly up and then down. "To give you the short version, I must admit that I've not managed my life very well through the years since I last saw you. And the situation at home has become increasingly difficult."

Meri knew it had *always* been difficult, but she sought to clarify. "I assume you mean the discord between you and your siblings."

"Yes," he said quickly. "And my mother, to be truthful. That should be no surprise to you. I know I talked with you a great deal about how I never felt like I fit in—and I believe everyone else in the family felt the same way. I really thought it would get better with time; that when we became adults we would have enough maturity to get beyond our differences. But it only got worse. I kept finding excuses to leave home; I've done a great deal of traveling—which was nice in some respects, although I quickly grew weary of it. I suppose you could say I've just felt somewhat . . . lost. Angus and Annabel have been very kind and encouraging—of course; one would not expect them to be anything less. A year or so ago I came to an extremely low point; I was weary of traveling but I couldn't bring myself to go home. They told me I was welcome to come and go as I please, and to consider this my home. I've been in London the last couple of months, staying with a friend and taking care of some business. I got in late last night." He chuckled softly and looked at her again. "That wasn't really a very *short* version."

Meri sensed there was a great deal more to his story. His very countenance radiated a heaviness she'd never seen in him before, and she felt deeply concerned. She squeezed his hand and said, "Feel free to tell me as much as you like; or perhaps more accurately . . . if you need to talk about . . . anything . . . I'm here. I know it's been a long time, but . . . you can trust me now as you once did; I would never betray your confidence. I just want you to know that."

As soon as Meri finished stating her sincere offer, she realized there was a great deal about herself that she didn't necessarily want to share with him—or anyone else. But if she could sense the darkness in Elliott, he could surely sense the same in her. She knew him to be sharp and perceptive, and it would be ridiculous to think that he wouldn't know there was *much* more to her story that she'd not told him. He proved her assumptions right when he looked directly into her eyes and said with sincerity, "That offer goes both ways, Meri. I mean it."

"Thank you," she said and looked down, certain that part of the reason they were now reconnecting so strongly was the fact that they were both carrying dark secrets regarding all that had happened in their lives since they'd last shared deep conversation—which had likely been about the time she had told him that she and Lord Sturgess were officially engaged. He hadn't been happy about it, but he'd told her he respected her decision and he would support her in it if that's what she'd wanted. At the time, she had believed she would be able to remain friends with Elliott—especially given that he was her cousin. But Lord Sturgess had quickly caught her up in his life so completely that he hadn't allowed her any time to continue *any* of her relationships with family and friends. Looking back, she knew it should have been an early sign that he was a controlling and selfish man. However, she had allowed herself to believe it was right for a woman to become involved in the life of the man she loved and intended to marry.

Meri forced her thoughts away from one of a thousand regrets she had regarding the choices she'd made that had brought her to this day. She smiled at Elliott and said, "It's so very good to see you, and I'm glad to know you'll be around. I've missed you; I've missed our conversations."

"As have I," he said eagerly. "So," he added, finally letting go of her hand to spread both of his arms across the back of the sofa, "our mutual aunt and uncle have told me very little about you these past years, but I *do* know you have children. Forgive me for not remembering *anything* about them. Of course, they must be here with you."

"Yes," Meri said and laughed softly just thinking about them; Crispin and Elaine were the *only* positive results of these terrible years, and their mere existence lightened her heart. "Elaine is six. She's very smart, and very observant. She's always surprising me, and she keeps me on my toes." She laughed again. "And Crispin is four. He too is very sharp for his age."

"How delightful," Elliott said. "How are they doing with the big changes in their life? Losing their father? Moving here? That's a lot for young children."

"Yes, it certainly is," Meri said. "And I've had a great deal of concern about how all of this might have impacted them. But they've settled in nicely here; everyone is so kind to them. The family. The staff. They're getting quite spoiled, actually." She looked at her hands in her lap and couldn't resist admitting what she considered an important point, even if it did offer a clue to the awful truth. "They deserve to be spoiled, I think. Life is far better for them here than it was before. Everyone was so . . . cold and forbidding there. And children were treated like . . . a necessary inconvenience."

"That's terrible!" Elliott said, validating her words with the sincerity of his statement.

"Yes, it is," Meri agreed. "And I had no control over the way the household was run; my husband's mother made certain of that." She sighed loudly. "Which is one of many reasons I'm glad to be here, and that my children have an environment where they can *be* children and be treated well."

"Amen to that!" Elliott said. "I look forward to meeting them." He chuckled. "I've not been around children much, so I don't know that I'll have any idea how to win them over, but I'd like to try."

"Just be yourself." Meri smiled at him. The mere thought of her children having Elliott in their lives to any degree felt soothing. "I'm certain they'll love you."

"I hope so," Elliott said and looked at her with a penetrating gaze that seemed to have some hidden meaning. Meri wanted to look away but couldn't. She was trying to discern what silent message he might be conveying. She'd once been able to read his emotions so easily, even when he didn't voice them. But at the moment, she had no idea why he would look at her that way.

"Is everything all right?" she asked, still returning his gaze as if she were in some kind of trance.

"I hope so," he said again and looked away abruptly, as if he'd just realized he'd been staring.

If only to dispel the sudden tension between them, Meri stood and said, "Would you like to meet the children now? They're playing with all the toys that *we* used to play with once upon a time."

"How delightful," Elliott said. He got to his feet as well, and Meri led the way even though she was well aware that he knew how to navigate through this house just as easily as she did.

Meri opened the door to the playroom and the children both jumped up to come and hug her, but they quickly returned to the puzzle that Alice had been helping them put together on the floor. They didn't even notice that someone else had entered the room with their mother.

"Elaine, Crispin," Meri said, "I would like you to meet someone." Their heads popped up and their eyes focused on the man at Meri's side. They looked both skeptical and curious. Meri impulsively took hold of Elliott's hand, certain it would illustrate to her children that she liked and trusted this man.

"This is Elliott Rosewell," she continued, noting that Alice too was curious but trying to be discreet. She had been here long enough that she might have seen Elliott on his previous visits, but it's possible that the work she'd done had not brought her into direct contact with him. "He is my cousin; well . . . sort of." She laughed softly. "He spent a great deal of time here during the years we were growing up, and we were very good friends right from our childhood. Now he's come to visit again." Meri looked at Elliott while she motioned toward the children. "Elliott, this is my daughter Elaine, and my son Crispin."

"It's very nice to meet you," Elliott said, bowing slightly as if he were addressing royalty.

The children said nothing and Meri prompted them. "Can you say hello?"

"Hello," they both said together, still staring at Elliott as if they were performing some detailed assessment.

"And this is Alice," Meri added, motioning toward the young woman. "I suppose we would officially call her the nanny, but she is much more than that. She does a very good job of helping me take care of the children; she's quickly become like family."

"A pleasure to meet you, Alice," Elliott said, nodding toward her respectfully.

"And you, sir," Alice said and put her attention back to the puzzle pieces she was sorting on the carpet.

Elaine stood up and moved a little closer. Looking up at Elliott she asked, "How can you be *sort of* a cousin to Mama? Are you a cousin like the sisters?" Meri smiled at the directness of her daughter, and at the way she'd picked up on calling her cousins *the sisters.* Meri had always referred to them that way when speaking of them as a group; it was much easier than referring to each of them by name.

"That's a very good question, Elaine," Elliott said, squatting down so that he met Elaine eye to eye. "Do you know how people have to be related to be cousins?"

Elaine nodded and said, "My grandmama who died is Auntie Annabel's sister, so my mama and Auntie Annabel's daughters are cousins."

"That is exactly correct," Elliott said. "Your mother told me that you were very smart; I can see that she's right. So, my father and Uncle Angus are brothers, and that's why I'm a cousin to his daughters. Even though Uncle Angus and Aunt Annabel are an uncle and aunt to both me and your mother, we are not actually related. So, we are *sort of* cousins. Does that make sense?"

Elaine thought about it for a long moment, then nodded. Meri noted that Crispin's expression was humorously distorted while he attempted to understand Elliott's explanation, but Elaine—as usual—was quick to comprehend just about anything. In her typical way of behaving more maturely than her age, she asked Elliott, "Where is your father who is Angus's brother?"

"He died a very long time ago," Elliott said, still looking directly at her and speaking to her with respect. "That is one of many reasons I always enjoyed coming to stay here. My aunt and uncle were always very good to me. Do you like living here?"

"I like it very much," Elaine said and returned to playing with Alice and her brother, as if she'd gotten all the information she needed to be comfortable with this newcomer. Crispin had apparently stopped trying to figure out Elliott's explanation and had returned his full attention to the puzzle.

"I'll let you get along with your project," Meri said to Alice, who smiled and nodded.

Meri escorted Elliott out of the room, but not before he could say, "It was very nice to meet you all." Alice looked up and smiled at him. The children both smiled and waved; Meri considered that a good sign. Given the way their father had treated them, she'd noticed they were sometimes hesitant about trusting strangers—men especially. But they'd come far in the short time since they'd begun this new life.

"They're delightful and adorable," Elliott said as soon as Meri closed the door. "But I would expect nothing less, knowing their mother as I do."

"Well," Meri laughed, ambling toward the stairs with Elliott at her side, "I've certainly tried to be a good mother, but I quickly learned—as any parent does—that children come to this world with their personalities, their gifts, their tendencies toward certain things already intact. I often feel more like I'm guiding them as opposed to actually teaching them much."

"It's evident they know you love them . . . and that you have confidence in them," Elliott said. "What could be more important than that?"

"And how could you possibly discern such a thing in only a few minutes?" she asked.

"I don't know how to explain it, Meri, but it seemed fairly obvious to me."

"Well, you're very kind, but—"

"I'm not trying to be kind, Meri. I'm just stating what I observed. You're obviously a very good mother."

Meri was surprised by a surge of emotion that tightened her chest and stung her eyes. She knew its source but didn't necessarily want to talk about it. Not once in the household of Lord Sturgess had anyone ever said or even hinted at the possibility that she was a good mother. In fact, it was quite the opposite. She'd been criticized and reproached continually. Since she'd come here, she'd felt respected as the mother of her children, but only Annabel had actually commented on her belief that Meri was doing well as a mother. For some reason, now, with Elliott, his words touched something inside of her that was painful and insecure. His validation meant a great deal to her, but now she was more concerned with not wanting him to see any evidence of the tears that were threatening to burst out of her.

Elliott barely kept himself from gasping aloud as he was overcome with a sudden wave of memories, a familiarity that made it difficult to breathe. He'd been wrestling with the feeling ever since he'd looked over his newspaper to see Meri standing in the solarium, the sun accentuating the slightly reddish hue in her otherwise brown hair. Her very presence had taken him back in time, consuming him with so many memories that he couldn't possibly expect his mind to process them all. And yet they were here in the present, with so many changes in both their lives. Still, he had once known Meri better than anyone else in his life; she had been his dearest friend, and he had been hers. They'd kept no secrets from each other, and they could talk about anything. He was glad to feel as comfortable with her now as he always had—almost. There was a mysterious air about her, something intangible that made him certain these years apart had not necessarily been good to her. He had sensed that she was haunted somehow, or perhaps that was a misguided projection resulting from his own haunted thoughts. Whatever it was, something deeply familiar struck him there in the hallway, not far from the nursery, when Meri discreetly put a hand over her mouth and increased the speed of her pace in order to get a few steps ahead of him. He knew the telltale signs very well. She was trying not to cry, and she didn't want him to know.

"Wait," he said and stopped, taking hold of her arm to force her to do the same. "What's wrong?"

Meri only looked down and kept a hand over her mouth.

"You *never* got away with trying to hide your tears from me, Meri; never. Why would you think you could get away with it now?" She shook her head but didn't speak, didn't look up.

Reverting to old habits, Elliott just put his arms around her and guided her head to his shoulder, offering a silent invitation for her to cry as much as she needed. He couldn't count the times she'd cried in his arms; and he'd cried in *her* arms more than a few times. It was only a moment before she took hold of his arms and buried her face against his waistcoat and wept. He put one hand to the back of her head and just let her cry, while that strange sensation of trying to connect the present to an ongoing flood of memories increased.

When Meri's emotion calmed down, she took a step back and let go of him, forcing him to let go of her despite his preferring not to.

"Forgive me," Meri said, wiping her hands over her cheeks. Elliott offered her a clean handkerchief from his pocket and she took it. "I don't know what came over me."

"Don't you?" he asked. "I suspect you do know, but perhaps you just don't want to talk about it. And that's all right, Meri. We haven't seen each other for years. I don't expect you to instantly be able to pour out your heart to me the way you once did. But I do want you to know that you can trust me as much now as you did then. If you *do* need someone to talk to, please. . . ."

"Thank you," she said. "It's not a matter of trust. I just . . . don't feel up to talking about it; about many things. Not yet. But . . ." She looked up at him with tears still glistening in her reddened eyes. "I'm very glad you're here."

"So am I," he said, hoping not to sound as overtly eager as he felt.

Meri laughed softly, seeming embarrassed. "Some things never change, I suppose," she said. "I remember so many times when I felt sad or upset about something, but I wouldn't shed a tear . . . until I was alone with you, and then I'd burst into tears and cry like a baby."

"As I recall, it was sometimes the other way around," he said. "I'd like to think it was because we felt safe with each other . . . perhaps more than we did with anyone else."

"That certainly makes sense," she said and began walking again. Elliott followed, hoping the fact that she'd just cried in his arms meant that she *still* felt safe with him. He wanted more than anything to take hold of everything they'd once shared and build upon it as the mature adults they had become. But there was so much that had happened in both their lives, and he reminded himself that it would be naive to think they could just pick up where they'd left off. She had two children, for heaven's sake. And he had hidden thoughts and memories he would prefer to never tell her.

Elliott followed Meri to the parlor where their aunt and uncle and all five of their cousins were chatting or reading or doing needlework. It was a familiar and comfortable situation, one that contributed to his feelings that nothing had changed despite the years that had passed. He'd spent a great deal of time here between his travels over the years, but he could always come back here and everything would be exactly the same, except for everyone growing a bit older and showing changes in their appearance.

"Oh, hello," Annabel said, looking up from her needlework. "I see the two of you found each other. I was going to tell you, Meri, that Elliott arrived late last night, but I haven't seen you yet this morning."

"And still I found him," Meri said, tossing a smile in Elliott's direction that made his heart quicken. "I just took him up to meet the children."

"Oh, how lovely," Annabel said. Angus, lost in his reading, didn't comment. The sisters each greeted Elliott kindly but nonchalantly, as if they were accustomed to his comings and goings. Then they each commented on how precious the children were and how much they enjoyed having Elaine and Crispin in the house. Meri and Elliott sat down to join the conversation. Elliott would have preferred not to have Meri sitting on the other side of the room, although her doing so made it easier for him to look at her without letting on that he thoroughly enjoyed doing so.

After a few minutes of casual conversation, lunch was announced. Elliott was delighted when he realized that Elaine and Crispin always joined the family for the midday meal. During the meal, he came to see more and more how Elaine was like a miniature adult, whose conversation with those around her often provoked humor. But Elaine always laughed with everyone else, as if she fully understood how funny she was. Crispin's personality was entirely different; he was more reticent and quiet—but he had trouble sitting still, which often led to his engaging in some mild mischief that appeared to have no other intention than to ease his own boredom. He put his head beneath the tablecloth, which was fine until he inadvertently snagged the cloth somehow and all the dishes on the table began to move. Meri was quick to solve the problem, but it evoked a great deal of laughter, to which Crispin appeared to be oblivious. After managing to sit still for a few minutes, he began putting his peas into his water glass one at a time, watching them with great interest. He seemed lost in deep thought while he was apparently performing some kind of experiment. He rearranged his silverware more than once, and created patterns with the food on his plate. Meri handled him calmly and with a smile. At one point, she smiled toward Elliott and said, "Yes, he's like this every day."

"How very entertaining," Elliott said.

"And exhausting," Meri replied with a melodramatic sigh that made everyone laugh.

Annabel made a comment about how delightful it was to have children in the house again, and both Hope and Comfort said something about how much they'd grown to love the children. Elaine ate her meal like a little lady and was praised for her good behavior in a way that let her know her efforts at good manners had not gone unnoticed, but at the same time, making it clear that Crispin's behavior was not being criticized. Elliott wondered what it might have been like for him if such distinctions had been made in his childhood, as opposed to continually being confronted with unfair comparisons and continual criticism. Neither Elliott nor his siblings could ever do anything right, but they had all been made to feel like they had to compete for favor and attention.

Elliott pushed away uncomfortable thoughts regarding his own family and focused on his enjoyment of the present. After lunch, it became evident that Meri sometimes took the children for a walk in the gardens or to the beach before their nap time on days when the weather was favorable. She declared that the fresh air and exercise were surely good for all of them, and that it also helped Crispin wear himself out somewhat so he might take a better nap and be calmer throughout the remainder of the day.

"May I come along?" Elliott asked, directing his question to the children. "Only if it's all right with your mother, of course. I don't want to intrude on your family time or—"

"We're only going for a walk in the garden," Elaine said, as if the idea of any intrusion was silly.

"Can he come, Mama?" Crispin asked Meri as if he'd never wanted anything so much in his entire life—even though he'd used the same tone when he'd asked for cake at lunch.

"Of course he can come," Meri said, smiling at Elliott as he followed them outside, secretly delighted by such an opportunity. When he'd made the decision a few weeks ago to return to England and stay with Annabel and Angus for a while, he'd been planning to do what he usually did—mostly keep to himself and show up occasionally to share tea or a meal with the family. But Meri and her children being here had changed everything. He'd missed Meri even more than he'd allowed himself to admit, and her children were delightful. He had every intention of being wherever they might be as much as he could possibly manage without making a pest of himself. As eager as he felt for their company, he knew he had to be very careful to avoid wearing out his welcome with them. For now, they were on their way to the gardens where he and Meri had played as childhood friends. Before they stepped outside, Elaine took hold of his hand as if she didn't want him to get lost. He smiled down at her and she returned his smile with an added sparkle in her eyes that reminded him so much of Meri. He felt like he'd truly come home.

Chapter Four
THE MISTAKE

MERI COULDN'T HELP NOTICING HOW much more pleasant her days had become since Elliott had returned. As much as she loved her aunt, uncle, and cousins, she couldn't spend too much time with them on any given day without feeling a certain frustration over the tedium of how they spent their hours. Annabel always had a sewing project to keep her hands busy while she sat with her husband and daughters, listening to their chatter more than contributing to it. When Meri had time alone with Annabel, their conversations were comfortable and loving, but when they were with the family, Annabel remained somewhat aloof, which felt mildly confusing to Meri—especially given that she hadn't spent any time alone with her aunt in weeks.

Angus mostly read, seeming completely oblivious unless he heard something in the conversation that provoked him to make a comment—usually a negative one. He obviously paid attention more than he let on; it was as if he purposely kept himself disconnected so he could choose not to be involved unless he wanted to be. His enthusiasm toward her and the children on the day they'd returned had completely disappeared.

The five sisters loved each other and their parents, and they had a strange dependency on each other that was difficult to define. They were like bees and flowers; one could not exist without the other. If one of the sisters was absent due to not feeling well, or in the rare event of them having somewhere else to be, the conversation lost something of its natural flow, like a stream with a large rock thrown in that forced the water to divert around it.

Upon Meri's return, she had quickly realized she felt more like an observer of this natural order of things in the Rosewell household. At first, she attributed it to having been away for so many years, but on further examination she realized now that she'd *always* been somewhat on the outside looking in. For all that she and her cousins were close and loved each other—and Meri was in their same age group—she was dramatically different in many ways. She often found herself thinking at a deeper level regarding their topics of discussion, but she kept her thoughts to herself because she knew from experience that trying to analyze literature or local happenings or emotions too deeply would only make her feel slightly odd and out of place, as if the established dynamic of the family was to keep everything at a certain shallow level. It was as if they were all on a little fishing boat, sailing aimlessly along, never caring to look up or down and see the vast sky above them or the depths of the ocean beneath, failing to consider that the world was so much larger, more amazing, and vastly more complex than any of them cared to acknowledge.

All of this settled in more clearly to Meri when Elliott returned and became a part of their family gatherings every day. After the two of them had ended up discussing one topic or another in depth while the rest of the family looked on, appearing confused and disinterested, Meri realized that Elliott was in the same position, and he likely felt the same way. The reasons they had been so close in their younger years made more sense now that she could look back and see all of this from an adult perspective.

Four days after Elliott's arrival, Meri found herself growing agitated over a lighthearted argument taking place between two of her cousins and their father about whether people born into privilege were naturally more intelligent. Meri disagreed so strongly that she wanted to burst out and say that more than one of them had attitudes that were judgmental and ridiculous and perhaps even contrary to the Christian beliefs they claimed to uphold. To avoid saying something that would only cause a fruitless dispute, Meri stood up and declared, "I'm feeling a bit restless. I believe I'll go for a walk."

"Enjoy the fresh air, dear," Annabel said without looking up from her stitching. Her light tone implied that she was completely detached from the conversation going on around her.

"Thank you; I will," Meri said and hurried out of the room. Knowing that the children were enjoying their playtime with Alice, she went directly out to her favorite section of the garden.

Meri stopped walking when she heard Elliott call, "Wait!" She watched him run toward her, noting how the wind tugged at his hair. He'd trimmed his beard since he'd returned, and she couldn't deny that it suited him; he looked more handsome than he ever had—and he'd always been handsome.

Elliott chuckled as he stopped next to her and took a moment to catch his breath. "If you get to escape all that nonsense, there is no way I am going to sit there and be subjected to it."

Meri laughed softly and they began to walk slowly, side by side. "And you don't think anyone will think it strange that you followed me out?"

"We always left together when we were younger. In fact, Annabel said as much when I got up to leave—as if she'd expected it. No one seemed to care. I wonder sometimes if they are more comfortable when I'm *not* there."

"I'm sure none of them would ever want us to not feel welcome."

"I'm sure of that too," Elliott said. "But we never really did fit in with them, did we?"

"No, I suppose we didn't. I hadn't thought of it that way until recently. I suppose when you're young you just accept things as they are. Now I find their conversation tedious and sometimes annoying."

"And shallow," Elliott added.

"Yes, shallow," she agreed. "Was it always shallow?"

"I think so, yes. In my opinion, they've all remained in their very small world all these years, while you and I have experienced life in different ways. Perhaps that's why it's become more difficult to sit and listen to their narrow views."

"I couldn't have said it better myself."

Alone with Elliott, Meri could freely express everything she'd been thinking, and she wasn't surprised to hear that he very much shared her perspective. While there was a great deal about their years apart that Meri never wanted Elliott to know, she could admit, "Even though my time away has been difficult in many respects, I would never want to remain that naive and oblivious to the plight of others."

"I agree," he said and stopped walking between two long rows of pristine shrubbery that created the effect of a long hallway. Meri stopped and turned to face him, wondering what might be on his mind. His next words were mildly surprising. "How is it that you keep saying things that perfectly express my own thoughts?"

Meri thought about this for a long moment while she considered the intensity of his gaze and her own inability to look away. "That's the way it's always been, hasn't it?"

"Yes," he said. "Yes, Meri, it's always been that way."

A tremor erupted in Meri's stomach and rushed up through her heart, coming out of her mouth on the wave of a lengthy sigh. She didn't want to compare Elliott to her husband, but as much as she tried not to, it kept happening inside her head almost continually. In that moment, she realized her husband had *never* looked at her the way Elliott was looking at her right now. Without saying a word, his gaze implied that he believed her to be beautiful and strong and valuable. He'd always looked at her that way, but until she'd experienced years of marriage to a man who hadn't ever really looked at her at all, she had never noticed enough to fully appreciate what it meant to her.

Another tremor went through her, this time creating a knot of emotion in her throat. Once again, just being with Elliott was spurring some inexplicable urge to cry, when tears normally refused to come to the surface no matter how much pain she might be feeling. Hoping to hide her emotion until she could get control of it, she resumed walking and assumed he would join her. But he caught hold of her arm to stop her, saying with confidence and compassion, "I know very well you're on the verge of tears and you're trying to hide it . . . again. You should know better than to think I'd let you get away with that."

For a long moment, Meri vacillated between relief and embarrassment, but she had no desire to give in to the temptation to cry. She successfully fought back her tears but didn't resist the way that Elliott wrapped her in a soothing embrace that made it easier to suppress her sorrow and feel calmer. She became keenly aware of the fine texture of his brocade waistcoat as she pressed her face against his chest and breathed deeply. She tried to think of a way to explain her reasons for accepting his comfort, but she honestly didn't know what to say because she hardly knew why herself. Or perhaps she knew, but she was determined to never tell him or anyone else how bad the last seven years had really been.

Elliott couldn't help wondering over the source of Meri's obvious need for succor. Her lack of tears could never fool him into believing that she wasn't struggling with a great deal of sorrow and grief. He only wished he knew why. The last few days had absolutely been the best of his adult life. He'd shared many long conversations with Meri, which had been stimulating and enjoyable—even though he knew they were both avoiding any discussion of certain facets of what had occurred during their years apart. Not only had he enjoyed being able to talk to someone who truly understood him, he'd fallen head over heels for Elaine and Crispin. He loved playing with them, and he loved the way they had so quickly become comfortable enough with him to fully allow him into their childhood world where they could laugh and play, and they would talk to him, each in their own way, about all the wondrous thoughts that were going through their inquisitive minds. But it was their mother he felt concerned about. He wondered what he might say when she inevitably separated herself from this momentary need she had to silently accept his supportive embrace. He concluded that he had no idea, but he couldn't deny how much he enjoyed holding her close, and how grateful he was that she felt safe enough to share her sorrow with him.

When Meri sighed deeply as if to conclude whatever she might be struggling with, Elliott expected her to let go of him and step back as she had done before, but she tightened her arms around him, and he couldn't help but respond to her embrace by returning it. She finally eased away and looked up at him; for a long moment, their eyes connected and he saw something there that reflected his own feelings. He couldn't be sure, but he defaulted to his deepest instincts and leaned forward slowly with the intent to kiss her. He wanted to give her fair warning in case she had no interest, but he still felt starkly disappointed when she stepped away and turned her back to him, making it clear that his advance had been unwanted. He felt both embarrassed and taken off guard. But he wasn't going to leave his feelings unspoken and subject to any kind of misinterpretation or distortion. He'd spent years regretting the fact that he'd not shared his feelings with her before she'd ever had a chance to be courted by any other man. He would not face such regrets again. The very fact that they were both here now—and she had become unexpectedly widowed—seemed nothing less than a miracle to him. He never would have believed it could happen, but he wasn't going to deny how blessed he felt to be given a second chance.

Considering the most obvious reasons for her refusing his kiss, he said gently, "Forgive me, Meri. I know you're in mourning still. It's not been so terribly long since you lost your husband, and . . . sometimes I forget.

It was not my intention to offend or upset you, but . . ." He considered his next words carefully, and decided he would rather risk having her possibly be upset with him, as opposed to holding the truth inside and wondering when or how he might ever get back to a place where he could say what he was thinking. "I thought you wanted me to kiss you, Meri. The . . . way you looked at me; the way you've been . . . behaving around me. I really thought that . . ." He cleared his throat, wishing he could see her face. "If I misread your feelings, you need to tell me. I need to know where we stand." Still she didn't speak and he began to feel decidedly uncomfortable. He'd exposed his deepest feelings, and the vulnerability he felt was far from pleasant. After more silence, he decided again that he just needed to state his concerns and be done with it. As he'd just told her, he needed to know where they stood.

"Meri, listen to me," he said in a voice that was quiet but firm, "if you're simply not ready for anything romantic in your life right now, just tell me; I'll wait. I'll wait for as long as it takes. If . . ."—this option was more difficult to put into words and he hesitated—". . . you have no interest in that kind of relationship with me, then . . . tell me. Just tell me. We can forget this ever happened, and . . . go back to being friends. I pray you don't let my foolishness come between us. Not now; not ever."

Meri still said nothing, and still her back was turned to him. But he noticed the way her shoulders moved up and down, indicating that she shared his present difficulty to breathe. The possible reasons for it left him terrified.

"Meri, please speak to me. I beg you to say something and put me out of my misery."

Meri turned so abruptly to look at him that it startled him. She met his eyes directly but he had no idea if she was about to give him hope or break his heart.

"I'm not mourning, Elliott," she said.

"What?" he asked, not because he hadn't heard her, but because he didn't understand.

"I never loved him," she went on. "I thought I did, but whatever I felt quickly faded when his lack of love for me became evident even before the honeymoon was over. How can I mourn for someone I didn't love? His death was a relief to me." She looked down and laughed uncomfortably, with no hint of humor. "That's an awful thing for a woman to say about her husband; I always thought it was an awful way to feel. But that's the truth of it." She looked back up at him. "Does that shock you? That I would admit to such a thing? Are you disappointed in me?"

"No, Meri; it doesn't shock me, and I'm not disappointed. I'm glad you told me."

"Of course, there are certain social expectations that are required of a widow. I don't want to cause any stir in the community by behaving inappropriately—for the sake of the family."

"Of course," he agreed, hoping now she would tell him that with time there might be hope of their sharing a future together.

"But . . ." her gaze tightened on him, ". . . it's only fair for you to know that . . . I *did* want you to kiss me." He took in a trembling breath. "I just wanted you to know *why.*"

"Of course," he said again, expecting her to repeat her concerns about social propriety. And he could live with that; as long as he had the hope that she might one day be his, he could live with almost anything.

Elliott pulled in his breath and held it when she stepped toward him and took hold of his arms, lifting her face toward his, openly inviting him to kiss her. "Meri," he whispered before he closed his eyes and pressed his lips to hers. Their lips touching sent a wave of light rushing to every nerve and cell of his body, filling his spirit with such remarkable joy and peace that he could almost believe if he opened his eyes he would see light shooting out of his fingertips and emanating from him with a distinct glow. He felt as if his entire life would be measured by this moment; he'd wanted this moment for more years than he could count, and now that it had happened he believed that every event he'd experienced would be put into compartments of before or after he'd finally kissed Meri.

He had barely concluded his first kiss before he kissed her again, urged on by the way she softened in his arms and responded to his affection as if she too were experiencing a life-altering moment. Reminding himself to be a gentleman, he eased his lips reluctantly from hers and slowly opened his eyes to see her face so close to his that he could feel the breath that slowly escaped through her lips. He watched her eyes come hesitantly open, which set free the tears that spilled down her cheeks.

"Why are you crying?" he asked in a whisper, pressing his hand over the side of her face while he wiped away a tear with his thumb.

Considering how hard she had fought to keep from crying not so many minutes ago, he wondered why she would allow herself to do so now.

"I never imagined," she whispered in reply, "that a kiss could be so . . . pleasant."

Elliott took that in as one more clue that her marriage had not been what it should have. But he chose not to think about that; he wanted to enjoy and appreciate every facet of this moment. To him, her husband's death—which had set her free—was nothing short of a miracle.

"I need to tell you something," he said, following his instincts, which were encouraged by the dreamy warmth in her eyes.

"Tell me," she urged and he wondered if she already knew what he needed to say, or perhaps she suspected.

Elliott took a deep breath and just said it, "I made a mistake, Meri. You were always my best friend, but in my mind—and in my heart—you were much more than that. We've been close since we were children, but from the moment I knew how it felt to be attracted to a woman, it was you and only you that consumed my thoughts. But we were so young, and I was afraid to tell you." His breath trembled as his confession became more difficult. "I was waiting, Meri; waiting until I was old enough to be a respectable husband." He saw wonder in her eyes, and perhaps confusion, but he saw nothing there that made him afraid to keep going.

"I was waiting for my inheritance to come, and then I knew that I could offer you a good life. I just didn't expect anyone else to come between us. Your being seventeen made you old enough as a woman to be married, but my being twenty did not make me old enough to be considered a suitable husband. And I had just assumed you felt the same way . . . that you loved me the way I love you. But I should have asked; I should have said something. It's the biggest mistake of my life, Meri. I thought I would get over it, but I never did. No matter how far I traveled, or the new friends I made, or the things I've experienced, I could never stop thinking of you. I never stopped feeling jealous of him, and I never stopped being angry with myself for not telling you how I felt. I should have never let you marry him. I should have told you to just wait for me. We could have been together all these years, Meri. Your children would be my children. It shouldn't have been this way, and it's my fault. I made a mistake, Meri, and I'm so sorry. I'm so very, very sorry for everything you've been through. I love you now more than ever, and you need to know that."

Elliott forced himself to take a deep breath that would fill his lungs when he realized he'd been talking so fast that he'd barely been breathing at all. He was glad to have finally said what he'd wanted to say ever since he'd come home to find Meri here, but now he had to wonder what her reaction might be. Her eyes were still soft and warm, but he had no idea what she was thinking. He held his breath when she put a hand to his face just before she said, "It was no more your fault than mine, Elliott. I knew you loved me, and I loved you. But I was afraid of the disruption it would cause in the family if you and I were to marry."

"Disruption?" he echoed, having no idea to what she referred.

"It doesn't matter now," she said softly. "I can look back and see that in the grand scheme of life, such disruption would be nothing compared to other challenges. I made a mistake too, Elliott. I should have been braver; I should have spoken my feelings. I was naive and gullible, and Lord Sturgess led me to believe that he loved me and could provide everything I would ever want or need. I chose what seemed the easiest path at the time, having no idea that it was all wrong."

Elliott just looked at her, feeling momentarily frozen while he considered which question he wanted to ask first. His mind was stuck on her mention of the *disruption* that would have been caused in the family if they had married. He had absolutely no idea what she meant by that, and it made him decidedly uncomfortable. But he was also caught up in all she'd just confessed about her feelings for him. While he'd been contending all these years with his love for her, he'd never imagined that she could have been in a loveless marriage and experiencing her own regrets. It was clearly going to take some time and pondering for his mind to catch up to everything that had just been said—especially when he was practically giddy over the way she'd returned his kiss. He'd been dreaming of such a moment for years, and it had finally happened. He was so overcome he could barely breathe.

Elliott was relieved to hear the children's voices calling for their mother. Despite wanting more time alone with her, he was glad to have a distraction that would give him time to mull over such a huge wave of information. Meri hurried toward the sound of their voices as they came closer, and Elliott just watched her go. When she emerged from the long rows of shrubbery, Elaine and Crispin launched themselves toward her with such force that she almost toppled over, but she only laughed and knelt to wrap them in her arms. Alice appeared as well but no one noticed Elliott standing some distance away where he just watched the happy reunion and tried to comprehend how deeply he loved Meri, and how quickly he'd grown to love her children. He never wanted to be away from Meri again; not ever! He wanted to care for and protect her and her children. He wanted Crispin and Elaine to come to see *him* as their father. It was only right for him to respect the social propriety of her being a widow. But as soon as it was possible to publicly court her without bringing any scandal to the family, he intended to do so. He felt no reason to ever leave here again, and if he did he would be taking Meri and her children with him.

* * *

Meri sat on the patio watching Elliott play with her children on the lawn nearby. They were all chasing each other around chaotically and laughing as they played some kind of made-up game that made absolutely no sense whatsoever. Meri still felt overcome by the conversation—and the affection—she and Elliott had shared the day before, and they'd not had a minute alone since to even comment on how they were each feeling. With Meri trying to spend as much time with her children as she could, and not wanting to alert anyone in the household to this budding romance with Elliott—for several reasons—being able to have a private conversation with him would have been awkward and surely would not have gone unnoticed. Now, as Meri watched him playing with the children, she doubted that she had ever felt so content. Knowing how Elliott felt about her—along with his growing affection for Elaine and Crispin—gave her a hope for the future that she'd never thought possible. She reminded herself not to be presumptuous or hasty. They certainly needed to give the matter some time. Still, there was hope.

Meri laughed when Elliott put Crispin on his shoulders and ran, as if to protect him from Elaine, who was chasing after them like a wild beast. A few minutes later, Elliott put Crispin down and pretended to collapse from exhaustion—although she felt certain the children had surely worn him out. They could do that well enough. While the children kept running, Meri saw Elliott look toward her from where he was laying on the lawn. He smiled with a glimmer in his eyes that implied they shared a wondrous secret. And they did. Her stomach flipped over and her heart quickened as she returned his smile, and a moment later Elaine and Crispin catapulted themselves on top of him, which took him off guard, after which he laughed and managed to tickle them both at the same time.

"He certainly has taken to the children," Charity said, startling Meri to the realization that her cousin had just come out of the house.

"He certainly has," Meri said.

"I'm sure it's good for them to have a grown man who will play with them," Hope said, and Meri realized that *two* of her cousins had come out.

"They must miss their father terribly," Comfort said, and all *three* of them sat down to watch the antics taking place on the lawn.

Meri didn't comment. Elaine and Crispin couldn't miss a man they had hardly known, and what they *had* known of him had been only frightening. They'd *never* played with an adult the way that Elliott had taken to playing with them. Meri did well at reading stories and playing on the floor with any numbers of toys that didn't require her to move much, since doing so in a dress was nigh to impossible. Alice was a little more active in her play than Meri, but men obviously played with children differently—and wearing breeches certainly made it easier to do so. Meri finally said, "Yes, I'm sure it's good for them to play with a grown man. They're clearly having a wonderful time."

Meri listened to her cousins exchange small talk while she kept her focus on the entertainment taking place on the lawn. After a short while, Elliott convinced the children that he needed a rest and he walked over to join Meri and the cousins. "Hello, ladies," he said. "Don't you all look lovely this morning."

"I never imagined you would be so good with children," Charity said to him as he sat down.

Meri wondered whether that was meant as a compliment or a mild criticism, but Elliott just said, "I never imagined it myself, but I do believe I like being able to act like a child at my age." He chuckled at himself, and the ladies all joined him. Meri tried not to look at him directly, fearing one of her cousins might notice the affection she felt for him that surely had to show on her face. She kept her focus on the children and participated very little in the conversation. A short while after Elliott had sat down, a maid came out to tell them that lunch was being served. Meri called for the children and they came running straightaway, probably because they were hungry. Elaine and Crispin went into the house with her cousins, who were all asking them questions about what they'd been playing. The sisters had all taken well to the children too, even if they didn't actively play with them. Meri followed behind the little crowd and gasped softly when she felt Elliott's hand on her back. There was no one behind them to notice, and she could feel nothing but grateful for a reminder that she'd not imagined their time together yesterday in the gardens.

"I'm hoping you will join me in the library this afternoon," he said in a normal tone of voice, almost as if he hoped the others would overhear. "I'm dying to talk to you about the book I've been reading."

Such an activity had been common between them in their youth, and no one would think a thing of it. Meri quickly replied, "I would very much like to hear about it."

Elliott then whispered close to her ear, "And if I don't get some time alone with you, my darling, I will lose my mind."

"We have been kept rather busy, haven't we," Meri whispered back.

"It's like a conspiracy," he said lightly and they all went into the dining room where Hope and Joy were helping the children get situated on their chairs. As always, Crispin's chair had a couple of very large books on it to increase his height so he could more easily reach his meal.

Lunch was pleasant despite the typical shallow conversation among the adults. But Meri didn't mind so much when the children were there, since they remained the center of attention, and the adults were less likely to gossip or discuss certain topics in their presence. After the meal was over, Alice came to ask if Meri would like to take the children for a walk before nap time, or if she would like Alice to do so. Meri was glad to relinquish the care of the children to Alice, knowing they would rest better after a good walk, and Meri felt the need for some time with Elliott. Alice would then take the children upstairs for a nap, which would give Meri even more time. Elaine rarely if ever actually fell asleep, but she did have quiet time in her bed with picture books to look at, and Crispin always needed a nap. He was full of so much energy that if he didn't rest in the afternoon he would be immensely cranky in the evening.

The family all went to the parlor for coffee, as they always did after lunch, but Meri felt impatient to be able to slip away and have some time alone with Elliott. The previous day, unexpected company had arrived at about this time and it would have been rude to leave. Today Meri couldn't keep herself from glancing at the clock, just waiting for a suitable amount of time to pass before she could excuse herself.

Elliott fought to keep himself from looking at Meri any more than he looked at anyone else in the room, but oh how he wanted to kiss her! He noticed her frequently glancing at the clock, which made him smile, secretly hoping her thoughts were the same as his. He was willing to politely remain here a few more minutes, and then he intended to be off to the library, taking Meri with him.

While Angus was hidden—as usual—behind a newspaper, he made a comment about something he was reading. An estate in the next county had been sold to a wealthy American because there had been no progeny of this very old family to whom the property would be bequeathed. Angus was astonished that an estate which had been in the same family for many generations would be sold, and he was downright appalled to know that it would be purchased by an American.

"I'm just glad it's not near enough to cause any stir around here," Angus concluded and turned the page of his newspaper.

"It might be exciting to have Americans in the community," Faith said with enthusiasm, but her father turned down the corner of the paper to glare at her and she looked at the floor.

Some silence passed as if no one else wanted to comment for fear of having Angus glare at *them.* Elliott wondered if it had always been like this—with Annabel hardly saying a word and Angus criticizing much of what his daughters said—and he realized that it *had.* He'd simply been too young to notice that it was awkward and not necessarily pleasant. And during his visits through more recent years, he had mostly avoided these family gatherings. Now this strange interaction only made him even more impatient to leave the room.

The silence was broken when Angus spoke without taking his eyes off his newspaper. "I'm glad to know we don't have to worry about ever losing *this* estate."

"We don't?" Comfort asked, practically taking the words right out of Elliott's mouth. Angus had only daughters; surely he had to be concerned about the laws regarding such things.

"We all know," Angus added, "that when I'm gone this house and all of the estate will legally belong to you, Elliott. It was set up that way when you were still a child."

"What?" Elliott exclaimed, astonished. Angus tipped his paper down only long enough to gaze directly at Elliott. As the implication of Angus's words set in, Elliott tried not to feel upset. He glanced at Meri and noted the alarm in her eyes, but it was also evident that she had known about this. She looked away, and he turned to glare at his uncle, wishing the fire in his eyes could burn through that stupid newspaper. "*I* didn't know," Elliott declared. "That's preposterous! This house is for your daughters, and you surely—"

"Daughters do not inherit property, young man," Angus said in a tone that implied Elliott was inane. "And you've surely noticed," he added with a subtle but biting criticism, "that none of my daughters have produced any kind of heir." Angus tipped down the corner of the paper again and looked directly at Elliott as if this was somehow his fault. Elliott stole a quick glance at his cousins, noting varying degrees of shame and embarrassment in their expressions.

Elliott looked back at his uncle, glaring at him in a way he hoped would convey that he would not be manipulated or forced into whatever ridiculous notion Angus was implying. "Let me make myself clear, Uncle," Elliott said. "I have never been made aware of any expectation of my inheriting Rosewell Abbey, and if such is the case, I will of course be certain that your family is well cared for and they will want for nothing. This is their home. However, I will not tangle matters of inheritance or any other legal nonsense into matters of the heart. When I *do* marry it will be for love—the kind of love that should exist between a husband and wife. I love my cousins dearly; they are each precious to me. But I will not humiliate or degrade any one of them—or myself—by allowing some ancient ritual of arranged marriages to be a part of my life, or theirs."

Feeling decidedly angry—especially when his uncle looked so disappointed, or perhaps disgusted with him—Elliott stood and bowed politely toward his cousins, who all looked both sheepish and astonished. "Forgive me, ladies, for being so brash. I wish to reiterate how I love and respect you all with sincerest affection." They each nodded, seeming to understand, but it occurred to him that it was possible they had all known about this for years, and perhaps more than one of them had been secretly hoping he would marry them. He wanted to run from the room and hide. But he forced his dignity to remain intact as he turned toward his uncle and said firmly, "I mean you no disrespect, sir. Forgive me if

I've disappointed you. And I hope you'll understand the difficulty of my position, especially when I've never had any knowledge of the situation. I hope we can discuss this privately at another time."

Angus said nothing and Elliott hurried from the room, fearing he would explode—and he needed to do so far away from anyone who might hear him, and anything he might be tempted to break. He headed to the library where he knew he could find solitude and respite, and he knew that Meri would seek him out there if she was able to get away from the drama that had just erupted in the parlor. He desperately wanted to talk to her—because she could always help him see reason, but also because she had obviously known about this for a long time. Despite wanting to talk to Meri, he hoped she wouldn't show up until he'd had time to calm down. He felt utterly furious! He felt as if his place in this home, among his uncle's family, had just been tainted and the taint could never be washed away. And to think that everyone else had known about this since his childhood—except for him—made him feel like an absolute fool.

Elliott was relieved when Meri came into the room and closed the door, but he still felt angry and he had to remind himself to remain calm and not get upset with *her.* He barely glanced at her over his shoulder before he turned back to the view out the window.

"I told them I would talk to you," she said, adding more lightly, "And so we finally have some time alone."

"Not exactly what I was hoping for," he said, his tone acrid.

"I sincerely believe they all thought you knew; that your mother would have told you."

Elliott turned and leaned against the windowsill, folding his arms over his chest. Meri was leaning back against the door, her eyes filled with concern. He decided to just get to the point and get it over with.

"Is *that* what you meant by *disruption*?" he demanded. "When you told me the other day that you were afraid of the disruption that would be caused in the family if you and I were to marry? Is that what you were talking about?"

"Yes," she said in a voice that indicated it had taken courage for her to admit it.

Elliott shook his head, unable to believe it. "So . . ." he asked hesitantly, "you knew that our aunt and uncle expected me to marry one of their daughters?"

Meri wrung her hands and looked at the floor. "Annabel told me years ago that it was understood Lawrence would inherit the home he'd grown up in, and you would inherit Rosewell Abbey, and that it was expected—or at least hoped for—that you would marry one of Angus's daughters to keep the estate securely in the family."

The reference to his older brother provoked a shudder that ran down Elliott's back, but he pushed thoughts of Lawrence away to focus on the present.

"Remarkable," Elliott said with an angry sarcasm that he didn't attempt to conceal, "that no one *ever* bothered to tell *me.* Now it's become embarrassing and awkward in more ways than I can possibly count." He groaned and pushed his hands into his hair. "How am I ever supposed to be in the same room with them again and not feel this hovering over us like some dark cloud threatening to break open and soak us all with these ridiculous assumptions and speculations? Do you suppose my cousins banter about me and place bets on which one of them might catch my eye?" He'd said the last with sarcasm, thinking of it as a joke, but Meri's countenance tightened and he felt a little nauseous as he said incredulously, "They do? Please don't tell me they do!"

Meri sighed. "They always have."

"Oh, this cannot be real!" Elliott growled.

Meri finally looked at him. "How could I have possibly declared to my cousins that I loved you and I knew that you loved me? I wasn't born here. Angus and Annabel are not my parents. For all that my cousins loved me and treated me like a sister, I believed that setting my sights on you would have alienated me from them for good. This is the only home and family I have, Elliott, and I just wasn't brave enough to take on whatever repercussions might have occurred."

"Well, this is the only home that ever felt like home to me; the only family that I believed loved me without condition. And now I wonder what motives might have always been a part of their making me feel so welcome and comfortable. It's all ruined now, Meri. If I'd known about this years ago I could have made my feelings clear and put all of this to rest, but now I realize these ridiculous speculations have been going on for years, and I have no idea where I really stand in this family."

"I can understand why you feel the way you do," Meri said, "but you cannot possibly believe they are so shallow and selfish that their entire motive has been about this. They all sincerely love you and care about you; I know they do. And for all that Angus speaks his mind so boldly—far too boldly most of the time, as we both know—I believe that Annabel and the sisters have a far more realistic view of all this. I believe their speculations have been more in a spirit of humor than any serious intent—at least it's become that way now that we are all well into adulthood. From what I've heard and observed, every one of them has accepted the likelihood that they will remain unmarried, and they've made peace with it. You mustn't allow this to make you uncomfortable here; this is your home."

"Yes," Elliott said with increased sarcasm, "literally and legally, it seems." He sighed and looked toward the window. "I don't think I can stay here, Meri."

"What?" Meri countered and moved to where she could look at him directly. "This is where *I* am—and the children! What of us? Am I to take your recent declarations to be sincere or not? Is your own discomfort more important than what we've come to share? Than the hope we have of sharing a future together? You've made yourself a part of my children's lives! Would you leave now and break their hearts? And mine? You can't keep running and hiding, Elliott. This will only remain awkward if you avoid it or allow it to be that way. If Angus chooses to remain huffy, so be it. He hides behind his newspapers anyway. Surely you can appropriately clarify your feelings and we can all go forward."

Elliott felt decidedly put in his place—and grateful for it. He took a minute to let her words saturate his bruised pride before he said, "You're right. Forgive me." He pulled her close and wrapped his arms around her. "And what of you and me, Meri? Will they truly be happy for us when they find out? Or will there be resentment?"

"I don't know," she said, tightening her arms around him. "It doesn't matter. When the time is right we will explain our feelings—and our intentions. It will be up to each of them to determine how they will respond." She looked up at him and he saw the glisten of tears in her eyes. Her chin quivered as she said, "Don't ever leave me, Elliott. Promise me. I never imagined it would be possible for us to be together, but now that you've come back into my life . . . now that I know you love me as I love you . . . I could never bear to be without you again. Promise me."

"I promise," he said firmly. "If I ever *do* leave here, I'm taking you and the children with me. Wherever we go from here, Meri, we go together.

I promise." She nodded, clearly relieved by his promise, which made him even more regretful for his immature outburst.

Chapter Five

A Version of Matchmaking

"Come here," Elliott said and eased Meri closer before he kissed her the way he'd been wanting to ever since their conversation in the garden two days ago had been interrupted. "I love you, Meri," he said, looking into her eyes while he touched her face, simply because he could. For years he'd remained behind an invisible barrier that had kept them apart, and now he'd finally been able to break past that wall and express his true feelings.

"And I love you," she whispered and kissed him again.

An idea sprung into his mind clearly and abruptly and he knew he needed to address this *disruption* here and now. He wasn't going to spend a single hour with any potential assumptions or awkwardness over this. He kissed Meri once more, then took her hand and headed toward the door.

"Come along," he said.

"Where are we going?" she asked, sounding a little frightened.

Elliott stopped and turned to look at her, knowing she deserved an explanation. "As much as I would like to remain here and just spend some time with you, I am not going to feel comfortable until this is addressed."

"What do you mean?" she asked, more curious than afraid.

"I'm going to take your advice, Meri. I'm going to appropriately clarify my feelings so we can all go forward."

"Right now?" she asked as he resumed his path toward the door.

"Right now," he said and opened the door, letting go of her hand once they were in the hallway. "I assume you will support me in my declarations."

"Of course," she said, walking at his side, in step with his brisk pace. "I assume you will be polite."

"Of course," he said, tossing her a little smile to let her know that his anger had been soothed. The shock of what he'd learned had dissipated, but he knew he needed to act on the need he felt to clear the air before the issue had time to evaporate into silent tension and uncomfortable assumptions. He'd experienced enough of both in this household that he knew exactly how that could be, and he didn't want it happening over something that involved him so directly.

Elliott entered the parlor with Meri at his side to find everyone exactly as they'd been when he'd left the room in a huff.

"There's something I need to say," Elliott declared, and the women all looked up. Angus grunted but remained behind his newspaper. Meri sat down and folded her hands in her lap, implying that this was up to him. "Uncle," Elliott said, "this is important. Could you please set the paper aside long enough for me to say what needs to be said?"

Angus folded his paper with a vehemence that implied his dislike of being asked to do so. He set it aside and looked at Elliott as if he were a naughty child. Elliott knew the look well, but he also knew from many other experiences that Angus loved him. For all his gruffness and even his inability to know how to be kind and respectful at times, Elliott knew that his uncle was a good man, and he believed that they would come to terms with this. But that would never happen if Elliott didn't act like a man and stand up appropriately against these strange assumptions his uncle had apparently been harboring for years without Elliott's knowledge.

"What is it, son?" Angus asked impatiently, and it occurred to Elliott that this man was dreadfully uncomfortable with any kind of confrontation or discord, and perhaps that was the very reason he chose to hide behind his newspapers.

Elliott took a deep breath and blew it out slowly. A quick glance at Meri enhanced his courage. "I just need to make it absolutely clear—even at the risk of repeating myself—that I had no knowledge of this stipulation regarding the ownership of your estate. And I meant what I said: I will *always* make certain that your daughters are cared for and that this remains their home—no matter what. I will meet with a solicitor and make certain that it's all taken care of legally in the event that anything should happen to me. I don't want any of you to ever worry about your security in that regard."

Elliott took a moment to gauge the temperature of the room. A quick glance at each face showed him that the women all seemed relaxed and comfortable in their expectation of what else he might say. Angus still looked a little miffed, but he was listening, so Elliott pressed on.

"I also want to make it clear that while I love each of my cousins dearly, they are like sisters to me. I have never felt the kind of love for any of your daughters that should be present in a marriage. I must follow my heart when it comes to marriage, Uncle. I know you love Annabel dearly, and I believe you understand what I'm saying. This is feeling terribly awkward for me at the moment, and I don't want it to be that way. You all know this is more of a home to me than my own home ever was. I don't want this to become an issue that creates discomfort for any of us."

"Oh, my dear," Annabel said and came to her feet. She put her hands on the sides of Elliott's face. "We all just assumed that you knew, but you mustn't feel out of place over this. We love having you here."

"Thank you, Aunt," he said and she went on her tiptoes to kiss his cheek before returning to her seat.

A terrible silence settled over the room while Elliott tried to think of what else he might need to say. He was hoping for reassurance from his uncle, but realized he likely wouldn't get it. Angus looked less defensive, but he wasn't one to speak words of comfort or kindness. It was more likely that over the next few weeks Elliott would be able to slowly discern Angus's acceptance from their simple interactions.

Elliott was considering how to simply thank them for listening when Faith surprised him by saying, "I think I speak for my sisters when I say that we all knew many years ago that marriage would never be a possibility for any of us. You know that we all love you, and we're very fond of your company, but it's as you said—you are like a brother to us. There is no need for you to feel discomfort over this with any of us." She glanced at each of her sisters as if to assess whether they agreed with her and they all nodded in a way that seemed to give their vote of approval and to encourage her to go on. Faith looked directly at Elliott as she added, "We are very grateful to know that you will let us live out our lives in our home, but let me clarify that we never feared otherwise. We know you well enough to know that you would always see us cared for, and that our needs would be met. You've always had a good heart, Elliott, which is why we care for you as we do, and we certainly don't want there to be any cause for awkwardness among us."

"Thank you, Faith," Elliott said, more grateful than he could say for her willingness to speak up and say what he needed to hear. He appreciated the fact that Faith had taken on the role of speaking for her sisters—some of them being too shy or naive to articulate complicated thoughts and feelings. It was as if Faith had at some point made a conscious decision to say the things that her parents most often wouldn't say. He looked at the other women and added, "Thank you . . . all of you . . . for being so kind and understanding." They all offered tender smiles and gentle nods that silently bridged any potential gaps in their relationships.

"Also . . ." Faith said, seeming a little hesitant—as if there was something else she believed she needed to say but it might be difficult. She cleared her throat and continued. "We've all known since our youth that none of us could ever compete with your feelings for Meri, and none of us ever wanted to get in the way of that. Even after she married Lord Sturgess, it was evident that it would take a remarkable woman to ever heal your heart. We wondered if you would ever marry at all if you couldn't marry her."

Elliott stared at Faith in astonishment, feeling his mouth fall open but unable to close it or make a sound. He glanced at the sisters and saw that they were all in complete agreement with Faith's statement. They had all clearly talked about it—probably a great deal. Annabel's face reflected the same expression as that of her daughters; she'd known and had never said anything. Meri too had her mouth open in astonishment, staring at her cousins in disbelief while her face glowed a warm pink. Only Angus shared Meri and Elliott's shock and surprise. Before Elliott could form any words to respond, Angus bellowed at Faith, "My dear girl! What in the name of heaven and earth are you talking about?"

Elliott felt proud of Faith as she looked directly at her father and said, "If you weren't always hiding behind your newspapers, Papa, you might have noticed what's been obvious for many years."

Angus stared at Faith as if he were searching for a retort but couldn't find one. He then glared at Elliott, once again implying that he had done something wrong. "What do you have to say about this, young man?"

Elliott took in a breath of courage and drew back his shoulders. He glanced at Meri as if he could silently warn her of what he was about to do. She still just looked as shocked as if someone had thrown cold water in her face. Elliott turned back to face his uncle, cleared his throat and said, "I could tell you the long and complicated version of this story, but I'll just keep it simple for now and tell you that I love Meri with all my heart, and I have for as long as I can remember. It broke my heart when she married another man, and I certainly never believed that I would get a second chance, but now that we're both here and circumstances have changed, you should all know that I intend to marry her as soon as it's socially appropriate to do so. We've known each other so well for so long, that the need for a lengthy courtship hardly seems relevant."

Angus stared at Elliott in stunned silence while Annabel and the sisters all made noises of happiness and glee, as if they couldn't have been told anything more exciting. He glanced at Meri to see that she was still in shock, but a sparkle of happiness showed in her eyes—and he couldn't miss the relief in her expression. He too felt relieved. They would need to keep their courtship a secret in public until some time had passed, but they no longer had to pretend and try to hide their feelings here at home with their family.

"Oh, it's wonderful!" Annabel said, and the girls all agreed with her.

Angus finally cleared his throat loudly and said, "Well, this certainly hasn't been a boring day." He then took up his newspaper, unfolded it, shook it out, and said nothing more. The cousins all decided that Elliott and Meri each needed to be hugged as an expression of their congratulations, and Elliott felt touched by the sincerity of their genuine happiness on behalf of both Meri and him. Annabel hugged them both as well, showing a glimmer of tears in her eyes, and he wondered if she had hoped for this all along. Had she just been waiting for this to happen ever since Meri had become widowed? Had she considered it inevitable that they would both end up here and their old feelings would spark back to life? He wanted to talk to her and ask those questions, but now was obviously not the time.

After Annabel and each of the sisters had declared their happiness at least twice, Elliott took hold of Meri's hand, saying, "Thank you . . . for your love and understanding. I think Meri and I need some time alone to . . . talk about all of this."

"Of course you do," Annabel said. "Run along. We'll not disturb you."

She practically ushered them out of the room and Elliott hurried toward the library, bringing Meri along by keeping her hand tightly in his. Even after they were alone with the door closed, neither of them had anything to say for a full minute or more. Meri finally laughed and said, "What on earth just happened?"

Elliott laughed as well. "I'm . . . not sure." He wrapped his arms around her and lifted her feet off the floor, twirling her around before he set her down and kissed her. "Does this really mean we don't have to hide and pretend? At least not here at home?"

"I believe that's what it means," she said brightly, then her expression became especially sober.

"What's wrong?" he asked.

"Do you think we're moving too quickly? We're both just taking for granted that marriage will be a part of our future, but . . ."

"But what?" he asked.

She wanted to say, *I've become so damaged; perhaps you wouldn't want me if you knew the truth.* Instead she said, "We know each other well, Elliott, but . . . a great deal has happened during these years apart. Surely we need time to . . ."

"Yes, we need time, and we will take all the time we need to both move forward with confidence, but Meri . . . no one knows you better than I do; and the other way around. We both know that life comes with challenges, but you and I have what it takes to face anything as long as we face it together."

"And how do you know that?" she asked, easing away from him.

"Because we not only love each other, we share a deep mutual respect. And we have so very much in common. Hey." He touched her chin and lifted her face so she could see that he meant it when he added, "I love you. Everything is going to work out exactly as it's meant to."

Meri nodded and smiled, but he saw hesitance in her eyes, or perhaps a deep sorrow that he didn't understand. He knew they *did* need time, but he also had great confidence in the love they shared.

"I love the way you play with the children," she said, as if to lighten the subject. "And I love the way they've taken to you. I don't think I've ever seen them so happy."

"Elaine and Crispin have already given me more joy and fulfillment than I've ever experienced in the whole of my life. I want to be a part of their lives."

Meri smiled again and said, "I still can't believe what Faith said. Did you ever know she had so much confidence hiding inside of her?"

"No, I did not," Elliott said and sat down, patting the sofa beside him to indicate that she should join him. They spent the next hour or so revisiting all that had come to light with the family that day and analyzing every detail. They'd always been like that. Most people just took an event or a conversation to be simply what it appeared to be, but they had always had the need to analyze and ponder and speculate over the possible deeper meanings.

Deciding they couldn't hide away too long without Annabel declaring that they might need a chaperone, they went upstairs to play with the children until supper. Elliott entered the dining room with Meri's hand in his, loving the fact that he could do so. Everyone was apparently in good spirits, and even Angus seemed to be his normal self. It seemed the drama and announcements of the day had all settled very quickly and comfortably. After they finished their meal, Charity suggested that Elliott and Meri go for a walk in the gardens, which were so lovely in the evening. He noticed a conspiratorial glance pass among the five sisters and decided that they were finding some delight in their version of matchmaking. It was as if in lieu of having romance in their own lives, they were thrilled to see it blossoming between Meri and Elliott. And they obviously had not liked Lord Sturgess at all. Elliott decided he could be considered good husband material in comparison—even given what little he knew.

Elliott didn't protest Charity's suggestion. While the sisters were inside playing with the children, he held Meri's hand in his and ambled slowly through the many lovely displays of nature, all kept in pristine condition. They talked a little about the future—which made him feel impatient for time to pass so they could be married. And they talked about the years they had been apart, although he could tell she was skirting around things she didn't want to tell him. But he couldn't criticize her for that when he knew he was doing the same. This alone showed him that he *did* need to be patient. They both surely had a great deal of healing to do before they could start over together officially.

Elliott went with Meri to help get the children ready for bed, and he was thrilled when they told their mother they wanted *him* to read their bedtime story. The four of them squished together onto a small sofa in the sitting room off Meri's bedroom and he read aloud from a picture book, doing funny voices for the animals that talked, which made the children laugh. When the story was done, they reluctantly went to bed, and Elliott helped tuck them in. When he and Meri were in the hall outside of the children's room, he whispered to her, "I want it to always be this way."

"So do I," she said and eagerly accepted his kiss.

Over the next few days, a new routine settled into place as Elliott and Meri shared time with the family and time with the children. And they always made time to be alone together so they could just talk and get to know each other again. They went together to the beach for the first time since they'd both returned. In their younger years, they had come here together more times than they could count. Now, just as then, they removed their shoes and stockings so they could more fully enjoy the experience. Elliott rolled up the legs of his breeches and Meri held her skirt just high enough to be able to walk in the waves without getting her dress wet.

The following day they took the children to the beach for a picnic. Elliott loved playing in the waves with the children, and he loved the way Meri laughed when he splashed water on her. During such moments, the course of his life seemed perfectly laid out before him, and he prayed that they could overcome any obstacle that might keep them from enjoying this nearly perfect existence together.

The family's acceptance of this new situation was readily evident. Angus's acceptance wasn't so apparent; he simply made no negative remarks, but both Elliott and Meri knew him well enough to know that was the best they would ever get out of Angus.

When Sunday came and they all went to church—as they always did—Elliott felt frustrated with the need to keep his distance from Meri. The family all knew this needed to be the case, since Meri was officially in mourning. At home, she wore whatever she pleased, but going out into public, it was only appropriate for her to wear black. She'd told him how hypocritical it felt, but she knew that social acceptance was important to her aunt and uncle, and so she heeded society's expectations in this regard.

Elliott sat at one end of the family pew, with Crispin on his lap, trying to keep him occupied and quiet. Meri sat at the other end, with three of their cousins between them. On the pew in front of them sat their aunt and uncle and the other two cousins, who had Elaine seated between them. At one point during the service Crispin became especially full of wiggles. Elliott just carried him outside to let him run around, not caring what anyone might think.

After church, they all enjoyed the finest meal of the day before Alice came to get the children for their nap time. Angus stood from the table and declared, "I believe I could do with a nap myself. I feel especially tired for some reason."

Annabel and the sisters all left the room in Angus's wake, agreeing that a nap was in order—except for Charity, who announced that she was in the mood for a long walk. Elliott noted that she'd been leaving the house for long walks a great deal since he'd returned home, and he wondered if there was some purpose to her leaving the house, beyond a desire for exercise and fresh air.

One moment the dining room was noisy and full of people, and the next almost everyone had left the room and it was silent. Elliott looked across the table at Meri. They watched each other while the silence became mildly strained. Meri looked away and laughed softly, as if she couldn't bear the tension, which made him laugh as well.

"Whatever will we do with our afternoon?" Meri asked.

"You tell me," he said. "Whatever you're doing, that's what I'll be doing, because I want to be with you."

"I was thinking that a nap *does* sound nice, but . . . we can't do that together; it wouldn't be appropriate, and—"

"We could just hurry and get married," he suggested, hoping she could tell by his tone that he was serious. She looked at him in a way that let him know she'd picked up on just how serious he was. "Since when do wc really care about social propriety? Let's just . . . get married."

"You really mean that," she said.

"I really do."

"Well . . . the idea certainly warrants some discussion, but we can't get married today, so it doesn't solve the immediate problem."

Elliott stood up and walked around the table, holding out his hand toward her. She stood and took it before he kissed her quickly and led her out of the room to the library. He left the door open and escorted her to one of the two long sofas that faced each other, with a long glass and wrought-iron table in between. He sat on the opposite sofa as he said, "I can tell you from much experience that these sofas are very comfortable for napping." He stretched out on the sofa and chuckled. "You can nap over there, and I'll nap over here, and we'll be napping together without the need for a chaperone."

"You're very clever, Elliott Rosewell," she said and laid down. "I too have taken many naps in here, usually because I got sleepy while reading."

"As I recall, this isn't the first time we both napped in here at the same time. I believe it happened many times."

"That's true," Meri said, "but we were very young and we were merely friends. It was different."

"Yes," Elliott said, his eyes connecting with hers, "it was different."

Meri smiled and closed her eyes, already looking relaxed enough to fall asleep. He too closed his eyes, enjoying his awareness that she was in the room.

Elliott came awake to the sound of a high-pitched scream. It had been such a terrified and pitiful sound that he felt sure he'd been dreaming; a frightening nightmare he couldn't remember. Then he heard it again—a cry for help—and he sat up abruptly, realizing that Meri was awake and alert, looking as fearful as he felt.

"What on earth?" she muttered just before Elliott rushed out of the room, with her following close behind. He heard that cry for help again and followed the sound up the stairs where he found Annabel sitting on the top step, holding to the bannister post as if for dear life. Her expression was unlike anything he'd ever seen on her in his entire life.

"What's happened?" he asked, kneeling in front of her, aware of Meri's footsteps coming up the stairs behind him. "What's wrong, Aunt?"

On the wake of a tearless sob she muttered, "He's . . . cold. I . . . woke up and . . . he was cold." She looked directly at Elliott. "I think he's . . ." She shook her head and squeezed her eyes closed, as if she couldn't bring herself to utter the word.

Elliott turned toward Meri to see his own shock and concern mirrored in her expression. "Stay with her," he said to Meri, who immediately sat next to Annabel and wrapped her arms around their aunt. Elliott rushed toward the bedroom his aunt and uncle shared, knowing he should hurry but feeling his steps drag as he approached the open doorway. He took a deep breath and walked into the room, seeing his uncle face up on the bed as if he were sleeping. But as Elliott got closer he didn't even have to touch him to know that he was dead. His eyes were only partly closed in an unnatural way, and even though the expression on his face was relaxed, even peaceful, it had a strangeness to it. Elliott touched his uncle's face just to be sure, and just as Annabel had said, he was cold. He took a sharp breath and softened his hand against Angus's face in some meager yet tender farewell gesture.

Elliott went more slowly back to where he'd left his aunt and Meri. He found all his cousins now there—except for Charity, who apparently had not returned from her walk—all sitting on the floor or the stairs, huddled around their mother, fearful and expectant as their eyes all focused on Elliott. He wondered what they might hope he could tell them after the obvious information that Annabel had already divulged. But it was evident they needed to hear it spoken; they needed to know the truth. And somehow it had fallen on him to be the official bearer of bad news.

Drawing courage, Elliott just said it. "He's dead; he must have gone in his sleep."

A chorus of wailing came in response to his words as the women all collapsed into sobbing and clung to each other more tightly—except for Meri, who had her arms tightly around Annabel. But her tears rolled silently down her cheeks as she looked up at Elliott and they shared a silent moment of trying to mutually accept this loss that had come so unexpectedly. He knelt and wrapped his arms around the huddle of women as much as it was possible. "I'm so very sorry," he whispered and pressed a kiss to his aunt's face.

Annabel seemed snapped out of a trance as she looked up at him and said, "I need to . . . tell the staff, and . . . we can't leave him there like that, and . . ."

"I'll take care of it," he said, glad for the way he felt presently numb and unable to feel anything at all. If that made it possible for him to take charge and make certain everything was taken care of, then he would consider it a huge blessing. He wanted to be able to properly care for these women he loved so dearly; he could acknowledge his grief later.

"Bless you," Annabel said as if it hadn't occurred to her that anyone besides her could do what needed to be done. As soon as Elliott stood up to leave, his aunt pressed her face to Meri's shoulder and resumed her weeping.

As Elliott headed down the back staircase, he wiped a few stray tears from his cheeks. For all that Angus could be difficult at times, he had a good heart and Elliott loved him. He was like a father to Elliott, and learning to live without him would not be easy. He also considered how difficult this was going to be on the seven women who lived in this home, and he felt a weight come down upon his shoulders as tangible as if someone had placed a burden there for him to carry. He recalled how recently he had declared to Angus that he would always make certain his cousins were cared for. He never could have imagined at the time how quickly his need to care for them would become literal. It occurred to him that legally this house and the property around it could not be bequeathed to Angus's wife or any of his daughters. If the estate did not officially belong to Elliott, he wondered what might have happened to them. He marveled that what had upset him not so many days ago now came as a relief. Considering how it might have been if his brother had inherited Rosewell Abbey, he shuddered. Lawrence would have seen their aunt and cousins relocated with a meager allowance before he would have ever considered their real needs and comforts.

As he became more upset, Elliott pushed away any thoughts over what might have been and focused on his need to take on some difficult tasks. He found the housekeeper and the head butler and asked to speak to them together and privately. As soon as they were all seated he told them that the master of the house had died. These people had been running Angus's household for many years, and they had a keen respect and fondness for their employer; therefore, they were naturally upset by the news. Despite Angus's brash personality, he had always been a fair employer. They quickly regained their composure and agreed to inform the rest of the staff and begin making proper arrangements.

Elliott himself went out to the stables to inform those who worked there of the death. They too took it hard, but they were eager to offer their assistance. Elliott sent one of the men to fetch the doctor, believing that even though it was obvious Angus was dead, having the doctor examine him, sign the appropriate documents, and speak to Annabel might give her some comfort. Elliott sent another man to fetch the undertaker, and another to inform the vicar and ask that he come to the house at his earliest convenience to offer comfort to the family and to help with arrangements for the funeral.

Having done all he could do for the moment, Elliott returned to the house and found all the women right where he'd left them. Charity was now there as well, having returned from her walk to be confronted by the dreadful news. He was glad he didn't have to tell her himself.

"Come along," he said in an authoritative voice as he approached. "You can't sit here all day. Let's go where we can be more comfortable."

The women reluctantly stood and followed Elliott. Logically he believed they should all stay together for the time being, but they shouldn't be too far from the room in which Angus's body still lay—at least until after the doctor and the undertaker had come. At the same time, he didn't want any of them to have to deal with anything that might upset them further; therefore, he wanted to remain with them. He took them to the large sitting room that was just next to Angus and Annabel's bedroom, and he quickly closed the door that led into the bedroom without anyone noticing as they all sat down on the sofas there. Some of the women were still crying—albeit more quietly now—and some appeared to be in shock.

"I can't believe it," Faith declared. "I just can't believe it." This began a conversation of sharing similar feelings, until Faith stood and said, "I need to see him. I won't believe it unless I see him."

Elliott shot a concerned glance toward Meri, hoping she could help him determine if this was wise. He honestly didn't know whether it would be more difficult for her to see the body at this point. But it only took him a moment to know that he could never prevent any of these women from doing something if they were determined to do it.

"Are you certain?" Elliott asked Faith, standing to block her way only long enough to let her think about it.

"Yes," Faith said and nodded with courage. She turned back toward the others and asked, "Does anyone want to join me?"

"I do," Comfort said decidedly and stood.

"As do I," Hope added and stood to take hold of Comfort's hand.

"I don't want to see him," Charity declared. "I don't need to. I have no reason not to believe what Mother and Elliott have told us."

"I'll stay here," Joy said. "I agree with Charity."

Meri stood and took Elliott's hand but said nothing. He wondered if she felt the need to see for herself that Angus was dead so she could more fully accept it as truth, or if she was trying to be a support to him. "Are you sure?" he asked her quietly, not wanting her to do this for the wrong reasons.

"Yes," she said firmly.

Elliott opened the door between the sitting room and the bedroom and he led the way in, keeping Meri at his side. Faith, Comfort, and Hope moved hesitantly to their father's bedside and held to each other as the evidence became clear. Only Faith reached out to touch Angus's hand, saying quietly, "He *is* cold." They all stood there for a few minutes and wept, as did Meri, who put her head on Elliott's shoulder. He put his arm around her and waited for his cousins to leave the room before he followed with Meri and closed the door behind them. They were both hugely grateful that the children's rooms were far enough removed from this part of the house for them to have heard anything. It would have been too difficult for them to experience the initial trauma of the situation. There would be time enough to explain to them what had happened in a more appropriate setting.

Elliott sat for a long while with Meri at his side, listening to the women expressing their grief and going through bouts of crying. He still felt numb, and he couldn't think of anything to say, but he felt the need to be there. A maid brought tea and cakes and sandwiches to the sitting room, and they all ate a little, but no one had much of an appetite.

Elliott was glad when one of the maids came to announce that the doctor had arrived, and she had taken him to the master's bedroom. Elliott had told the women his reasons for having the doctor come, and Annabel had seemed relieved with his insight. It was as if despite the obvious evidence that Angus was dead, she would indeed feel more at peace if a doctor declared him so. At the maid's announcement, Annabel looked at Elliott and said, "Should I . . ." She didn't finish, but he knew what she meant, and he also knew from her expression that she did *not* want to deal with this.

"I'll take care of it," he said and hurried out of the room to join the doctor.

"Hello," the doctor said kindly when Elliott entered the bedroom.

"Forgive me," Elliott said, "I know your face but I don't recall your name."

"Dr. Sheddon," he said. "And you're Elliott. We've crossed paths here as you've come and gone through the years."

"Yes," was all Elliott could think to say.

"I'm glad you're here now," the doctor continued. "I can only assume that the women who love this poor fellow are taking it hard."

"Indeed, they are," Elliott said, noting the way that the doctor was discreetly looking at and touching Angus's eyelids, his arms, his hands, his chest. Becoming nervous with the silence, Elliott asked, "Is there any way of knowing what happened?"

Dr. Sheddon looked mildly surprised. "He didn't tell you, did he." It wasn't a question.

"Tell me what?" Elliott asked, his skin prickling.

"I suspect he didn't tell anyone except his wife. Although she knew, because I told her myself."

"Knew what?" Elliott asked, his voice rising in pitch.

The doctor turned to face Elliott, apparently finished with his examination. "I assume you want me to be honest and direct."

"I do," Elliott said.

"I assume that if you choose to convey any of this information to the rest of the family, you will do so more delicately than what I'm going to tell you."

"Of course," Elliott said, appreciating the man's sensitivity but growing steadily more nervous.

"His heart was bad; it has been for a few years. He ate poorly and way too much. He made no effort to get any exercise, and he's been carrying around a great deal of excess weight—which is hard on the heart and cannot be remedied without good eating habits and exercise."

"Then this cannot be too much of a surprise for my aunt," Elliott said, trying to fully take in what he'd just heard.

"Not a surprise, perhaps," the doctor said, "but still a shock. Unfortunately, I have seen this kind of thing a great deal in my profession. When people receive a diagnosis they don't want to hear, they often go about their lives as if their heart is not failing, as if cancer or any other number of diseases are not actually there. Unless a person is experiencing pain or discomfort—or even sometimes when they are—they won't accept what is too uncomfortable or frightening. I don't believe your aunt or your uncle ever really heard what I told them." He sighed. "But there is no good to be found in regret, and there is no going back." He put a hand on Elliott's shoulder. "I'm going to tell your aunt that his heart stopped beating while he was asleep, and he felt no pain at all. That's the only information his wife and his daughters need to know."

"I understand," Elliott said, appreciating this man's insight and wisdom. He was glad to know the whole truth, but he could understand why such knowledge might only make this loss more difficult for Annabel and her daughters. He believed that Meri would want to know the truth, but he needed to give that some thought.

"Thank you," Elliott added.

"Shall we get this over with?" Dr. Sheddon asked, and Elliott led him to the sitting room.

Annabel moved to the edge of her seat when the men entered the room, but the doctor said to her, "No, no. Don't get up. I know this is a very difficult day for you." He stood directly in front of Annabel and took her hand into both of his. "I'm so very sorry for your loss." Annabel nodded and pressed her handkerchief underneath her nose with her free hand. The doctor then told her exactly what he'd informed Elliott he would say. Annabel expressed her appreciation. The doctor offered further condolences to her and to the others before Elliott escorted him out of the room, down the stairs, and to the door.

"If there's anything else I can do," Dr. Sheddon said, offering a firm handshake, "please don't hesitate to send for me."

"Thank you," Elliott said, wondering what that might entail since the patient was already dead.

As if the doctor had read his mind, he added, "Sometimes when people are afflicted with heavy grief they have difficulty sleeping or they become especially anxious. If that happens with anyone in the family, I can give them something to help."

Elliott nodded his understanding. "Thank you. I'm glad to know that's an option."

"Take care of yourself, young man," the doctor said. "I will be at the funeral."

The good doctor left and Elliott took a few minutes to just sit in one of the parlors and take in all that had happened that day and all he had learned about Angus's medical condition—and the way both his aunt and uncle had apparently ignored and avoided the issue. He wondered if heeding the doctor's advice might have extended Angus's life, but obviously that was a question that would never be answered. Steeling himself to be strong for his aunt and cousins, he went back upstairs to join them, wondering how they were all going to come to terms with this dramatic change in their lives.

Chapter Six

HOUSE OF SECRETS

IN THE DAYS LEADING UP to the funeral, Meri came to hate the gloominess that had fallen over the house. The sun was shining outside, but inside there seemed to be invisible storm clouds making everything gray and chilly. It was easier to spend time with the children, since everything felt mostly normal with them. Neither of them had been terribly close to Angus. He'd teased them a little here and there, but very seldom. He'd rarely shown his gruff side around them, but his absence hadn't left any kind of void in their lives. When Meri told them Uncle Angus had died, they had many questions, but Meri felt confident that she had answered them well enough to satisfy their curiosity and to offer reassurances. Her own faith in God had always been an innate part of her, and her belief in life after death had been strengthened after she'd lost her parents and her brother.

It was difficult to put into words the peace she felt that let her know of a surety that her loved ones lived on. Meri had many times talked to the children about her family, and about her belief that they were now angels who watched over them. It was therefore not too difficult to explain Angus's death, and both Elaine and Crispin each had their own measure of faith that came from within themselves. They were very matter-of-fact about Uncle Angus being an angel now, and Elaine even commented that he was probably happier as an angel. Meri asked what she meant but Elaine's answers were vague. It seemed, however, that even as young as she was, Elaine had picked up on something about her great-uncle that had made her believe he hadn't necessarily been a very happy person. Meri had never looked at it quite that way, but she couldn't dispute that Elaine's insight was accurate.

Meri wished that talking to her aunt and cousins about Angus's passing could be half as easy as talking to the children. The reality was that none of them wanted to talk about it at all, and yet it seemed somehow disrespectful or inappropriate to talk about anything else with the funeral pending. Therefore, mealtimes and their usual time together in the parlor were filled with little else except dreadful silence. Meri was glad for any time that she could legitimately excuse herself and be anywhere but beneath the pall that shrouded her aunt and cousins. She felt like she should be available to offer support and compassion, but when no one wanted to talk about it, she felt her presence was useless.

Thankfully, Elliott felt much the same as Meri, and he was also eager to slip away whenever she could. He often spent time with her and the children—just as he'd been doing before Angus's death. And when the children were in Alice's care, Elliott and Meri would walk in the gardens or go to the beach or lounge in the library or the solarium where they could talk about their uncle's death as much as they needed to and even cry if necessary, which was often the case.

Sitting on one of the library sofas with Elliott's arms around her and her head on his shoulder, Meri said earnestly, "I'm so grateful we've crossed this line in our lives, Elliott. I don't know what I'd do without you. And," she looked up at him and he kissed her, "I'm so glad we're more than friends."

"Oh, I'm grateful for that too," he said and kissed her again before she once more settled her head comfortably against his shoulder.

"I'm worried about Annabel . . . and our cousins."

"I'm worried, too," he said. "I think I'd prefer to have them shouting and sobbing rather than all this gloomy silence. Holding it all inside surely can't be good for them."

"I agree," Meri said. "And as much as some of them cried the first day, I can't believe there aren't still a great many more tears bottled up inside."

"I suppose we just have to give them time," Elliott concluded.

"Perhaps they are crying when we're not around."

"Perhaps," Elliott said, "but I'm not getting that impression."

"I'm glad the doctor told you what he did," Meri said, "and I'm glad you told me. But I'm equally glad the others don't know. I think they would be . . . I don't know what, but . . ."

"Angry," Elliott stated. "I've thought about it a great deal, and I think they would be angry with him. I've felt a little that way myself, but . . .

well, does it sound arrogant or out of line to say that I think I can handle knowing better than they would?"

"No, I think it's a fact. And now that you mention it, I've felt a little angry with him myself. But you're right; Annabel and the girls would likely not take it so well. But Annabel knows, does she not?"

"She knows whatever the doctor told her in the past about Angus's health, but who's to say how much of it she has chosen to remember?" He sighed. "I've thought a lot about what the doctor said . . . about how people won't accept what is too uncomfortable or frightening, and therefore they don't even really hear or accept difficult news when it's given to them."

"Didn't you tell me he said that unless a person is actually experiencing pain or discomfort—or even sometimes when they are—they often just won't accept it?"

"Yes, that's what he said," Elliott explained. "And it's occurred to me that the same is likely true concerning any kind of emotional pain or trauma." Meri noticed by his tone and the thoughtful silence that followed that he seemed to be referring to something personal, and she wondered what might have happened in his life that he'd not shared with her, but she didn't want to probe when there was so much she didn't want to talk about regarding her own life. Elliott sighed and added, "I wonder if there are uncomfortable feelings about all of this in the family, and that's why no one is talking."

Meri looked up at him again. "I think you might be right, Elliott Rosewell. You know, I do believe you're a rather smart man. I'd do well to never let you go."

He looked at her and chuckled. "I don't know how smart I am," he said, "but I won't argue with the latter."

"I suppose we should get back," Meri said with a heavy sigh.

"Yes, I suppose we must." Elliott stood up and took her hand to help her to her feet. "Back to the mausoleum."

They both returned to the parlor to find everyone either reading or doing needlework, all of them completely silent. But tea had been served and Meri distracted herself with the fact that she was hungry, and her favorite carrot cake was on the tea tray.

Meri was proud of Elliott when he broke the silence by saying, "Does no one have even a word to speak? We are family and we are all in this together. Surely it is a good thing to share our feelings over what's happened."

No one spoke; they all just looked at Elliott as if he'd gone mad, which incited him to get up and leave the room, saying over his shoulder, "I'm certain that Elaine and Crispin are much better company." Meri finished her cake and followed him.

The day of the funeral came as a relief to Meri, mostly because she wanted to have it over with. The service was lovely, and the vicar was very kind, as were people from the community who were in attendance. Meri noticed that her aunt and cousins were frequently tucking their handkerchiefs beneath their veils to dab at their tears. At least they were crying. But then she was reminded of how she'd *pretended* to cry in the same manner at Lord Sturgess's funeral, which only heightened her empathy.

After the funeral, there was a gathering at the house, and it was evident the entire staff had put their best efforts into preparing and serving a fine array of food. Once the guests had all left, Annabel and the girls quickly departed to their own rooms, declaring the need to be alone—except for Charity, who went for a walk. Alice had taken the children upstairs a while earlier for nap time, and Meri found herself alone in the parlor with Elliott.

"This has been an interesting day," Elliott said, and she waited for him to clarify what he meant exactly. He looked deeply thoughtful for a minute or two before he added, "Does something feel . . . strange to you . . . or is it just me?"

"Strange how?" Meri asked.

"I don't know how to explain it," he said, still thoughtful. "I've seen people grieving before, but . . . this doesn't feel like . . . normal grieving." He chuckled humorlessly. "Is there a *normal* way to grieve?"

"I would think there are certain commonalities to grief among all human beings."

"I would think so too," he said. "But . . ." he looked around the room, even though no one else was there, as if he could further assess what he was trying to explain, ". . . well, this doesn't feel like grieving as much as . . . everyone is just . . . different. Our chattering cousins who are rarely quiet for a moment among the five of them have now taken to silence as if they had become monks. And Annabel seems . . ."

"Unaffected?" Meri provided.

"Yes," Elliott agreed with enthusiasm. "Unaffected. How is that possible?"

"I don't know," Meri said, "but I think you're right. This whole thing just feels . . . strange. But truthfully, I don't want to talk about it right now. All of this has been terribly exhausting, and I don't even want to think about it."

"Fair enough," he said and they went to the library to take naps on separate sofas.

The following day, the mood among the family was as if nothing at all had happened to disrupt their lives. During afternoon tea, Comfort and Joy were full of silly conversation again. Hope was preoccupied with the novel she was reading and hardly seemed aware that she wasn't alone. Charity and Faith were more subdued than usual, although they seemed more angry than sad. But most astonishing was the way that Annabel was downright chipper. She was initiating conversation and smiling a great deal—two things that Meri hadn't realized she'd rarely done during these family gatherings until she now saw the contrast.

Meri was glad to have Elliott in the room, and the way they occasionally exchanged discreet glances let her know he was as bewildered as she over the strangeness Angus's death had provoked.

Meri was surprised when Elliott said, "Annabel, I wonder if I could speak with you privately when it's convenient." Everyone turned curious eyes toward him and he added, "I have some questions about the estate."

"Of course, dear," she replied with an unusually bright smile. "Now would be fine," she added, which surprised Elliott but he stood and motioned toward the door.

The girls all returned their attention to their previous activities as Annabel stood and walked across the room.

"I'd like Meri to join us," Elliott said, tossing Meri a discreet glare that seemed to convey a subtle warning.

"Whatever you wish, dear," Annabel said and exited the room.

Elliott followed with Meri at his side. He hurried to whisper in her ear, "Forgive me. This is all rather impulsive, but . . . I need to talk to her, and I need you there."

Meri nodded to indicate she'd heard, but she felt nervous over whatever it might be that had incited Elliott to impulsively request this conversation with their aunt. She had a feeling it didn't have much—if anything—to do with the estate. But Annabel led the way to the office where Angus had conducted estate business, and where all the associated records were kept. Once in the room with the door closed, they were all seated, but Elliott remained at the edge of his chair, directly facing Annabel.

"Everything with the estate should be in order," Annabel said. "Did the solicitor not—"

"I met with Mr. Browby before the funeral," Elliott said. "Everything *is* in order. The house and the estate—as Angus told me—all now legally belong to me, which is something I had not anticipated and I am still adjusting to, but . . . I wanted to let you know that I have asked Mr. Browby—this man Angus has relied on for years—to draw up a legal document that will ensure security for you and your daughters if something happens to me. It's just a precaution, of course, but I don't want any of you to have any concerns for the future. While there is the stipulation that women cannot inherit property, there is more than enough money to be divided among all of you that will quite comfortably see you through the remainder of your lives. I just wanted you to know that it will soon be taken care of."

"Thank you, Elliott," she said. "I'm very grateful."

"It's the only right thing to do." He looked down, seeming mildly embarrassed.

"You say that," Annabel said, "but many people would not agree, and would not necessarily address the situation so generously; therefore, it's only right that you know how very, very grateful I am . . . to know that my girls will be all right."

"Of course," Elliott said before an awkward silence descended over the room.

Annabel broke it by saying, "I appreciate knowing that everything is in order legally, Elliott, but I know that's not what you wanted to talk to me about."

Elliott cleared his throat nervously as if he'd been caught in a lie. He glanced at Meri as if she might give him courage, but she had no idea what he had impulsively decided he should speak to Annabel about.

"Forgive me, Aunt," he began hesitantly, "but . . . I feel concerned; *we,"* he corrected, motioning to Meri, "feel concerned. About you . . . and our cousins. Something seems to have changed dramatically since Angus's death, but we are having trouble understanding what it is. Meri and I have talked many times about how—for as long as we can remember—we could come to you privately and talk about anything, and you would be straightforward. You've always been a wise and insightful woman, Annabel. We just . . . want to help; we want to understand. People have different ways of grieving, I'm sure, but—"

"My dear Elliott," Annabel said in a voice that was kind but firm. "Meri," she added, nodding toward her as if to be certain Meri knew she was officially included in whatever Annabel was about to say. "I don't want to shock or disillusion either one of you; you're both so precious to me. But you've asked for the truth and I'm going to give it to you. Angus is gone now, which means it's no longer necessary to keep secrets in this house."

At the word *secrets,* Elliott and Meri exchanged a brief, alarmed glance, then they both turned back to look at Annabel. Meri's heart was pounding as she waited for whatever their aunt intended to say.

"It's not possible to grieve for someone when his death is nothing but a relief to me. Love cannot grow when it has been continually choked by so much hurt," Annabel stated with calm confidence. Meri took in a sharp breath, startled both by what this meant about the marriage of her aunt and uncle, but also because it so accurately described how she had felt when her own husband had died. Annabel had offered perfect compassion to Meri then, but Meri had had no idea just how perfectly Annabel had understood Meri's feelings.

"You both know that Angus had a kind and tender side, but he was also very negative and critical. You're also both mature enough to understand that a marriage relationship is different from any other. I believe that Angus came into this marriage thinking it was my responsibility to make him happy, even while he himself brought a great deal of unhappiness into the marriage, and he would never let me get close enough to him emotionally to even allow me to help him become happier. On the rare occasions that he was more soft and open with me, it would inevitably end with him saying or doing something utterly cruel, as if to declare that I had no business getting anywhere near his heart. For years I blamed myself; I wanted it to be my fault so that I could fix it. And then I finally accepted that there was absolutely nothing I could do to help my husband when he was not interested in becoming a better man. While I was continually striving to improve myself, and learn more about wisdom and happiness, he remained emotionally stuck in the same place he was in when I married him. Perhaps I married him because I believed I *could* fix him; I quickly learned that I was wrong."

Annabel sighed, brushing her hands over her skirt before she clasped them in her lap. "So, that's the truth of it. Every day of my life with Angus was difficult, and many days were downright painful. He broke my heart over and over—because I allowed him to, always believing that perhaps this time he would finally take hold of the love I was trying to offer him. But in reality, he was never capable of loving me the way I deserved, and as much as I know he *did* love me and our daughters—and the two of you—love is not a feeling alone; it is action. Love is shown by the way we treat people and care for them; and he had none to give. In his heart he was penniless, all the while believing we should be satisfied with his own distorted belief that he was showering us with riches. The girls have all suffered greatly from his attitudes. I've tried over the years to have private conversations with them and teach them that their father's remarks and behavior toward them were not necessarily correct—even while I tried not to express disrespect for their father. But I could never undo his damage. And you all know the results. I know how sharp you both are, and I know how much you love and care for your cousins. But there is so much you don't know about."

She sighed again, and this time it was a painful sound. Her face tightened, and her eyes became distant and deeply sad. "Of course, I was legitimately shocked and upset to find him dead, and change can be difficult even when it may be for the best. But now that he's gone I will endeavor to love my daughters and try to make up somehow for the damage that cannot be undone. That's all I can do."

She took a deep breath in a way that indicated she had more to say. "Concerning the reasons for his death, you must realize that he knew his health was not good, and perhaps you've wondered if I might not have taken seriously what the doctor has told us a number of times. I sincerely tried to encourage Angus to make the necessary changes the doctor suggested. He wanted nothing to do with it. After several attempts on my part to be supportive, he called me a nag . . . and a few other more unfavorable things . . . and I told him that his health was up to him; I was done trying to help him."

Apparently having said what she felt the need to say, Annabel looked at each of them squarely and concluded, "So now you know. I'm done pretending. I feel happier and freer than I have since I married him. I will not speak ill of him to his daughters or anyone else, but there is no one else beyond the two of you who will ever be able to help your cousins find happiness in this life. You should not take that on as a burden by any means, but I'm glad you asked me, and I'm glad you are aware. True happiness can only be found when it's based in truth. It could take time for the girls to each find their own truth, but I will be there to help them, and I'm glad to know that the two of you will be here, as well. And I'm glad that you know the truth."

Meri couldn't think of anything to say, and Elliott too responded only with silence. Annabel chuckled tensely and said, "I must have shocked both of you. Forgive me if I've imparted far too much information."

"No," Elliott said, "I'm glad you told us." He glanced at Meri. "I admit to being somewhat shocked, but . . . I agree with you . . . about happiness being based in truth; in fact, I believe you taught me that." He leaned forward toward Annabel and said with compassion, "I'm terribly sorry your life has been so difficult, Aunt." Tears rose in Annabel's eyes and Elliott added, "I loved Angus, but I was not blind to his faults; clearly you experienced the brunt of those faults more than anyone. I wish for you nothing but happiness in the future."

"You are so dear," Annabel said, then looked at Meri as if to question her feelings on the matter.

"I agree with everything Elliott has just said, Aunt; truly. Even though I've not told you everything, you know my marriage was extremely difficult. I understand how you feel." She took a deep breath. "I confess that it brings up some anger toward Angus, and I believe it will take time for me to come to terms with that. But I would far rather know the truth and be able to come to terms with my feelings for the right reasons, rather than seeing the situation from a distorted perspective."

"Amen to that," Elliott said.

"The two of you are very kind," Annabel said. "And wise. It's only right that you should be together, and it makes me so happy."

"I don't know how wise I am," Elliott said, smiling toward Meri, "but I am certainly happy about Meri and me being together."

"Is there anything else?" Annabel asked. Meri and Elliott looked at each other then back at her, shaking their heads. Their aunt stood and added, "It's a beautiful day. I think I'll take a walk before supper."

"We'll . . . see you later then," Elliott said, and Annabel left the room.

Elliott closed the door and leaned against it with a heavy sigh. He looked as overcome and disoriented as Meri felt. He shook his head and sat down in the chair where Annabel had been sitting so that he could face Meri. "Am I a fool for having believed they were happy together?"

"If you're a fool, then I am too," Meri said. "I just assumed that for all of their outward . . . idiosyncrasies . . . they surely shared a certain closeness."

"As did I."

"I'm somewhat in shock, I think. A part of me wants to believe she's making it up, perhaps because I don't want to think their marriage was something of a . . . farce all these years. But I know she's telling the truth."

"Yes, I'm certain of that. It doesn't take much thought to recount in retrospect the evidence of everything she's said. And what about the—"

"Secrets?" they both said together.

"Secrets?" Elliott repeated. "What did she say exactly?"

"That it was no longer necessary to keep secrets in this house," Meri recalled. "Do you suppose she means something more than her lack of love and respect for Angus?"

"I don't know," Elliott said, "but I sense a great deal of . . . unhappiness and . . . I don't know what . . . with our cousins."

"Disquiet," Meri said as the recent strange behaviors of the sisters made more sense. "It's as if they are feeling unrest because their emotions are so confusing. It doesn't take a vivid imagination to consider that they have each been negatively impacted by their father."

"I've believed that for a long time," Elliott said. "But . . . *secrets?* Do you think they have secrets? Things they don't want us to know?"

"Only time will tell, I suppose," Meri said and shook her head. "I don't think I can talk about this anymore right now. It's giving me a headache."

Elliott stood. "Do you think nap time is over?"

Meri followed him out the door, saying, "Sometimes I think you love the children more than you love me." She laughed at the notion, because she knew his love for all of them was genuine. And having a man step in to be a loving father to her children expressed a great love for her as their mother.

Elliott stopped long enough to quickly kiss her. "Only almost as much," he said, and they hurried up the stairs, as if he couldn't wait to get to the playroom and be with Elaine and Crispin.

* * *

Over the following week or so, nearly every time the family gathered in the parlor following lunch or tea—a time when they had always visited for a long while—Annabel and her daughters quickly made their excuses and left. Charity always went for a long walk if the weather was favorable, and sometimes when it wasn't. The other sisters were off to their rooms. And Annabel had taken to going to town to shop or to visit friends at their homes—both of which Angus had protested. None of Annabel's daughters accepted their mother's invitation to go shopping with her, even though some of them had once enjoyed shopping very much.

When Elliott and Meri found themselves alone, Elliott said, "And here we are again." He sighed. "It wasn't so long ago that we couldn't get away long enough to *ever* be alone, and now we have apparently become unfavorable company."

"Apparently," Meri said, her concern growing about how her cousins were coping with their father's death—or perhaps they weren't.

The following day while the family was gathered in the parlor, drinking tea and enjoying the delightful little cakes and sandwiches that had come from the kitchen, Meri felt so deeply unnerved that she knew she had to say something in order to prevent an unseemly outburst at some future time. Knowing that as soon as everyone had finished their tea they would likely scatter, she cleared her throat and just forced the words out.

"Forgive me if I'm being presumptuous," Meri said, and all eyes turned toward her, some curious, some silently daring her to say anything they might not want to discuss openly, "but everything has changed so dramatically. You are all behaving so differently. We don't have conversations the way we used to. It's as if none of you want to even stay in the same room together any longer than necessary."

Meri looked to Elliott for encouragement and was glad to see it in the way he nodded subtly, and something in his eyes told her he was pleased with what she was saying.

"We're family," Meri hurried on, fearing she would lose their attention if she didn't. "We've been close throughout most of our lives. Surely your father's death shouldn't change that. Can't we . . . talk about him? Can't we talk about difficult feelings related to his death . . . or even his life?" She added the last with some trepidation, but instinctively she believed that each one of Angus's daughters had very mixed emotions about their father's death, and the way he had not necessarily been a very good father when he'd been alive. She feared that if they didn't acknowledge those feelings soon, they would gradually become more and more permanent and impossible to move beyond.

The girls all stared at Meri as if not one of them knew what to think of her suggesting such a thing. Annabel looked proud of Meri, as did Elliott, but that didn't mean she hadn't provoked something that might not have positive results.

"I think you're right," Faith said and broke the tense silence. Her sisters all turned to look at her with varying expressions of fear and astonishment. Faith's voice took on a tinge of anger. "I'm sick to death of not being able to talk about how we really feel. All that chattering we did when he was sitting here among us was mostly nonsense; it was trivial conversation for the sake of it, mostly because I think remaining silent in his presence made us all nervous. And sometimes it took everything I had not to just scream and tell everybody to shut up unless they could actually say something meaningful."

Faith paused, but had her eyes closed, as if seeing her sisters' reactions would prevent her from being able to finish. Meri noted that they all looked astonished—perhaps horrified. Was speaking so openly considered to be improper and appalling? Apparently. Again, Meri and Elliott exchanged a glance. They'd become very good at their silent communications as these strange events in the family kept evolving in surprising ways.

Faith took a trembling breath and went on. "I believe we all have things we need to say, and that we should stop hiding things we knew we had to keep hidden from our father." Another faltering breath. "I'm the oldest and I'm going first, because I have to say it or I'm going to lose my mind. I'm *sick* of keeping it inside! *Sick!*"

Meri reached for Elliott's hand and felt him squeeze it. Faith's vehemence was making it evident this was no small thing. The potential secrets that were being kept hidden suddenly felt frightening. Still Meri never could have been prepared for what Faith was about to say.

"I loved my father and I know he loved me, but I only knew it by impersonal logic. I rarely if ever actually *felt* loved by him, and it was difficult to feel any love for him when he wouldn't even look at me, and . . . if . . ." She squeezed her eyes shut more tightly as if she could block something out, and a sob burst out of her mouth as she pressed both hands over her chest. Meri looked at Elliott in alarm before they both looked back at Faith with concern.

Faith's confession—whatever it might be—became stuck behind the emotion that it was forcing to the surface. She sobbed again and hung her head, and Meri instinctively crossed the room and sat on the sofa beside her, putting an arm around her as she said gently, "Whatever it is, Faith, it's all right. We're your family and we'll love you no matter what. You mustn't feel all alone in whatever is causing you so much pain." Meri glanced at Annabel, hoping she might have some answer on how to help Faith, but her aunt only nodded with approval and Meri continued to encourage Faith to finish what she'd begun. Whatever it was, Annabel already knew.

"If . . ." Faith said again, her voice steadier but her eyes still shut tightly, "if he had died a year ago . . . maybe I wouldn't have been forced to give my baby away, and . . ." She dissolved into helpless sobbing in Meri's arms, while Meri looked at Elliott over the top of Faith's head, glad to see that he was as utterly shocked as she. A glance around the room made it clear that everyone else knew what Faith was talking about, but they were all looking at the floor or toward the window, as if they didn't want to acknowledge what Faith had said. Only Annabel seemed emotionally present, gazing at her daughter with compassion, while silent tears trickled down her face.

"Aunt," Meri said to her quietly while Faith continued to cry as if this baby she had referred to had been taken from her arms this very moment, "can you help us understand?"

"Faith, darling?" Annabel said. "Is it all right if I tell Meri and Elliott what happened? I won't if you don't want me to."

"Please tell them," Faith muttered. "They need to know . . . but I don't want to say it."

"Very well then," Annabel said, wiping away her tears. "Faith, like her sisters, has suffered greatly from the daily comments made by their father that led them to believe they would never find suitable marriages, that no decent man would ever be willing to take care of them. He told them they were too thin, or too fat, or too silly, or too smart. And despite my efforts to teach them otherwise, they have all taken their father's beliefs very much to heart. I'm not saying anything I haven't discussed with my daughters a great deal. We are all aware of the damage that's been caused, but none of us are certain how to undo it; I suppose that's why we avoid it and don't talk about it. But obviously *that's* not helping." She looked again at Faith who couldn't stop crying. "So . . ." Annabel went on, "Faith was . . . taken advantage of by a man who led her to believe he would marry her, but once she got pregnant it became evident he'd been lying. She came to me as soon as she knew she was pregnant. To get to the point, I wanted to keep the baby within the family; I didn't care what people thought of us. But Angus wouldn't have it; he wouldn't even consider it. He put Faith into hiding, refused to listen to any of my reasoning, and had the baby swept away for adoption before Faith even had a chance to see it."

Annabel became teary again, saying softly, "However wrong the circumstances might have been, I don't believe Faith's actions can be judged too harshly. Who are we to cast stones, especially given what I believe was her need to simply feel loved, and to perhaps prove her father wrong?" Her voice quivered. "He is Faith's son . . . my grandson; and we will never see him again. We know he's in a good home, and he will be well cared for. But we will never see him. He might as well be dead to us. Perhaps adoption was the best alternative, but I believe Faith should have been allowed to make that decision for herself. She's a grown woman. But Angus bribed the people who knew about it to keep quiet, and once it had all been taken care of, he wouldn't allow us to ever speak of it in his presence."

Annabel stood abruptly and turned her back to the group as if she didn't want them to know how upset she was. "I told myself I would not speak ill of Angus. I tried to feel no ill will toward him, despite the challenges. But for the sake of my daughters, I cannot remain silent any longer. I must speak the truth—the facts." She turned and knelt next to Faith, who was still crying in Meri's arms. "My darling girl," she said, taking both of her hands. "I'm so very sorry . . . that you had to go through that . . . and I'm sorry that I couldn't protect you better . . . that I couldn't have done something differently so that—"

"It's not your fault, Mother," Faith said, sniffling as her sobs softened. "You were always there for me, always made me feel loved and accepted."

"But I should have had more courage to stand up to him," Annabel said.

"You *did* stand up to him," Faith said. "He was the man of the house; he had all the control and the power. There's nothing any of us could have done to change that." Faith sat up straight and wiped at her tears with her hands. "But I'm glad he's dead, and I'm glad I don't have to be silent about it anymore. Meri's right. We're family. We should be able to talk about our heartache and help each other through. Perhaps if I could talk about him . . . my son . . . I could eventually find some peace over losing him."

"I believe that's possible," Meri said, her hand on Faith's shoulder. "Did you know that I lost a baby?"

Faith looked at Meri, astonished. "No! How could we not know that?"

Meri realized then that Elliott didn't know either. She looked at him to see his silent echo to Faith's question, but she would have to talk to him later. For now, she turned her attention completely to Faith.

"I wrote and told your mother, but I asked her not to tell anyone else. It's not her fault. I didn't want to talk about it, but some months have passed . . . and I think that I *should* talk about it. He died within minutes after he was born. He was taken away and they wouldn't let me see him. My husband was very . . . controlling, and . . . he ignored my requests to see my son. Even though he was dead I wanted to hold him and at least be able to say goodbye."

"Yes!" Faith said, taking hold of Meri's hand. "I wish I could have just said goodbye; I wish I at least had the memory of knowing what he looked like."

"Yes," Meri agreed, and Faith embraced her tightly.

"Thank you," Faith said, easing back, "for forcing us out of this ridiculous silence. I'm tired of the secrets." She looked around at her sisters as if to imply that they *all* had secrets. "It's time to make a new beginning . . . to heal . . . together."

"I agree," Meri said.

"As do I," Elliott asserted, and everyone turned to him as if they'd forgotten he was in the room. "And I'm here for you . . . all of you . . . no matter what you might need."

"Thank you," Faith said, almost sounding like a different person. It seemed that by openly sharing a portion of her grief, and speaking of her true feelings to the entire family, she felt somewhat calmer. Meri hoped that her sisters might follow her example, although she knew it wasn't necessarily all going to come out into the open today.

They were all startled when Charity came to her feet, declaring, "I need to go for a walk. If I don't get some fresh air I'll . . . break something." The way she said it made Meri wonder if her brisk walks were somehow her means of letting off steam about whatever *she* might be holding inside. Whatever it might be, she was making it clear she had no intention of talking about it today—and perhaps not ever. Meri needed to be realistic about the fact that she could not help her cousins if they had no desire to share their painful secrets with the family and seek their support.

Charity stepped toward Faith and kissed her sister's brow. "I love you, dear sister," she said. "You know I do."

"I know you do," Faith said. "And I love you, as well. Be careful," she added, as if there might be wild beasts in the woods, and Meri saw a glance pass between them that left her certain there was more to Charity's walks than what they were all being led to believe. Another secret. And how many more might they yet uncover?

Meri looked around the room at these women she loved so dearly, and she felt a distinct heartache and concern for every one of them. She marveled at how much damage one selfish, critical man could cause, even if he'd never consciously intended to do so. He'd certainly never put any effort into curbing his bad behaviors, even when they'd been appropriately pointed out to him. In Meri's mind, that still made his unintentional criticism and judgment—and even cruelty—something for which he was certainly guilty.

Meri felt heartbroken and overwhelmed. After Charity left the room, Meri expressed her love for all her cousins, and her gratitude for Faith having the courage to openly share her experience and her feelings.

"I hope we can talk more," Meri said. "I think it would be good for all of us."

"I agree," Annabel said, and a couple of her daughters nodded slightly to indicate their hesitant agreement.

"I should check on the children," Meri said and hurried out of the room, suddenly feeling like she might suffocate if she didn't leave. The enormity of heartache in the room was almost palpable. She hurried up the stairs and wasn't surprised to hear Elliott's footsteps behind her, although with his long legs she knew he was taking the stairs three at a time, and he quickly caught up to her. She couldn't deny being glad for his ongoing support. She would have been disappointed if he *hadn't* followed her.

"Are you all right?" he asked, but at least he wasn't demanding to know why she hadn't told him about the death of her baby. She hoped to put off that conversation until another time.

"Not really," she admitted as they came to the top of the stairs and started down a long hallway. "You?"

"Not at all," he said. "And I can't even find the words to tell you why." It seemed he'd forgotten about her baby for the moment; or perhaps that was also included in his reasons for not being all right.

"No words are necessary," she countered. "I know how you feel because I feel the same; we both love them, and we are . . . in such a strange situation—a part of the family and yet on the outside of this strange . . . moral farce . . . that has existed in the family, which seems to have grown much worse in the years since I left."

"And apparently I've been oblivious to it in my comings and goings over the years. Clearly, they were all on their best behavior for me."

Meri stopped walking and Elliott did the same. She turned to face him and took hold of his arms. "It's difficult to know what to do . . . how to go about helping them . . . but I feel like we should . . . like we have to."

"I agree."

"But I could never do it alone, Elliott. I want you to know that just having you in the room gives me strength, and it helps me believe that we'll all get through this."

Elliott pulled her into his arms and embraced her tightly, wordlessly assuring her that they were in this together. If not for him, Meri believed she might go to her room and lock the door and be tempted to never come out again.

Chapter Seven

THE PLAGUE

MERI SLIPPED OUT OF ELLIOTT'S arms and hurried to find the children. Elliott followed, but she was relieved to be with Elaine and Crispin, knowing that Elliott wouldn't initiate any serious conversation in their presence. While she sat and observed Elliott and the children playing, a heaviness began to descend upon her. All that had come to light since Angus's death was swirling around in her mind, tapping into facets of her own life that were feeling more uncomfortable than they had since she'd left the prison of the Sturgess home to come here.

Meri didn't realize her breathing had become shallow until she heard Elliott say, "Are you all right?"

Seeing the concern on his face, she had to acknowledge her growing internal discomfort. "Actually," she said, "I'm not feeling very well. I think I'll go and lie down . . . if you don't mind watching out for the children."

"Of course I don't mind," he said, jumping to his feet. "Is there anything else I can do?"

"No, thank you," she said, hurrying to the door. "I just need to rest."

Once Meri had left the room and closed the door, she practically ran to her own room, wanting to be alone before a sudden, inexplicable wave of emotion erupted out of her. She kicked off her shoes and burrowed beneath the covers, pressing her face into a pillow where she wept uncontrollably.

* * *

Elliott couldn't help but feel concerned when Meri rushed out of the playroom, clearly upset. He distracted himself by remaining engaged with the delightful antics of the children, but he was relieved when Alice appeared and asked if he would like her to take over now. He left Elaine and Crispin each with a tight hug and a big, excessively loud smooch on the cheek that had become a lighthearted ritual between them.

Elliott went to Meri's room and knocked lightly on the door. He didn't hear a response so he opened it slightly and could see from a distance that she was beneath the covers and appeared to be sleeping. He closed the door quietly and left her to rest, relieved at least to know where she was. But he wished he knew what was troubling her. A great deal of difficult information had come to light recently, but he sensed that whatever troubled Meri was more personal than her concern for her aunt and cousins.

Elliott went downstairs to Angus's office, knowing that it was now supposed to be his. He'd spent a little time here since his uncle's death, looking through estate records and going over the current books that indicated the financial workings of the household and the tenant farms he had now inherited. It all still felt very strange to him, but he was glad to have received sufficient education to understand what all these facts and figures meant, and even though he didn't feel prepared to oversee all that had been bequeathed to him, he felt confident that he could manage well enough—especially with the guidance of the senior members of the staff and the overseers, who were loyal, trustworthy, and hard-working.

Leaning back in Angus's chair behind the desk, Elliott's thoughts simmered with the recent confessions of Annabel and Faith, and he felt decidedly more concerned about his feelings of responsibility for their well-being, along with that of his other cousins—and that of Meri and the children, of course. He wondered for a moment how it might have been if Meri and the children weren't here. If she had not been widowed . . . if she'd not come back here with her children with the intention of never going back to her deceased husband's home. Would Elliott have chosen to stay here? Or would he have simply made certain that everything was in order and continued to come and go as he'd done for years? There was no point speculating over *that.* Meri *was* here, and he found it easy to think of them staying here forever. It wasn't that they couldn't afford to move elsewhere and find a new home; they certainly could. And his aunt and cousins would be able to continue living in the comfort and security to which they were accustomed. But Elliott felt better about actually living in the same home as these women, most of whom seemed fragile and perhaps lost in a way. He wanted to be able to help care for them, and he knew Meri felt the same way. Instinctively, they had become partners in wanting to be certain all was well with Annabel and her daughters. And the thought of *not* living under the same roof with them seemed a little too boring and quiet. The house was huge, and there was plenty of space—and love—to go around.

Elliott looked around the room and recalled being told by more than one of the servants that he needed to make this place his own now that Angus was gone. He noted the shelves of Angus's collections—an odd array of things that Elliott had enjoyed looking at when he'd been a child. He decided they shouldn't be done away with; he knew Elaine and Crispin liked to look at them. But they should be moved elsewhere—perhaps to one of the parlors where they could be enjoyed as a tribute to Angus; and he thought that a cabinet with glass doors would keep all the little pieces safe and in need of less dusting.

Hearing the clock chime he realized it was time for supper and he hurried to the dining room, anxious to see how Meri was doing. He was disappointed to find her absent. A maid announced that Meri had chosen to have supper brought to her room.

"Is she all right?" Faith asked, looking at Elliott.

"I believe she's just very tired," he said with a reassuring smile, even though he felt inwardly concerned.

Elliott noticed during the meal that Annabel and Faith both seemed much better than they had for a very long time—or perhaps ever. He could see now that the Annabel with whom he'd shared private conversations throughout his life was not the same woman she had been in Angus's presence. And now that Angus was gone, it was as if she had the freedom to be completely herself. She was trying to engage her daughters in conversation, but it was mostly Faith who seemed to respond. She too was more free and open than he'd ever seen her. Sharing the burden of her secret had obviously been therapeutic for her. It was evident that her sisters had all known about it, but they'd never been allowed to talk about it in front of their father, and he wondered if that had led to them not talking about it at all.

Elliott felt relieved and satisfied to observe the obvious boost of spirits with Annabel and Faith, but it only added to his concern for the others.

Hope was—as usual—preoccupied with a book she was reading, and she barely managed to eat while it seemed difficult for her to take her eyes off the printed pages. But Charity, Joy, and Comfort were almost as quiet as Hope, as if their minds were equally far away. He wondered what burdens they were carrying, and if they would ever be able to follow Faith's example and share them in a way that might help them heal and openly allow themselves to be supported by the family.

As soon as Elliott could politely excuse himself from the dinner table, he hurried up to Meri's room, needing to know if she was all right. Instinctively he knew she wasn't, but he needed to understand why. He felt worried about her, and it didn't seem right to leave her on her own when he knew she was troubled. He was dismayed to discover that she was not in her room, and the supper tray that had been brought there showed that she had eaten very little. He found Alice watching over the children, and she reported that Meri had gone for a walk to the beach.

"She told me she wanted to watch the sun go down," Alice said, "and I was to put the little ones to bed."

"Thank you, Alice," Elliott said and took a few minutes to talk to the children and reassure them that all was well, and both he and their mother would see them in the morning.

Not certain when Meri had left, or how long she might have been walking, Elliott went to the stables and bridled a horse but mounted without a saddle, not wanting to take the time. He rode toward the sound of the waves, loving the way they became louder as he got closer. It was an experience that connected him to many good memories. He guided the horse down the steep decline to the beach and scanned the area to see Meri a good distance up the beach, much farther than she usually went. She was standing with her shawl wrapped tightly around her arms, looking out over the ocean while the breeze coming off the water teased at her hair and clothing. She looked so beautiful that for a long moment he just watched and waited, overcome with an indescribable joy at the prospect of spending his life with her. He felt enormously blessed, and a quiet peace settled over him, as if some source beyond himself wanted him to know that everything would be all right. Elliott took that peace in and held it close for a long moment before he recalled his reasons for coming here in search of Meri. He heeled the horse toward her, and as he got closer, she turned to see him approaching.

"What are you doing here?" she asked as he halted the horse and dismounted.

"Looking for you, obviously," he said, holding to the horse's reins with one hand while putting an arm around her shoulders. "You were upset, and then you didn't come to supper. I've been worried about you."

"No need for that," she said and looked toward the horizon with an expression that contradicted her words.

"Meri," he said gently and tightened his embrace, "I know you better than that. Talk to me."

He felt her relax a little and put her head on his shoulder. She sighed deeply and he wondered if she would tell him she didn't want to talk about it, or if she would actually let him know what was troubling her.

"Do you think," she began, "that *you* were influenced in any negative way with all the time you spent here growing up?"

"I've never really thought about it," he said. "Until recently I'd never given much thought at all to the potential challenges of growing up under the influence of Uncle Angus with all of his personal difficulties. Why are you asking me this?"

"Because I realized somewhere in between crying myself to sleep and walking down here that the things that have been said . . . the truth that's coming out . . ." She sighed again and seemed to be struggling for the right words. "It's all very personal, Elliott. I couldn't see it before, but I can see it now. I believe I married a harsh and unloving man because somewhere deep inside I believed it was the best I could hope for and I should be grateful for an offer of marriage that would provide for me financially. I remember now how our uncle had made many comments that at the time had seemed innocent enough, but now I realize that he'd made me feel like a burden . . . another mouth to feed . . . another female to care for. By getting married I was eliminating his obligation of having to care for me."

She wiped a hand over her cheeks and sniffled. "And I think that I've suffered from the same kind of feelings that Annabel described regarding her daughters. I keep hearing her words over and over . . . that they had suffered greatly from the daily comments made by their father that led them to believe they would never find suitable marriages, that no decent man would ever be willing to take care of them." Meri looked up at Elliott. "Did I not believe the same thing about myself? I look back and I can see signs that Lord Sturgess was not necessarily a kind and tender man. But neither was Angus. Was I drawn to him because it was . . . comfortable somehow? And yet my husband was far worse than my uncle."

She blew out a trembling breath and looked back toward the horizon. "I feel . . . disoriented, Elliott. I feel as if I've just realized so much about why I have done what I've done, and that so much of it was because of the influence of growing up with such distorted and negative attitudes. I don't know whether to feel angry or just . . . well . . . I don't know."

"I can certainly understand why you'd feel angry. It saddens me to say that everything you're telling me makes perfect sense. It's difficult to look back and see that someone you loved and looked up to actually created so much damage in your life."

"And what about you?" Meri looked at him, her eyes piercing him with a question that seemed far deeper than he understood. "Were you not impacted by all of this?"

"I don't know, Meri. It's certainly something to think about."

"I believe it was different for you."

"Different how?"

"For one thing, you never actually *lived* here. You spent intervals of many weeks, sometimes months, but it was never your actual home."

"And yet I always considered my actual home to be far worse than anything I experienced while being here."

"It's also different because you are a man," Meri said as if she resented it.

"How so?" he asked, trying not to sound defensive. "Obviously I can't help the fact that I'm male."

"No, of course not," she said more softly. "But it's impossible for a man to fully comprehend what life looks like from a woman's eyes . . . especially when life is controlled so much by men. There is a vast amount of complicated differences that could be discussed a great deal, but I could sum it up by simply stating that a woman is required both by society and the law to be completely reliant upon men. If a woman is lucky enough to have good men in her life, that's not so bad; but it's often the opposite. I'm certain it's not easy for you to have suddenly been given the responsibility of caring for seven women, and I'm not trying to negate how that feels for you. My point is that we are all very blessed to know that you are such a good man. What if you weren't? What if things had worked out differently regarding Angus's property? Neither our aunt nor any of our cousins have any control whatsoever regarding their future security. But it's as if such laws have sanctioned the way people behave in society. Women are subjected to life, whereas men have the right to make certain choices."

Elliott listened to the woman he loved express thoughts that had never before crossed his mind. Since Meri seemed to be finished saying what she needed to say, he told her, "You've certainly given me a great deal to think about, but I hope you know that I don't see you—or any of the other women in our family—as anything less than my equals."

"I know that," she said, turning to him with soft eyes. "You are the best of the best, Elliott. I was merely trying to make a point."

"And given the fact that you were treated unfairly in your marriage, combined with this new perspective of our uncle, I can understand why you feel unsettled."

Meri looked away and Elliott once again felt unnerved to realize there were things she'd never told him. He wondered when they might get to the point where they could stop keeping secrets from each other. As much as he preferred to hold onto his own dark experiences, he was beginning to see how damaging that could be. But they'd had enough drama for one day, and he could see that Meri was tired—in body and spirit.

"Let's go home," he said. "We can talk some more tomorrow. I'm certain it will take time to come to terms with all that's happened."

"Yes," she said somewhat acridly, "and I have a feeling we've not yet begun to see the truth of everything going on in that house."

"Then we'd better get some rest," he said in a tone that he hoped would lighten the mood.

Elliott helped Meri mount the horse and he mounted behind her, reaching around her to take control of the reins. As he eased the horse into an easy gallop along the edge of the ocean, he heard Meri laugh and was glad for the evidence that her mood had brightened.

"We should do this more often," she said.

"Yes, we should," he agreed and turned the horse around to run the length of the beach again before they returned home.

* * *

Meri determined firmly—after a great deal of prayer—that she needed to do everything in her power to help her cousins openly discuss their challenges, with the hope that they could experience the kind of healing Meri was witnessing with Annabel and Faith, now that they were no longer hiding the truth, pretending to feelings they'd been forced to assume. Meri also talked her feelings through with Elliott in great detail—in a way that had always been comfortable and natural between them. He agreed that they should lovingly do all they could to encourage their cousins to share their true feelings and try to heal.

Less than a week after Faith had openly talked about the illegitimate baby she'd given birth to—and had been forced to give away—Meri's concern for her cousins was growing. She'd had some wonderful conversations privately with Faith in which they'd talked about the babies they'd lost, shared many tears, and worked through many difficult emotions. Meri knew it was not only helping Faith, but was helping her as well. She also knew that her aunt was doing well. But the other sisters were as closed off as they'd ever been. Determined to create some change in this damaging pattern, Meri interrupted the strained silence that had become typical of teatime by saying, "I think it's time we all stop pretending that everything is all right when it clearly is not. I believe it would be wise for all of us to follow Faith's example and talk about the things we're holding inside."

Following a long moment while everyone stared at Meri as if she'd turned purple, Hope snapped at her in a tone of voice Meri had never heard come out of her cousin's mouth. "That's easy for you to say when you've been blessed with the privilege of marriage and children. When you've been cared for and loved by a fine man, you have no business telling us what we may or may not be allowed to feel."

Meri was so stunned that it took her a full minute to respond. But she did so with honesty and confidence. "First of all, Hope, I am not telling any of you what you are allowed to feel. You are all entitled to your own feelings, whatever they may be. I am only concerned that keeping these feelings to yourself—especially when they are painful and volatile—will only make you more and more miserable. And as to your reference to my being *blessed,* please allow me to set the record straight. I feel *very* blessed to have two beautiful children, but my life with Lord Sturgess was anything but blessed. He was a harsh and cruel man, and there was not a person in that house who was willing to offer any tidbit of kindness." She saw surprise in the eyes of all her cousins, and she hurried to finish.

"You have no idea what I have been through or how it has affected me, just as I have no idea about *your* experiences. But I think it's time we stopped keeping secrets from each other—especially when those secrets are creating walls of silence and tension that are affecting all of us."

No one spoke for a minute or more, then Charity stood up and said, "I'm going for a walk."

Charity huffed out of the room and Hope stood up, slamming the book closed that she had been reading before Meri had made her declaration. "I'm going to my room where I can read in peace."

Comfort stood up and said with less disdain, "I just want to be alone."

Before Comfort was out the door, Joy stood up and followed her, saying over her shoulder, "I'd best make certain my sisters are all right."

Meri took hold of Elliott's hand and looked at Annabel and Faith, who both appeared as downhearted as she felt. The only two who remained were those who had already been willing to let go of their disillusionments and share their pain.

"Well," Elliott sighed and said with light sarcasm, "I think that went extremely well, darling."

"I believe it needed to be said," Annabel added. "And even if they didn't take to it today, it's given them something to think about."

"I'm glad you said it," Faith interjected. "I *wanted* to say it, but I didn't know how."

Meri exchanged a wan gaze with Elliott, wishing she didn't feel so weighed down by the challenges being faced by her family members. She cared for each of them deeply and wanted them to be happy. Besides that, she couldn't deny that their struggles had tapped into her own. Realizing what she'd just confessed to her cousins made her feel a little queasy. And the whole thing was not resting well within her spirit.

* * *

Meri both wanted to talk to Elliott and didn't want to talk about it at all. She honestly had lost track of what she'd told him about her marriage, but she felt relatively certain he had heard her say things today that he'd never heard before. She was glad to be able to escape to the playroom and be with the children, and even though Elliott arrived there only a few minutes later, being in the presence of the children made it impossible for them to engage in any serious conversation.

When it was time for the adults to go downstairs for dinner, Alice took over the care of the children, and Elliott guided Meri into the hall and toward the stairs. He touched the center of her back and asked quietly, "Would you go for a walk with me later? After the children are put to bed?"

"So late?" she asked, if only to perhaps make an excuse that might make it possible to avoid any difficult conversation.

"You don't have to talk if you don't want to," he said as if he'd read her mind. "Just . . . come with me."

"Very well," she said and smiled at him as they headed down the stairs. Lightening her tone with the hope that it would lighten her mood, she added, "I suppose that I could tolerate your company for such a thing as a late-night stroll."

"How very gracious of you," he replied with the same light sarcasm.

Meri wasn't terribly surprised to find that three of her cousins were absent, having opted for supper in their rooms. Those who were present remained very quiet despite Annabel's efforts to initiate pleasant conversation, and Elliott did well at responding to their aunt's comments, which helped ease the silence if nothing else.

When supper finally ended and Meri had tucked the children into bed for the night, she was glad to be able to leave the house. She wrapped a shawl around her arms and shoulders, expecting to have Elliott guide her toward the gardens. But he headed in a different direction at a fairly brisk pace, and she wondered what his intentions might be.

"Where *are* we going?" she asked, holding tightly to his hand, glad for the way the children kept her active so that she could keep up.

"You'll see," he said and then said nothing else as they walked a very long while, and Meri completely lost her sense of direction, although she was keenly aware that they were mostly going uphill.

Suddenly Elliott stopped and declared, "Tah-dah!"

Meri had been mostly focused on looking at her feet to be certain she didn't misstep and trip. She looked up and around and gasped. They were standing in a lovely grassy spot at the crest of a hill, where the absence of trees made it possible for them to have a perfect view of Rosewell Abbey by looking in one direction. Looking in the other direction, they could see the distant lights of the village. "I'd completely forgotten about this place," she declared, still a little out of breath from their brisk walk.

"I've been wanting to come back here with you," Elliott said, "but things have been . . . complicated."

Meri hadn't even noticed that he'd been carrying a blanket over his free arm until he spread it out on the ground and sat on it, patting the ground beside him to indicate that she should join him, and her memories of their coming here together became clearer. Elliott lay back on the blanket and put his hands behind his head, and she lay back as well, a prudent distance from him, recalling now how many times they had come here together in their youth to look at the stars. Given how young they'd been, they'd often had to sneak out after everyone had believed they'd gone to bed, and it had been a great adventure.

"There's no moon tonight," Elliott said, "so I knew we would be able to see the stars more clearly."

"Oh, they're magnificent!" Meri declared, wondering how long it had been since she'd made the effort to just look up and admire the beauty and wonder of a starlit sky.

"Do you remember," Elliott said, taking hold of her hand, "how we would watch for shooting stars so that we could make a wish?"

"I do," she said, "although we didn't see them very often."

"Which made them more special, and the wishes even more likely to come true."

"You never told me what you wished for," she said.

"Nor did you," he added. "You can't *tell* anyone your wish . . . or it might not come true. Although," he added, "I'm wondering if it's all right to tell someone your wish after it *has* come true."

"I don't see why not," Meri said, still gazing at the magnificent view of the sky.

Elliott tightened his hold on her hand by threading his fingers between hers, and his voice softened with meaning. "*This* is what I wished for, Meri." She turned to look at him, not surprised to find him looking at her. "I wished for us to be all grown up, and to be together. I wished for us to be able to share our lives in every way." He drew her hand to his lips and kissed it. "My greatest wish is coming true, Meri, and I wonder how I could be blessed with such a miracle."

Meri looked at the sky and sighed. "It *is* a miracle," she agreed. "I just . . ."

"What?" he asked when she hesitated. "Please don't tell me you're having doubts . . . about us . . . or . . ."

"No," she said. "You are the best thing that ever happened to me, Elliott. I simply don't want the things that happened in my previous marriage to come back to haunt me . . . us. I want to be a good wife to you, but perhaps I don't know how."

"I absolutely disagree with that," he said, letting go of her hand to turn onto his side and lean on his elbow.

Meri drew the courage to look at him and say, "I thought you would want to talk about what I said earlier."

"What I want is for you to know that you can tell me anything, and it won't change how I feel. You keep hinting at the fact your marriage was dreadful . . . and I hope you can trust me enough to tell me more . . . but only when you're ready. And I will love you no matter what, Meri. However the past might have impacted us, we will work it out together."

Meri lifted a hand to touch his face. "It's no wonder I love you."

He smiled and kissed her and lay back down to look up at the sky. "I love you too, Grace Meriwether."

Meri loved looking at the stars and feeling the peace that settled over her as she did. She loved having Elliott by her side, and the fact that they didn't talk at all about the drama taking place with their cousins. There would be plenty of time for them to face such things. For now, she felt like the world with all its pain and drama was too far away to ever intrude on this magical moment.

* * *

Over the next few days, everything seemed almost normal when the family gathered for meals and tea. Almost. The underlying tension was impossible to ignore, even though everyone was clearly trying to do so. Meri was deeply grateful for the excuse of needing to spend time with her children, and she also took any opportunity she could arrange to spend time alone with Elliott. If her cousins weren't willing to talk about their struggles or difficult feelings, there was nothing anyone could do to help them. But it was impossible to avoid seeing the demeanor and attitude of those who were holding their pain inside; it was as visible as if they had pockmarks on their faces.

On the fourth day after Meri had tried to provoke her cousins into admitting to their secrets—and she had instead ended up confessing to her own—tea with the family felt especially strained. After several minutes of taut silence, Joy set her teacup down with a force that made it rattle in the saucer, and Meri worried for a moment that it might have actually broken. The sound turned everyone's attention toward her even before she said, "I cannot bear this any further. I feel as if I've spent my entire life trying to help my sisters . . . and protect them somehow." Her eyes scanned the room and Meri did the same, realizing that the other three sisters who had not already come forward with their confessions all looked utterly terrified. But Joy didn't seem to care. She looked directly at her mother, as if it was to her she needed to make her confession, yet it was necessary for everyone to be present.

"I've kept their secrets, Mother, and I've helped them do things I knew were not good, but somehow I convinced myself that these things could be justified. But I won't do it any longer." Joy glanced at Faith, who was the only one of the girls who seemed pleased with what was happening.

Faith nodded, as if to encourage Joy, who continued by saying, "I knew about Faith's pregnancy before anyone else, and I tried to convince her that Father would let her keep the baby." Tears rolled down Joy's face. "When he refused to even consider it, I somehow felt as if it was *my* fault that she had to give her baby away."

"No, of course not!" Faith insisted.

Joy nodded toward Faith in appreciation, but it seemed she didn't want to lose momentum. She turned again toward Annabel and said, "I think it's true that we should no longer have secrets in this house. Our secrets are like a plague, destroying us all from the inside out, when we should be bound together as a family, working to overcome our struggles. We should be helping each other get better instead of helping each other cover up what's really going on. I've been thinking a great deal about this, and I've realized that I'm the one who has done most of that covering up. I don't know why my sisters come to me for help, and why I go against my principles over and over to help them, but I have done it for years. Well, I'm not going to do it anymore." She hit a fist on the arm of her chair and startled everyone in the room.

"Don't you *dare,*" Charity snarled in a tone of voice Meri had never heard before, "think that you can speak on my behalf and spill my private matters in front of everyone. It's my business and mine alone."

"And it will see you nowhere but hurt," Joy said to her angry sister. Her voice firm with courage. "I'm not assisting you any further in this madness, and I am no longer keeping secrets for *any* of you!" Hope and Comfort both looked concerned as well, although Comfort looked more so.

"Mother," Joy said, and Charity erupted to her feet.

"I'm not going to sit here and have my sister demean me and—"

"Sit down," Annabel said to Charity with the kind of authority a parent would use with a very young child who had been caught doing mischief. "I will not tolerate secrets among us another day. I want to hear what Joy has to say, and you *will* stay here and listen. If you leave, how will you know whether what she's telling me is true?"

Charity sat down reluctantly but looked terrified. Joy took a deep breath and looked again at her mother. "When Charity leaves the house for her long walks, it is usually to meet a man who has taken a fancy to her. If they aren't meeting, they are leaving letters for each other."

Annabel took this in and turned to look at Charity. "If a man has taken a fancy to you, then why not invite him over for tea so we can become acquainted?"

Charity's face tightened and she looked at the floor. Annabel looked to Joy for the answer. Joy's words came with tears that made it clear her motives were based in concern for her sisters, as opposed to any intention to hurt them. "Because he's married," Joy said, and everyone in the room gasped except for Charity, who put her hands over her face.

Meri exchanged a discreetly astonished glance with Elliott while she waited for Annabel to say something wise and insightful. But instead, Hope said with excessive zeal, "Well, I don't have any secrets you need to tattle about to everyone else, so I might as well just go and—"

Hope rose to her feet and again Annabel said, "Sit down. No one will be excluded from this. No one is leaving this room until my daughters' secrets are out in the open. No one!"

Hope sat down and tossed Joy a daring glare that implied she *did* have a secret. Joy said to her, "Some might not consider the way you always need to have a book in your hands to be anything of concern; and maybe it's not. But you've become so obsessed with continually reading and getting lost in fictional worlds that the rest of us hardly even know you anymore. If you're not reading, you're talking about what you've been reading. Except for attending church, you don't even step outside of the house because you want to be reading. I'm concerned, Hope, that you're hiding from things you don't want to talk about, because I know that Father disapproved of your romance with the butcher's son, and now he's married with children. Can you honestly tell us that your heart was not broken? Is it broken still?"

Hope put a hand over her mouth as tears erupted. And Charity still had her hands over her face, with her head drooping more and more in shame. Again, while Meri waited for her aunt to say something that would help ease the awkwardness and tension of this unfolding drama, Comfort blurted out, "I suppose you're going to tell *my* secret too!"

Comfort sounded almost like a snotty child, but Joy responded kindly, "Not if you tell it first."

Comfort only turned and looked toward the window, silently implying that she would *not* tell her secret—whatever it might be. Joy looked at her mother and said, "Comfort is careful to not eat excessively—for the most part—when we share meals and tea. But she is continually sneaking food out of the kitchen—or trying to talk me into doing it for her—and she has food hidden in several places in her room where the servants wouldn't look when they clean. She eats almost continually when she is alone, and I'm deeply concerned for her health—especially after what happened to Father."

"Is this true?" Annabel asked Comfort in a kind voice.

"What difference does it make?" Comfort snapped.

"I want to understand why you feel the need to eat so much, darling," Annabel said. "I want you to be healthy so that you can live a good life. We can support you in changing your habits, but not if you keep the problem a secret." Annabel looked toward Hope and Charity, who were sitting close together. "And I want to understand what's going on for both of you. Hope, my darling, I don't want you hiding away from the world with a broken heart, and Charity, dearest, I need to understand why you would think that dallying with a married man is all right."

"What other man would have me?" Charity snapped from beneath her hands, and her crying became more audible.

"Well," Annabel said with a sigh that made evident the weight she felt on her shoulders as mother to these five struggling women, "it seems we need many private conversations, and we obviously have to figure out how to manage this family better in the future than we have in the past. Although," she sighed again, "I think we've had enough drama for the moment. I want you all to go to your rooms and rest, and I will come talk with each of you when I can. I'm certain it will take time to thoroughly talk these things through, and to find solutions. I think supper in our rooms would be best this evening."

The sisters all left the room, some as if they couldn't leave quickly enough. Meri and Elliott were left alone with Annabel, who began to cry only after her daughters were no longer present.

"If there's anything we can do . . ." Elliott said.

"You are both so very kind," Annabel said, wiping her tears with her handkerchief. "I know it can't be easy for either of you to be here amid all this."

"We're family," Meri said. "We want to help in any way we can."

"Yes," Elliott agreed.

"And I am very grateful for that," Annabel said. "But . . . you can't fix these problems. I need to try to help each of my daughters with their individual needs and heartaches. Your love and support is greatly appreciated, but you must not take these problems onto your shoulders or assume responsibility for them. Although I promise you that if I need a shoulder to cry on myself, I will be hunting one or both of you down."

"I should hope," Elliott said.

Annabel then looked directly at Meri and surprised her by saying, "I've feared ever since you began courting Lord Sturgess that you too had been impacted by being raised in this home. I know you have your own heartache to come to terms with, my dear. You must work on healing your own wounds."

Meri could only nod slightly, wondering what kind of outburst she might exhibit if all her own experiences were brought to light.

Chapter Eight
The Debacle

For more than a week, the drama that had been unleashed among the bruised family Angus had left behind seemed to infiltrate every crack and crevice of the house. The servants were all clearly aware that a great many private conversations were taking place. They also obviously knew that meals were being taken to separate rooms, since some of the sisters apparently didn't even want to be in proximity with each other.

Meri and Elliott each had some private conversations with their aunt and some of their cousins; it was evident that some of them were doing better than others. While Meri and Elliott frequently discussed the concern they felt for their cousins, Meri became increasingly uneasy about her own secrets. She didn't feel the need to tell her cousins any more than they already knew, but there was so much that Elliott didn't know, and she knew that holding back was beginning to create tension between them. She wasn't at all surprised when he asked her to join him in the library one rainy evening after they had put the children to bed. A part of her wanted to just openly spill her every secret, if only she could get past the wall of fear that was blocking her. She didn't know if that was Elliott's purpose for wanting to talk, but she both hoped and feared that it was.

Once they were alone with the door closed, Elliott guided Meri to a sofa and sat close beside her, holding her hand. "Meri," he began, "so much has been going on, but . . . all of this drama with our cousins should not be holding you and me back from pursuing a life together. We talk all the time about sharing a future . . . as if we've both come to accept that it will happen. And yet when I mention anything specific . . . about becoming officially engaged . . . or just getting married . . . you're hesitant and evasive. And I need to understand why, Meri."

Meri looked down, knowing how unfair she'd been in that regard. He was right, even if she didn't want to accept the reasons for it.

"I want to marry you," Elliott said. "I don't understand why we both have to be alone at night when we spend our days almost as if we were already married."

As always, Elliott's insistence on moving forward with their relationship left her terrified. But he was right, and he deserved some kind of explanation. Meri just forced herself to put a voice to words she knew she needed to say. "There is so much you don't know, Elliott; so much that happened. There are things I don't want to talk about; things I don't know if I can *ever* talk about. And yet . . . I don't believe that secrets should exist in a marriage—not if it has any hope of being a *good* marriage." Feeling suddenly exposed and vulnerable, Meri turned the attention away from herself. "And I know very well that I'm not the only one keeping secrets. There are things that haunt you, Elliott; things you've never told me. You can't expect me to pour out every detail of what's happened during our years apart when you're not willing to do the same."

"Every detail?" he countered. "*Every* detail? How can you be concerned about *every detail* when you have told me so little, Meri? I know it was horrible; and I know that it damaged you. But I have no idea what really went on, because you won't let yourself open up to me about it beyond a certain point *at all*."

"I can't deny that's true," she admitted. "I don't want to talk about it *at all*. I just want it to . . . go away." Even as she said this, Meri realized how contradictory her words must sound, considering her recent conversations with their cousins.

"And yet you're the one who just said we shouldn't have any secrets. It won't just go away, Meri; none of it. We *must* talk about it. I don't need to know every detail, but I need to know what happened and why."

Meri felt herself trembling at the very idea of talking to him about her marriage, even though she knew he was right. In a desperate attempt to ward off her fears, she turned to him and spoke in a tone that was far fiercer than she'd intended. "You're sounding like a hypocrite, Elliott. Again, I say that you can't expect me to spill all my secrets when you have secrets of your own."

"So, you want me to go first?" he snapped and stood up. "Is that it? If I bare my soul, then you'll bare yours?"

Meri couldn't respond. She wanted him to bare his soul, but she did *not* want to bare her own. However, she had just accused him of hypocrisy, and she couldn't be that unfair. In her deepest self, she knew he was right. She was tired of keeping these secrets from him. It wasn't that she didn't trust him, and she certainly didn't believe he would think any less of her. Or did she? Perhaps that was part of the problem. She knew that speaking of what had happened, and sharing it with him, would make it all feel more real. But perhaps her biggest reason for avoiding it had been her fear that he would see the evidence of what a fool she'd been, and he *would* see her differently.

When Meri said nothing, Elliott leaned more toward her and said emphatically, "Fine. You want me to go first; I'll go first." He looked at the floor and took a deep breath. He looked at her again and drew back his shoulders as if to summon courage. She saw his eyes darken, and her heart began to pound as she wondered what he might tell her.

"I had an argument with Lawrence," he said and she wondered why *this* would be so serious. Elliott had been arguing with his older brother all his life. "We both said some awful things, but . . . I was a little bit drunk . . . and I said some things I'd never said before; horrible things. You know he was selfish by nature, and he had never made it easy to get along with him, but . . . I still shouldn't have said the things I said, and . . ."

Elliott looked to the side, giving her a perfect view of his profile. She noted that the side of his face had tightened and she could see his chin quivering. She wanted to say something to encourage him, but she believed it was better to just remain silent and allow him to finish. For the life of her, she couldn't imagine what might be so serious. He cleared his throat and looked at her. He cleared his throat again and said with a quaver in his voice, "A few hours later . . . he . . . put a gun to his head and . . ."

Meri gasped just before she put her hands over her mouth to hold back the sound. Was he saying what she thought he was saying? No one had even told her that Lawrence had died. Did this family know how to communicate *at all?* Again, she just waited for Elliott to go on.

"My mother . . . uh . . . heard the shot and . . . she found him. She has . . . uh . . ." Elliott squeezed his eyes closed, as if he either couldn't bear to look at Meri, or he couldn't bear to even think about what he was saying; probably both. "She . . . has never recovered. She hardly gets out of bed.

My sisters . . . are all . . . in agreement that . . . it was my fault; that I drove him to it. Sybil overheard our argument. They . . . are also all in agreement that . . . they're glad our father wasn't alive to have to face this, and . . . that our mother's condition is . . . also my fault. They have been so crass as to accuse me of wanting him dead so that I would inherit everything. Given the fact that I *have* inherited all my father's estate only increases my guilt. I didn't want it; I never wanted it. But my sisters do not believe me."

Elliott sat down suddenly on the opposite sofa as if he'd lost all his strength. He hung his head and pushed his hands through his hair. "Clearly . . . I can never go back there. I keep up regular communication with the overseer and the housekeeper; thankfully they have not lost respect for me and I know I can trust them to make certain that all is well, and they would let me know if there's a problem that needs my attention. They always know where I am as much as possible despite all my moving around. I've been . . . running . . . and hiding . . . somehow believing that time would make it better. But it hasn't. Not an hour passes when I don't . . . think about it . . . and regret . . . everything I said to him." He sighed deeply and added with a false lightness, "I've never had a single drink since then; I suppose that's something."

"Elliott," Meri said and sat beside him, putting a hand on his back, "you must know that one argument between you and your brother would not have driven him to such a dreadful choice."

"I *do* know that," he said with a sadness so deep it spurred tears into Meri's eyes. The shock of what he'd told her had dissipated and now she could feel his sorrow. "I've rehearsed over and over every conversation I ever had with him; every encounter between us throughout my entire life—at least the ones I can remember. I've prayed and prayed to be able to understand and to find peace. I know he was always prone to being irrational . . . to distorting the truth so intensely that he could almost make me believe his lies. I know it sounds strange, but . . . I sincerely believe that something was not right with his mind. My belief is that he'd been considering suicide for a long time; he'd made comments . . . dramatic, ridiculous comments about how we would be better off without him . . . and that we didn't deserve him . . . that we would regret the way we'd treated him. He was completely self-absorbed, and everything was always someone else's fault; and yet . . . it was as if my mother and sisters could not see the evidence of his manipulation and . . ."

Elliott hung his head further and let out a heavy breath. "I don't know; maybe I'm just rationalizing to make myself feel better. But . . . I would swear he'd been planning on doing it . . . and he purposely did it after an argument with me so that it *would* make it appear to be my fault. Obviously, there's no way of knowing where his thoughts were; he's gone and nothing will bring him back. I think what's most difficult is . . . the way I've been more or less banished from my family. Even though I never really enjoyed their company, and I always felt more comfortable here than in my own home, I hate the very idea of how they think of me . . . and how they feel about me. It's almost like I can feel this . . . toxic cloud created by the way they probably speak of me disparagingly in every conversation . . . and it follows me wherever I go."

Meri examined his countenance and knew there was absolutely nothing she could say to convince him that while his grief and sorrow were valid, his guilt was not. She simply said, "I'm so sorry you had to go through that, Elliott. I wish I could have . . . somehow . . . been there for you."

Elliott looked at her with a lengthy, thoughtful gaze. "I wish that too," he said. His eyes became more fixed on her and he added, "Not only do I wish you could have been there for me, I wish I could have been there for you."

Meri's concern for him slipped immediately into an unbridled panic as she realized that he had just opened his heart to her and shared the dark and painful secret he'd been holding there. And now he expected her to do the same. The very thought of letting the words out of her mouth made her heart pound, and a strange buzzing filled her ears, as if she'd just been attacked by a swarm of bees.

"I need some air," Meri said and stood abruptly, counting in her mind how many seconds it might take her to get out of the house with the hope that it would free her of this smothering sensation.

But Elliott stood as well and grabbed her arm before she even took a step. "If you're not ready to talk about it, Meri, it's all right, but don't run away from me."

Meri reluctantly turned and looked up at him the same moment she became aware that she was trembling. He glanced down to where he was holding her arm as he became aware of it too. "Is it so terrifying?" he asked, looking at her with a furrowed brow. "Does talking to me frighten you this much?"

"You do not frighten me, Elliott," she said and took hold of his arms as she pressed the side of her face to his shoulder, which prevented her from having to look at him. "But I don't want to talk about what happened; I don't even want to think about it."

"And now we're back where we began," he said, but he said it with compassion.

"I agree that there shouldn't be secrets between us," she admitted, "and I know . . . that you need to know. I'm just . . . not ready. Just . . . give me a little more time."

Meri heard disappointment in his sigh, but he wrapped her in his protective embrace and she felt the unspoken evidence that he would love her no matter what. "Of course," he said and pressed a kiss into her hair. "We're both tired," he added, much to her relief. "I'm certain that what I just told you is enough drama for one day."

Meri felt calmer now that she knew he wouldn't expect her to tell him anything tonight, and even more so with having the attention turned back to *his* struggles. She looked up at him and took his face into her hands. "It wasn't your fault, Elliott," she said with firm resolve.

She saw in his eyes that he wanted to believe her, and a tightening in his face that implied he was trying not to get emotional. He nodded very subtly and said in a low, husky voice, "A part of me knows that's true," he said. "Still . . . I'm haunted by it."

"I'm here for you," she said and kissed him.

"I am so glad for that." He kissed her again and guided her out of the room and up the stairs. He kissed her once more at the door to her room and left her for the night.

Once she was alone, Meri practically collapsed onto her bed. She felt no motivation to change into a nightgown, or even to check on the children as she always did. The very thought of telling Elliott the truth about her marriage brought back that buzzing in her ears. But she knew she had to; somehow, she had to find the courage to just do it. For reasons she didn't fully understand, she couldn't even fathom allowing the words into the open. For the sake of distracting herself from what she simply could not take on right now, she pushed her thoughts toward all that Elliott had told her about his brother's tragic death and his own difficult feelings of guilt associated with it. Tears crept from Meri's eyes to think of Elliott's suffering. He was a good man; he did not deserve to carry such a burden, and he certainly didn't deserve the way his family members treated him. Her heart ached just to think of it. She *did* wish she could have been there for him throughout the course of those events. Perhaps if they'd been married Elliott wouldn't have even been anywhere near his family home when his brother had made such a terrible choice. But Meri knew that wishing for the past to be different was as pointless as wishing for snow not to melt beneath a warm sun. The past could not be changed. The future was filled with unpredictability. She could only hold on to the present. And even with the sorrow she felt, she was immeasurably grateful to be safe with her children here in this home and to have Elliott here. She just prayed that when she could no longer procrastinate telling him the truth about her marriage, he would be able to forgive her for being such a fool.

* * *

The following day, the tension in the household was more evident than it had ever been. Meri stayed close to the children and enjoyed, as always, the way Elliott played with them. When they had their nap time, she made a graceful exit to her own room to lie down, since she hadn't slept very well the previous night.

Meri and Elliott had supper with the children since they'd been told the rest of the family were all once again having supper in their rooms. They both knew that Annabel was spending time every day with each of her daughters, urging them to talk through their heartache and losses, and the reasons for behaviors in their lives that were causing them pain—or inevitably would. There was nothing Meri or Elliott could do to help at the moment, so they just kept each other company and enjoyed their time with Elaine and Crispin—who were both so full of energy and natural joy that being with them was a great distraction.

Elliott asked Meri if she would join him for tea on the patio after the children had gone to bed. She anticipated the opportunity, especially since he'd made it clear that he didn't expect her to tell him the things she didn't want to talk about—until she felt ready. And she certainly didn't feel ready.

As soon as Meri had the children tucked into bed, knowing that Alice would be nearby if they needed anything, she hurried down the stairs and out to the patio where she knew Elliott would be waiting. She enjoyed this new habit of ofttimes sharing late-evening tea with him either here or in the solarium, and just being able to share pleasant conversation and relax. Doubting that she had ever felt completely relaxed during all her years of marriage, she was enjoying the process of learning to do so again. Her hovering fear over not wanting to talk to Elliott about certain things was assuaged by his promise to let her tell him when she was ready. She couldn't imagine *ever* being ready, and she knew he would not wait indefinitely, but for tonight she didn't have to worry about that. She just wanted to be in his presence and enjoy his company.

The sun had gone down and it was dusk as Meri stepped outside and closed the door behind her. Elliott smiled and stood to greet her as she moved toward him with the intention of sharing a quick kiss before she sat down. But a strange debacle occurred with the little table on which the tea tray had been set. Meri didn't know which one of them tripped over it, causing it to tip, or if it was simply the result of the table being between them while they were too focused on looking at each other. Meri only knew that the sound of the teapot and china cups crashing onto the patio floor triggered something strange and awful in her mind, and for a long moment she was far away from there in another time and place.

The second Elliott realized the table and its contents had toppled, he reached out for Meri to prevent her from doing the same. He was entirely unprepared for the way she didn't fall but rather dropped to her knees and shielded her face with her arms. "Don't! Please don't!" she begged in a voice of perfect terror. "It was an accident. I'm sorry. I won't let it happen again."

"Meri," Elliott said gently, attempting to take hold of her to help her to her feet, but she cowered further away and whimpered. His heart pounded and a sick knot formed in the pit of his stomach. She didn't have to tell him what her marriage had been like; the evidence was here in front of him, and he wondered if he'd ever felt so angry or shocked or horrified in all his life. He'd known Meri most of his life. And he knew her well. But this strong, confident, remarkable woman was cowering on the ground as if she'd been reduced to a nothingness he couldn't even fathom.

Pushing his own roiling emotions down to a level where they would not impair his ability to think clearly, he repeated her name again in a gentle voice and added, "It's me, Meri. It's Elliott. You're all right. Meri, it's fine." He saw the trance-like expression on her face begin to soften and he repeated all the same words, reassuring her that everything was fine and he wasn't going to hurt her. When she finally came to her senses and looked up at him, he saw her countenance change as she came out of the past, fully aware of what had just happened. Shame and embarrassment clouded her expression and she scrambled to her feet without allowing him to help her. She ran as if some sort of monster was chasing her, but he wasn't going to let her run away from *him*. Not anymore, and not like this. He knew now that she needed him; she needed someone to prove to her that she no longer had any reason to live in fear. And she needed to know that she had absolutely no reason to feel embarrassed or ashamed—not with him.

Elliott called out to her with the hope of convincing her to wait for him, but she glanced over her shoulder, lifted her skirts, and ran faster, disappearing around the corner of the house. He was glad that his legs were longer than hers and that their many childhood races reminded him that he could always outrun her. Turning the corner to the back of the house, he could barely see her in the growing darkness, but he ran as fast as he could and caught up with her quickly. When she ignored his request for her to stop, he took hold of her arm and held it tightly despite her attempts to wriggle free.

"Meri, stop," he said, taking hold of her other arm. "I'm not going to hurt you. You know I'm not. Stop and listen to me." She stopped fighting, but she wouldn't look at him while they both tried to catch their breath. "Meri," he said again, careful to maintain a calm tone that wouldn't alarm her, "there's no need to hide the truth from me, and there's nothing to be ashamed of. Nothing! Do you hear me?"

He heard her sob just before she slumped right out of his grasp, like a rag doll being dropped to the ground. He tried to break her fall but barely managed to get one arm around her waist as her skirt billowed out around her and the palms of her hands went to the grass to keep her upright. He knelt beside her and quickly realized the shallow sharpness of her breathing was not from running. She was in a state of shock and terror, as if she had just faced the devil himself and had barely escaped with her life intact. And perhaps that was true. The little accident on the patio had obviously taken her back to a time that had triggered a terror in her he couldn't begin to understand—even though he was fairly certain of its source.

"Meri," Elliott said in the kind of voice he might use with a frightened animal to keep it from bolting. He sat carefully on the ground but thought it best not to touch her until she calmed down. "Talk to me, Meri," he pleaded gently. "You don't have to hold it inside any longer, my darling. You can tell me anything . . . everything. I'm not going to hurt you, and I'm not going to leave you. Not ever, Meri. Do you hear me?"

When she hung her head and started to cry, Elliott was glad to know that she was finally allowing her pain into the open. When her crying turned to heaving sobs, he had to fight to keep his anger at bay. There would be plenty of time for him to try to come to terms with such hateful and horrible feelings toward the man who had done this to her. Right now, Meri was his only concern, and he needed to be nothing but calm and loving and accepting. When she leaned toward him as if she were having trouble remaining upright, he gladly caught her in his arms and guided her face to his chest where she cried so hard he wondered how she could keep breathing. And he cried with her. Silent tears crept down his face as he considered the possibilities of all that might have happened to her. Whatever had happened, the results were evident, and in addition to making him sick, it broke his heart.

"Meri," he whispered after her tears had slowly dissipated into a stark silence. He could hear only her breathing as he pressed a kiss into her hair.

"I'm so sorry," she murmured.

"Why on earth would you apologize to me?" he asked, trying not to sound as surprised as he felt.

"So many things," she said on the wave of a long sigh. "I feared that when I told you the truth . . . I would either erupt . . . or crumble completely. And now I've done both." She sighed again. "I don't want to burden you with this, Elliott."

"You could never be a burden to me, Meri. Never! Share your pain with me, and let me help you come to terms with it."

"I'm not sure that's possible."

"Anything is possible, Meri. With God's help and the love we share, anything is possible."

"I want to believe that," she said, tightening her hold on him. "But . . . you don't even know . . . what happened . . . and why . . . and . . ."

"After what happened this evening, I think I have a fairly good idea," he said.

Meri groaned with self-recrimination. "I'm so sorry," she said again.

"Stop apologizing, Meri. You have nothing to be sorry for." She didn't speak, but he knew she didn't believe him. He wondered how long it might take, or how hard it might be, to convince her of that—and of so many other things she had clearly lost throughout the past seven years. But they would never get beyond this if they didn't start talking about it. He could understand why she didn't *want* to talk about it, and he could understand why it would be difficult. But he couldn't help her heal if she wouldn't confide in him. In that moment, it occurred to him that perhaps if he stated the obvious . . . if he spoke the words she didn't want to say . . . then maybe it would be easier for her. He took a deep breath and silently prayed for inspiration to know exactly what to say and how to say it.

"Meri," he began, "life is full of little mishaps and accidents. We all drop things . . . and break things . . . because we're human. And it's all right." He took another deep breath and hurried to just ask the big, ugly question that was hanging in the air. "How many times did he hit you, Meri, simply because you're human?"

He could almost feel her grimace by the way she tightened up and withdrew slightly. He heard her breathing sharpen again and feared another outburst. But she said with a quivering voice, "Too many times to count."

"Oh, Meri," he murmured and pressed a hand over her hair. "If I had known . . ."

"There's nothing you could have done," she said, and he sensed the need to keep his own thoughts to himself for the moment, if only to encourage her to talk more about what had happened.

"Tell me," he urged when she didn't go on.

Meri sighed, hesitated, and sighed again. "I don't know if I was completely blind and gullible when he was courting me, or if he was simply a very good actor. I know he certainly put effort into deceiving me . . . into playing the perfect gentleman in the interests of acquiring a wife. But looking back . . . I still believe there must have been some indication of his true character, and somehow I missed it." He felt her tremble in his arms as if she was getting closer to letting go of words that were more difficult. "As soon as we were married . . . almost within the hour . . . his true self began to show. I was confused . . . and terrified. But what could be done? Still, what I feared then became insignificant in light of how it came to be."

Meri moved suddenly away from him, as if for some reason she required distance. He feared that she would say nothing more about it, or perhaps even run away again. But she drew her legs up against her chest and rested the side of her face on her knees. Even in the darkness he could see the faraway look in her eyes, and what could only be described as despair in her demeanor. He'd sensed that something had changed in her ever since he'd returned to find her here at Rosewell Abby, but he could see now that she'd done a very good job at keeping the truth hidden. He knew for himself that there were things in life that were easier to pretend never happened, things you could choose to push away because it was too difficult to face. But what he had endured was nothing in light of all she'd been through. And she still had admitted very little; he was still putting the pieces together based mostly on his observations.

When he began to fear she'd said all that she would, Meri said in a toneless voice, "I remember the day I awoke and finally admitted to myself the truth about the man I had married. He yelled at everyone in the house—including his own mother. He whipped his horses. He kicked his dogs. And . . . he beat his wife."

Elliott took in a sharp breath to hear her finally give voice it. He was glad she hadn't noticed his reaction, and then he kept very quiet, hoping she would continue to unburden herself.

"If he hit my face he insisted that I not leave my rooms until the bruises healed—which meant days of confinement; sometimes weeks. Generally, he made certain the bruises wouldn't be seen; my arms and legs, my stomach and back. And if I screamed or cried, he hurt me more." She sighed as if she'd just told him she wasn't fond of eating whatever had been served for supper. Elliott felt so sick inside that he was struggling to subdue his nausea. And the nausea barely masked his growing anger.

"I tried so hard to do everything perfectly," Meri continued, "because I believed that if I did, he would stop hurting me. But he always found a reason to criticize me, to find fault, to justify his anger toward me. And the entire household knew it was happening; every single person—except for the children—knew how he treated me, and no one ever spoke a kind word to me, or offered any compassion or assistance, as if they too might be plagued by his wrath." Meri lifted her head and looked away, but she kept talking. "When Elaine was born, he would hardly look at her because she wasn't a boy, and he wanted a son. When Crispin was born, he got it into his head that the baby did not resemble him and was therefore evidence that I was guilty of adultery and should be punished for it. I lost a baby about halfway through the pregnancy after that—because he kicked me in the stomach."

Elliott found it increasingly difficult to remain quiet and calm. Only his desire to have her say all she needed to say kept him from erupting.

"I got pregnant again, and he was furious. He only complained about the children; he wanted nothing to do with them. He certainly didn't want another one. I remember wishing that I was *not* pregnant—if only for the sake of the baby. I was so worried about the impact it would have on Elaine and Crispin, and I didn't think I could protect still another child. After that baby was born, he . . ." She showed the first sign of emotion in her voice since she'd begun her wretched story. With a quivering voice she added, "He lived for only a few minutes, and . . . I felt so guilty, as if my wish had somehow brought this about."

When she was silent for a few minutes, Elliott finally forced a steady voice and said, "You know that's not true. No one can wish a person dead or alive, Meri. And you must know that the way he treated you . . . it wasn't your fault; none of it was your fault."

"I've tried to convince myself of that, but . . . his words haunt me as much as the things he did to me. He said such *awful* things to me."

"I can't imagine that he was even of sound mind," Elliott said, still struggling to keep his anger under control.

"I truly don't believe he was," Meri said, as if his validation of her belief was comforting to her.

"Meri," he put a hand on her shoulder, "I can't even imagine what you've been through. It's more horrible than I ever thought possible, but . . . I'm glad you told me. No one can dictate how long it might take to heal from such horrific circumstances, but I'm here for you, Meri. You don't ever have to pretend with me; you don't ever have to keep secrets. I want to help you heal from this, Meri. I want to give you a good life . . . the life you deserve."

Meri jumped to her feet so quickly it startled him. "And what do I deserve, Elliott?" she asked, sounding angry. "I *chose* to marry him, and I chose to stay with him."

"And in both cases, you had your reasons," he said, standing beside her.

"Maybe I did, but . . . that will never erase the damage that's been done." She turned to look at him. "Your kindness means more than I can say, but . . . I don't know if I can ever love you the way you deserve."

"You already do, Meri," he said, but she shook her head as if she didn't believe him. His fury rose as he considered what the supposedly esteemed Lord Sturgess had done to this fine, beautiful woman. He had broken her, heart and spirit. Elliott didn't know how to fix her—except to just love her—but he was going to give it everything he had.

"You can't tell me," she said, "that after everything I just said, you still see me the same way."

"You are the same woman you have always been," he insisted, "and nothing could make me love you any less. I am *furious* with this man, Meri. And if he was still alive I would want to kill him."

"Then it's a good thing he is not," Meri said, looking at the ground.

"No, he's not, Meri. He's dead. He will never hurt you again. And we have the chance to start over . . . to make a new life . . . together. I love you! There is nothing you told me . . . nothing you could ever tell me . . . that would change that. Nothing!"

Even through the darkness, her silence told him she wasn't convinced. And that too incited his anger. While he was wondering what she might say next, she walked past him, saying over her shoulder, "Please do not break my confidence and tell anyone else. Not anyone."

"You know I wouldn't," he said and watched her walk away. A part of him wanted to go after her and try to convince her that—if anything—he loved her more for all that she'd survived, for her courage and dignity in facing such horrors. But he knew they were both strained to the limit, and emotions were taut. It was better to wait until tomorrow, until they'd both had time to adjust to all she'd shared with him.

Now that he was alone and he didn't have to worry about frightening her or hurting her feelings, the anger seethed inside of him and quickly erupted to the surface. He turned and threw his fist into the stone wall of the house, then he dropped to his knees and groaned in response to the pain. And then he cried. He wrapped his arms around the sick smoldering in his stomach and wept like a lost child. Oh, how he wished he could go back! He should have told her how he felt about her; he never should have let her marry that . . . *monster*! But he couldn't go back; the past couldn't be changed. All they could do was attempt to heal from what had happened and make a fresh start. And he prayed with all his soul that such might be possible.

* * *

Meri blindly made her way to her bedroom, fighting to hold back the grief and sorrow and heartbreak that were threatening to explode because of everything she'd just told Elliott. She peeked in on the children and found them sleeping soundly, then she went to her own room and closed both the doors before she curled up in the center of the bed and sobbed the way she had in Elliott's arms not so long ago. She couldn't deny some measure of relief that he now knew everything. Keeping it from him had become more and more difficult; at least she didn't have to dread the conversation anymore. But the emotion that had accompanied her confessions was far worse than she'd imagined, and she wondered how she would possibly be able to show her face tomorrow and behave as if everything was normal and fine.

Memories paraded through her mind with haunting accuracy until she could barely breathe, and she had to force her thoughts toward more happy times and her gratitude that Lord Sturgess was indeed dead, and she was now here—safe and cared for.

Her crying finally calmed, and the next thing she knew she was coming awake to sunlight and the sound of birds singing outside her windows. She got up and looked in the mirror, only to groan at the sight of herself. Deciding that the best option for today was to claim illness, she changed into a nightgown and went back to bed. This way she could have her meals brought to her room and she wouldn't have to face Elliott or anyone else. Illness could explain her red, swollen eyes, and she could have at least a day to come to terms with the bridge she'd crossed last night in telling Elliott her darkest secrets.

She caught her breath, recalling that she'd not told him *everything*. But in her heart, she knew that if he knew the *whole* truth, it would indeed change the way he felt about her. She loved him so much and needed him so badly that she couldn't bear the thought of losing him now. Even though she'd been afraid of how he might react to the truth about her marriage, she wasn't surprised by the way he'd expressed his undying love for her. While she couldn't be sure yet if time would prove his love to be stronger than the depth to which she'd been damaged, she *could* be sure that if he knew the whole truth, everything would surely change. In her heart, she prayed that the remainder of her secrets would go with her to the grave, and he would never have to know.

Alice came to check on Meri when she didn't show up in the children's room at the usual time. She expressed concern for Meri but assured her that she would watch over the children. A short while later a tray arrived from the kitchen with some breakfast for Meri—delivered personally by Mrs. Biddle, who checked Meri's face for fever and grilled her with questions to ascertain whether she should send for the doctor. Meri assured her it was likely just a little cold and she simply needed to rest, and Mrs. Biddle left her to do so.

Meri ate very little of her breakfast, not feeling much appetite. She was just snuggling back into bed when Annabel came to check on her, and Meri had to give her aunt the same assurances she had given the cook.

"I just need to rest," Meri declared. "I haven't been sleeping well," she said, which was mostly true. "Perhaps I'm just overtired." Meri certainly didn't want to add any more burden to her aunt's shoulders, considering all that she was surely dealing with regarding all five of her daughters.

"Perhaps you are," Annabel said. "I'll leave you alone then. Ring when you need something, and we won't bother you otherwise."

"Thank you," Meri said as Annabel kissed her brow then left her alone.

Meri cried silent tears as the past and the future collided in her mind—and in her heart. Then by some miracle she was able to fall back to sleep. Perhaps all that crying had truly worn her out. She awoke to note that the shadows in the room had changed dramatically, and she knew it was afternoon. She couldn't believe she had slept so long. Her stomach growled with hunger and she rolled over, knowing she needed to ring for some food to be brought up from the kitchen. She gasped, startled, to see Elliott sitting in a chair near the bed, his booted ankle crossed over his knee, an open book facedown on his lap.

"What are you doing here?" she demanded.

He set the book on the floor, along with his foot, before he leaned his forearms on his thighs and looked closely at her. But there was a warmth in his eyes that helped her believe his feelings for her might have truly not changed.

"You might be able to fool the rest of them," he said with a wink, "but you can't fool me." He took her hand and squeezed it. "Don't worry; your secret is safe with me. But I wanted to know how you're *really* doing."

Meri took a minute to carefully consider her answer. She wanted to be completely honest—with him and with herself, something she realized she'd not been very good at doing. She tightened her hold on his hand and said, "I'm relieved that you know the truth. I'm weary of trying to keep it from you . . . of keeping it bottled up inside of me."

"There's no need for secrets between us, Meri," he said. "Ever."

Meri nodded while she methodically told herself there had to be one exception to that rule. But since no one knew the truth except her, and she was determined to put the matter away for good, she didn't have any reason to believe it would ever be a problem.

"And?" he asked.

"And what?" she countered.

"You're relieved, and . . .?"

"Exhausted," she admitted. "Obviously I have not come to terms with what happened nearly as well as I had convinced myself. I thought I could just . . . move on and . . . put it behind me and all would be well. Clearly that's not the case."

"Clearly, it's not," he said. "Not for either of us." He sighed and leaned a little closer. "I'm glad you know about Lawrence; about how he died . . . and how it's affected me. I still believe it will take time and effort for me to fully come to terms with it, but I want to find peace over it. Having you know . . . and being able to talk about it with you . . . helps me believe that peace is possible. I hope you feel the same way . . . that together we can find peace over *all* that's happened."

The very idea stung her eyes with tears and she nodded again. "I truly hope that's possible," she said, and a tear spilled from her eye and over the bridge of her nose. He wiped it away with his free hand and she couldn't help but see the redness and bruising on his knuckles, as well as several fresh scabs where they had been bleeding.

"What on earth have you done?" she asked, gently taking hold of his ailing hand with both of her own.

She heard Elliott take a sharp breath, as if he didn't want to tell her. But they had just committed to complete honesty, and she wondered if he might fail the test so quickly. "I told Annabel and Faith at breakfast that I'd been clumsy and had scraped it. No one questioned me further." Meri gave him a hard stare and he added, "Clearly you are more perceptive than the rest of the family." He sighed and admitted, "I was angry last night, Meri; I don't know if I've ever felt so angry in my life. Not at you; not at all. But angry with that poor excuse of a man you married. I hit the wall of the house. I didn't even think about it; I just did it."

Meri sighed and kissed his hand. "Obviously the results were painful."

"Extremely," he said with a little chuckle. "It would have been far wiser to come into the house first and hit a couch or a pillow or something equally soft. But anger doesn't generally allow a person to think rationally, does it?"

"No, I don't suppose so." She sat up in bed but remained under the covers. "I'm sorry."

"You're apologizing again for something that isn't your fault."

"I don't know how much of this is my fault, Elliott. I think it will take time for me to figure that out. I still believe I could have done something better somewhere along the way. Perhaps that's part of what I need to come to terms with. Even if I did make bad choices, I can't go back and change them, and I suppose I need to forgive myself."

"Yes, I believe you do," he said.

"And you should take your own advice on that," she countered firmly.

"Touché," he said with another little chuckle.

"Still, I do feel *very* sorry for bringing my burdens into your life. Perhaps it's not so much an apology as it is . . . compassion. I'm sorry for the anger and frustration you feel on my behalf, but at the same time . . ." her voice cracked and she could feel her chin quivering, ". . . I'm so grateful to have you back."

"The feeling is very mutual, Meri," he said and their eyes met. She knew that look well; he wanted to kiss her, but he was surely as aware as she that the present situation was likely not a wise or appropriate time to do so. He kissed her hand as he came to his feet, saying, "I know you didn't eat very much breakfast, and you slept through lunch. I'm going to personally go to the kitchen and get you something to eat."

"Thank you," she said.

Elliott smiled at her over his shoulder as he left through the open door.

Chapter Nine
Ghosts

Meri lay back down and closed her eyes, silently thanking God for Elliott's perfect love and acceptance and for all that had transpired to help free her of having to carry her burden alone. She hated the thought of Elliott being so upset that he would have hit a stone wall hard enough to injure his hand, but she felt better when she imagined him hitting her deceased husband instead. Finding gratification in such a thought didn't necessarily feel like a very Christian attitude, but given the innumerable times her husband had hit her, the very idea of Elliott hitting him—just once, good and hard—felt somehow comforting to Meri. She'd long ago let go of any guilt she'd felt over her relief that Lord Sturgess was dead; therefore, it was difficult to find any remorse in wishing that Elliott might have been there just once to intervene and inflict even a degree of the pain on Meri's husband that he had inflicted on her.

Realizing that Elliott would soon return, Meri hurried to freshen up and put on a robe and slippers. She felt barely presentable when he returned with a tray, which he set on the table near the window by which she was already sitting.

"Thank you," Meri said, eyeing with pleasure the savory biscuits, two kinds of cheese, fresh berries, a slice of apple cake, and a pot of warm tea. "Are you going to eat with me?" she asked as he sat down across the table.

"I ate while you were sleeping," he said, "but I'll keep you company . . . if that's all right."

"More than all right," she said, quickly realizing she was very hungry. She ate almost everything on the tray except the cake, and had enjoyed two cups of tea before Elliott even spoke.

He came out of a thoughtful trance and said, "May I ask you something, Meri? You don't have to answer if you don't want to, but . . . I want to understand."

Meri felt a little nervous, but they had agreed to work together to come to terms with the painful things that had happened in their lives. "Of course," she said and steeled herself for a difficult question.

"Did he ever hurt the children?" Elliott asked with such deep concern that Meri felt tempted to cry. This dear man cared for her children so genuinely that he was deeply troubled over the possibility of how all she'd told him might have impacted them.

"He never hit the children," Meri said in a toneless voice that allowed her to tell him the facts without getting upset all over again; she was too exhausted to get upset. "He mostly ignored them, and in fact rarely even saw them. He made it clear that children should be kept with their nannies and governesses. I strongly disagreed; I wanted to be the person that my children saw the most, but he wouldn't have it. He wanted me with him almost constantly, as if I might do something devious if I were let out of his sight. So, the children were cared for by women I detested; women who paid no heed to my requests on behalf of my own son and daughter because they were acting on his orders and they were terrified of him." Hearing the vehemence in her own voice, she took a deep breath to calm herself. "I'm very glad to now be able to have complete charge over the care of my children. I can't deny that I appreciate having assistance, and Alice is wonderful with them. But I'm their mother, and I should be the one who determines the structure of their lives."

"Absolutely," Elliott agreed with enthusiasm. Following a long moment of silence, he added, "You said he never hit them . . . he mostly ignored them . . . but . . . was there anything else? How did they feel about their father? How do they feel now?"

"They were terrified of him too. When they did see him, he most often shouted at them, and then he would be angry with me because the children clung to me when they were so frightened."

"The man was a—"

The abrupt way he stopped led Meri to say with confidence, "You were going to curse, weren't you?"

"Yes," he admitted, "but I'm in the presence of a lady so I'll do my best to refrain."

"I'd prefer that over having you do yourself any further harm by hitting hard obstacles." Meri observed his furrowed brow and the tightness of his face. He'd found no humor at all from her comment. "You're angry," she observed.

Elliott blew out a loud burst of air, as if he were blowing out a candle. He folded his arms over his chest and looked out the window. "I am *so* angry, Meri. And again, you need to know that I'm not angry with you. I'm angry with *him.* If I had known . . ." He shook his head but didn't finish the sentence. "If he were still alive . . ." Again, he didn't finish, and she felt sure he didn't want to admit to his desire to inflict violence on Lord Sturgess.

Meri saw Elliott squeeze his eyes closed, and the muscles in his cheek twitched involuntarily. "I'm so glad you told me, Meri. I needed to know. But I ask you to be patient with me. It's going to take some time for me to . . ." He cleared his throat, again not finishing his thought. "I keep seeing it in my mind; him striking you. And I keep thinking about how that must have been for you, and I . . ." Once again, he didn't finish the sentence. She saw him visibly attempting to calm himself before he turned to look at her. "I'm so sorry, Meri."

"Now look who's apologizing for something that isn't your fault."

"Maybe it is," he said far too zealously. "I should have told you how I felt about you. I should have told you to wait until it was suitable for us to marry. I should have . . ." His voice lowered to a rumble. "I should have *never* let you marry him!"

Meri leaned over the table and reached a hand toward him. He took it and she said, "Do you not think I have similar thoughts? There are complicated reasons why we didn't do things differently back then. Be angry if you must. I have certainly contended with a great deal of anger. But don't let yourself get caught up in wishing you could change things that can never be changed."

He gazed at her for what felt like minutes before he nodded, as if it had taken great willpower for him to agree to let go of his regrets. He squeezed her hand and murmured, "I love you, Meri. I love you more for the strength and courage it has taken for you to survive such atrocities."

Meri looked down, embarrassed. "I am *not* strong," she insisted. "Are you not the man who held me last night while I completely collapsed into a sobbing mess?"

"And rightly so," he said. "Are you not the woman sitting here now offering remarkable wisdom and insight? You have survived, Meri—both in body and spirit—things that many women would never be able to rise above. You are an incredible mother despite all that's happened. And I love you as much as I respect and admire you. Don't you ever forget it."

Meri looked up at him, allowing the sincerity of his words to wash over her. "You might have to keep reminding me."

"I will," he promised. "Every day, if that's what you need."

"I love you, too," she said and he smiled, showing no sign of anger in his expression.

"Do you want some of my cake?" she asked, and his smile broadened.

"Just a bite," he said. "I already had some at lunch."

"Perhaps later you could sneak more of it from the kitchen for me."

"Whatever you ask of me, my lady," he said as if she'd asked him to slay a dragon and he would gladly face death to do so.

Meri broke off a forkful of cake and held it in front of his mouth. He opened his mouth and took the bite from her, although some of the icing stuck to his lips, which made her smile. Instead of using a napkin, he stood and reached over the table to kiss her, transferring the excess icing to *her* lips, which made her laugh.

"And there's my sweet Meri," he said, sitting back down, sounding rather satisfied with himself. But Meri concluded he had a right to be. He had accepted her unconditionally with all her damaged history, and he loved her perfectly. He had given her the hope of a future far brighter than she'd ever dared to believe possible.

She ate the rest of her cake without sharing. He teased her about it and they laughed together. Given the state she'd been in not so many hours ago, she considered laughter in the midst of such a simple moment nothing short of a miracle.

* * *

The progress Meri felt taking place between her and Elliott—now that they'd unburdened themselves of their secret pain—seemed to be somehow contagious. All the hiding away and talking and crying her aunt and cousins had done must have been effective, given the way they all began to show themselves once again. Conversation over their meals and tea became more normal, reminding Meri of how it had been before Uncle Angus had died—except that now there were no strange undertones or snide implications that had to be ignored. Little by little, the sisters began to speak openly with the rest of the family about their personal challenges and their plans to make their own lives better. As a family, they agreed to work together to strive to become happier, each of them admitting they could not do it alone.

Hope committed to gradually reducing the time she spent reading each day so she could be engaged in other activities. Every member of the family was eager to spend time with Hope each day doing anything *except* talking about books in order to help her work toward a healthier balance. She also shared with the family what she had obviously already discussed with her mother—how brokenhearted she had been when she'd fallen in love with a kind and decent man, but because of his social standing her father had refused to give his consent for her to marry. And now this man had a beautiful family, and Hope had subsequently lost herself in the fantasy of fiction as a means of coping with her disappointment and heartache. The family validated Hope's grief over this loss, and she was given open permission to be able to express her emotions with members of her family with the goal of moving past what had happened, rather than just wishing life were different.

As if inspired by Hope's candor and her commitment to improve her unhealthy habits, a few days later Comfort began to talk during tea about the reasons she believed that eating food helped her to avoid thinking about her unhappiness in believing she was not lovable or of any value to anyone else. The conversation went on for a long while, with Comfort crying a great deal while her mother and sisters took turns sitting next to her so they could hold her hand or put their arms around her, offering compassion and reassurance. Meri and Elliott both expressed their love for Comfort, and their commitment to doing whatever they could do to help. They all contributed ideas on how they could each assist Comfort in seeking out other distractions to slowly help wean her away from her unhealthy eating habits. Comfort knew it would not be easy to make such dramatic changes, but she was deeply motivated, and the commitment of her family to help support her was something she admitted more than once made all the difference in the world. The simple fact that everyone in the family was astonished just to hear Comfort admit she didn't feel loved or valuable already seemed to have healed something in her. She declared that she could see she'd distorted the truth in her mind over things she'd not been able to vocalize.

While Hope and Comfort poured out their hearts to their family and formulated plans for making their lives better, Joy stated firmly that she would never again do *anything* to aid her sisters in covering up their less-than-desirable, unfortunate choices, habits, or unhealthy lifestyles. And she committed with eager zealousness to do whatever she could to support and assist them in leading better lives.

While miracles were unfolding among the sisters, Meri noticed that Charity said very little. She offered support and expressions of love toward her sisters, but it was evident she had no interest in talking about her own challenges. During multiple conversations spread over nearly a week, Charity was present and occasionally offered her input, but she mostly looked at the floor or out the window. Annabel had told Meri privately that no one could force Charity to change, and that she had spoken many times with her daughter about the reasons for what was going on in her life, and how changes *could* take place, but Charity had thus far only become depressed and perhaps even despondent. But no one was giving up on her.

Following the example of their cousins, Elliott shared with them the story he'd recently told Meri about Lawrence's death and the guilt he'd felt, as well as the way his family had come to blame him. Every one of the women shed tears and offered Elliott their compassion, and Meri was proud of him for being so open about something he'd not even wanted to speak of at all. Even Charity said more than she'd said to any of her sisters, which Meri hoped was a good sign toward her being able to candidly share the difficulties in her own life. Since Charity was still taking long walks each day, everyone had to assume she was still engaged in some level of involvement with this unnamed married man. They all felt concerned, but agreed that Charity was an adult and no one could force her to make certain choices.

Elliott said nothing to make Meri feel like she needed to follow his lead and share her own secrets with the rest of the family, but in her heart, she knew she needed to do so. It was clear that she and Elliott intended to live out their lives in this home, and she would be a hypocrite to have made such a fuss about her cousins hiding things from each other and then keep to herself all she'd experienced in her marriage. They didn't need to know all the details she'd shared with Elliott, but they did need to know.

On a day of thunderstorms that made the house dark and mildly chilly, Meri waited until they were nearly finished with tea. She didn't want to ruin anyone's appetite or infringe on their enjoyment of sipping a comforting beverage or finding pleasure in the yummy little cakes and sandwiches that always came like magic from the kitchen. Meri began to feel nervous long before the teatime ritual was winding down. But only Elliott noticed. She was sitting next to him on a sofa and he turned to look at her with discreet concern in his expression. She wondered why, until he glanced down to where he was holding her hand and she realized she was trembling. She met his eyes firmly and within just a moment she knew he had guessed what she was about to do. He offered a subtle nod of encouragement and squeezed her hand as if to reassure her that she was not alone.

Meri stared at the fire crackling in the fireplace until she knew she couldn't put this off any longer without risking that someone would leave the room. She cleared her throat unnaturally loudly and said, "There's something I need to tell you." All eyes turned to her, some with curiosity, some with concern. She took a deep breath and went on with a speech she'd tried to memorize. "I've been very adamant about the need for all of us to open up about our pain . . . and to share our secrets . . . so that we can help each other heal. Now it's time that you all know *my* secrets; things I've been too ashamed to admit. Aunt knows some of this . . . and she has been very supportive." Meri exchanged a wan smile with Annabel. "But there is much you don't know, Aunt," she added and Annabel's brow creased. Taking in the concerned and supportive faces of her cousins, Meri forged ahead. "Of course, it goes without saying that all the things we have shared here as a family will remain confidential among us."

Everyone in the room responded simultaneously with a few words of agreement and reassurance, which helped Meri to just say it. "My marriage to Lord Sturgess was not simply difficult; it was a nightmare." She looked at Elliott as a stony knot formed in her throat and tears stung her eyes. He nodded to encourage her, but she shook her head and said, "Please tell them. They need to know, but I can't say it."

Meri saw Elliott nod, but she also saw in his eyes how difficult it was for *him* to be able to say it. But he was willing to do so on her behalf if it would help her. She squeezed her eyes closed as she heard him say, "He treated her worse than his horses and his dogs, and he was cruel to his animals. He beat her," Elliott said with a quiver in his voice, and all the women in the room gasped. "And not just a little," Elliott added.

Meri didn't want to open her eyes, but she heard many sniffles in the room as well as a few more gasps. She finally looked at her aunt and cousins and found every one of them wiping away tears with their handkerchiefs.

Now that Elliott had said the worst, she was able to tell them the rest of what mattered. She told them how terrible it had been living in that house, and how cold and unfeeling everyone had been. She told them how terrified the children had been of their father, and how she had miscarried a baby due to her husband's physical abuse. She thanked them for offering her a haven to come home to and for their love and support. By the time she'd finished, Elliott's arm was around her.

When it became evident she had nothing more to say, each of her cousins took a turn sitting on the sofa next to her while Elliott remained on the opposite side. Faith, Hope, Charity, Joy, and Comfort each embraced her tightly and expressed their love for her and their sorrow for what she'd endured. Meri had never felt closer to her cousins, not even when they'd been children together and she'd truly felt like a sister to them. Opening her heart to them and allowing them to grieve with her had deepened their bond immensely. The fact that each of them were in the process of sharing their own burdens with the family added to a growing kinship. They were all working together to heal and become happier. She couldn't imagine any greater purpose to family than that. She only prayed—as she knew the others were doing—that Charity would arrive at a point when she could end her relationship with the unnamed married man and move forward in a way that would allow her to be happier.

* * *

Meri felt the need for a nap; her confession had drained away all her energy. Elliott encouraged her to rest and offered to give Alice some relief by taking the children outside to play. As soon as her head hit the pillow, Meri started to cry. But the tears felt cleansing, and she realized that the emotion that accompanied sharing her burdens with loved ones was far more light and peaceful than that of trying to keep it locked away and hidden. Her tears lulled her to sleep and she awoke to realize she had missed supper. Disoriented from how deeply she'd slept, she knew the rest had done her good but she also knew that late afternoon was not necessarily a wise time to take a nap. Now it was well into evening and she wondered if she would be able to sleep tonight.

Meri was glad to find a note from Elliott telling her that he would read the children their bedtime story and see that they were put to bed on time, and that Mrs. Biddle was keeping her supper warm in the kitchen. He added at the end: *After you eat, if you feel up to it, I would be honored to have you accompany me outdoors to gaze at the stars.*

Meri smiled and hurried to freshen up before she went to the children's room to find them both ready for bed and Elliott reading them a story. Their excitement made her laugh, and she laughed even more when they ran and both jumped into her arms at the same time.

"Oh, you're both getting far too big to do that," she said, going to her knees so she could hug them each more tightly.

"Elliott said you weren't feeling well," Elaine said with a concern that was far more mature than her years.

"I was just very tired and needed a nap," Meri explained. "I'm feeling much better now, although I'm very hungry because I missed my supper."

"Which is waiting in the kitchen," Elliott said and leaned over the children to kiss her cheek. He comically rubbed the tops of the children's heads in a way that made them giggle. "Kiss your mother good night and we'll finish our story. She needs to go eat her supper."

"Good night, Mum," Crispin said and gave her a loud smooch.

"Good night, Mother," Elaine added and offered a more lady-like kiss.

"I will see you both in the morning," Meri said, "and we will count the roses that are in bloom in the garden."

"There's too many to count!" Elaine declared.

"Then we'll see how high we *can* count," Meri said.

Elliott herded the children back to their story and shooed Meri out of the room, saying just before she left, "I'll meet you on the patio."

"I'll be waiting," she said, feeling a sudden urge for the two of them to move forward with their plans for the future. He'd been right when he'd said that it was ridiculous for them to be alone at night when they spent their days almost as if they were already married. He was already far more of a father to her children than their own father had ever been. And they had come a long way in taking steps to put the past behind them and being able to help each other heal.

By the time she got to the kitchen, Meri had decided she would tell Elliott tonight she was feeling ready for them to make some serious decisions about their future together. She wondered what exactly he had in mind. Would they have a more public courtship? A period wherein they were officially engaged? Or would they just toss convention aside and get married as soon as possible? Knowing Elliott, she guessed it would be the latter. But she was surprisingly fine with that. She loved him and he loved her, and they shared the kind of trust and respect she needed in her life. There was no man in the world except for Elliott who could ever help her recover and become strong. She would be a fool not to take hold of him and never let go.

After visiting with Mrs. Biddle while she ate her supper, Meri helped clean some dishes and chatted with a couple of the maids who were hard-working assistants to the cook. She then went out to the patio to find Elliott leaning back in a chair with his booted legs stacked on another chair. He looked up at her upon hearing the door, but she hurried to say, "Don't get up. You look far too comfortable."

Meri bent over to kiss him before she relaxed in a chair she had scooted close enough to Elliott that she could sit and hold his hand.

"How are you feeling?" he asked after a stretch of silence that allowed her to hear the crickets chirping nearby.

"Better," she said. "Rested and . . . relieved."

"Good," he said and turned to look at her.

Meri wondered if he wanted to bring up marriage again, and perhaps he felt hesitant to do so, given all the drama that had followed his last mention of it. Since she had been the one resistant to move forward, she tried to come up with the words to let him know that her feelings had changed on the matter, and she believed that the sooner they were able to get married, the better—for everyone. She wanted him to be her husband, and she wanted him to officially become a father to the children. Beyond that, she believed their marriage would help stabilize the entire household. He legally owned Rosewell Abbey and the estate, and he also felt personally responsible for the family Angus had left behind. They both wanted to live out their lives here, and their marriage would perhaps help the entire family feel more secure. Though she couldn't bear the thought of ever losing him, she knew that a marriage between them would help keep the estate in the family in the event of his death—even if it meant his legally adopting Crispin so he would have a male heir.

Meri didn't want to think about such things, but she did believe they should talk about them. However, her desire to marry him had very little to do with matters of estate or legalities. She loved him deeply, and he had proven himself capable of loving her in return, without any condition or reservation. Surely this was right for both of them.

Meri almost had the words assembled in her mind when Elliott said, "I want to marry you—at the soonest possible opportunity." He set his feet on the patio floor and turned more toward her. "I've wanted it ever since I came back and found you here. We've had some things to overcome, and we certainly needed some time to become reacquainted enough to know if this was right. But . . . I believe things are better between us now."

"I agree," she said and couldn't hold back a smile. The fact that he'd spoken her own thoughts so accurately seemed another witness that this was the correct course for her life. "I love you, Elliott. I want you in my life . . . forever. I want you to be a father to my children, officially. And I believe that our being in this home . . . and being married will help our aunt and cousins feel more secure."

"You and I have been having the same ideas, it would seem," he said, smiling back at her. He leaned over to kiss her before he said, "I don't want to wait. We've both waited long enough. We deserve to be happy."

"Then let's get married tomorrow," she said and laughed.

He laughed with her. "*That* might not be feasible—especially if we want the family to be involved, and I believe they should be."

"I believe so too."

"And I want Elaine and Crispin to witness our marriage, Meri. I want them to be involved, and to understand what our vows mean to them."

Meri got tears in her eyes in response to such a tender thought. "I believe you're right."

"So, we can't get married tomorrow . . . but I can go and see the vicar and begin the arrangements, and we can be married in less than a month."

Meri sighed and kissed him. "I'll be counting the days. If we—"

She stopped when the door came open and a maid exited the house and curtsied. "Forgive me, m'lady," she said, seeming mildly upset. "But there are some people here to see you; they were quite insistent, despite the late hour."

"Who on earth?" Meri asked on the wave of a gasp. Her fear of her dead husband rushed up inside of her and had to be talked down with the evidence that he was indeed dead, and she had nothing to be afraid of.

"It's two young women," the maid reported. "And one of 'em gots a baby. They said they've come a long way and they must speak with you."

"Very well," Meri said as she stood, but she kept Elliott's hand in hers, making it clear that she wanted him beside her while she dealt with whatever this strange situation might be.

Meri and Elliott followed the maid into the house and to the drawing room where she had taken the unexpected visitors to wait. Meri knew the maid's name was Susan, but she knew little about her, given that she was very quiet and shy. She often brought tea to the parlor, and their paths had crossed many times, but they'd never had any personal conversation. Still, Meri knew Susan to be a young woman of kindness and integrity and she felt increased confidence in having Susan with them.

Just before Meri and Elliott entered the drawing room, Meri said to her, "Thank you, Susan. Given the late hour, our guests might have needs. Will you stay nearby until we can figure out what this might be about?"

"Of course, m'lady," Susan said and curtsied slightly.

Meri was surprised by the way her heartbeat quickened as she entered the drawing room, still with Elliott's hand in hers. He closed the door behind them while she observed that the room was fairly dark, given there were only a few candles burning. Elliott apparently had the same thought as he quickly took up one of the candles and used it to light four lamps, which allowed Meri to see the faces of the two women who had stood up when she and Elliott entered the room. And just as Susan had reported, one of them was holding a baby who was wrapped in a blanket and sleeping in its mother's arms. Meri felt decidedly nervous when she recognized these women immediately. They were like ghosts from the past, their very presence taking her back to a time and place she had been trying so hard to forget.

Before Meri could speak, the woman holding the baby said, "Please let me explain our reasons for coming, my lady, and then you may ask any question of us. I beg you not to be afraid, even though I would understand why you might be."

"Please . . . sit down," Elliott said, motioning the two women back to the sofa upon which they'd been sitting. He guided Meri to a smaller sofa opposite their guests and sat down close beside her.

Meri took in this woman's sincere request for Meri not to be afraid; she wasn't entirely without fear, but she was willing to hear what they had to say, and she couldn't help being curious over the reasons why two maids from the Sturgess household would show up here like this.

"Go on," Meri said when it seemed evident they were waiting for her permission to speak any further.

"I know that you recognize us because we helped care for your children prior to the death of your late husband."

"I do recognize you," Meri said, "but I don't know your names. I never knew the names of anyone there who wasn't a member of the family."

"That's the way it was there," this woman said, "for reasons we both have trouble understanding." The two women shared a glance that seemed fearful but determined. The woman who was speaking turned again to Meri, an aura of forced courage emanating from her. "My name is Lara," she hurried to add. "Like Sara with an L. And this is Vera." She motioned toward the woman sitting beside her, who only nodded, looking upset but apparently not wanting to talk.

Lara and Vera both glanced hesitantly toward Elliott, as if his presence might make them afraid to state their purpose for coming, given the fact that they didn't know who he was. "This is Elliott Rosewell," Meri said. "He is my cousin via the marriage between my aunt and his uncle. This is his home, and we've been very close since we were children." She also felt compelled to add, "And we are engaged to be married."

Meri wondered how these women might take such news; she felt sure that the majority of the Sturgess household would be appalled over her getting married again at all, let alone so soon. But Lara said with a genuine smile, "Oh, how lovely!"

Vera added, "I'm so happy for you, my lady."

"Thank you," Meri said, wanting to get on with this conversation.

Elliott and the two visitors exchanged silent but cordial nods of greeting before Meri looked almost sternly at Lara, wanting to understand the reasons for this strange visit.

Lara continued as if she'd been thinking her words through very carefully long before this encounter. "I want you to know, my lady, that both Vera and I never agreed with the rules your deceased husband—may he rest in peace—inflicted on the household. In our care of your children we tried very hard to help them feel safe and comfortable and to have fun—at least when no one else was watching."

"Thank you for that," Meri said. "That means a great deal to me. But I'm certain you didn't come all this way to tell me that."

"No, my lady," Lara said and became slightly fidgety even while she made a great effort not to disturb the baby sleeping in her arms.

"If I recall correctly," Meri said when Lara hesitated, "you left months before my husband died . . . rather unexpectedly. There were all kinds of rumors as to your reasons for leaving, but I'm not one to give heed to gossip."

Tears glistened in Lara's eyes and her bottom lip quivered until she bit it. She visibly gathered her composure and said, "That is the very thing I wish to talk to you about, my lady. The truth that very few people knew is that Lord Sturgess sent me away. He gave me a great deal of money to remain silent about something I knew he didn't want the rest of the world to know. He made me promise to take care of what he considered a problem, and I agreed because I believed I had no choice without putting myself or others in danger. I know this sounds strange, my lady, but Lord Sturgess could be a very frightening man, and—"

"You don't have to convince me of that, Lara," Meri said, still confused over why these women would end up here like this. "Please go on."

"He promised to continue sending me money, and he did. And then it stopped. Vera had remained working in the house, helping with the children, but after you left she was put to work doing the most menial chores. Vera and I exchanged letters regularly, and so I knew of Lord Sturgess's death and of your leaving. When all my money ran out, I didn't know what to do. His lordship's death did not solve the problem he had commissioned me to handle. But there was no one else who knew or who could help me—except for Vera. She had been putting money away for many years, never buying anything for herself that wasn't absolutely necessary, with the hope of one day being able to leave that dreadful place. We decided the time for her to leave had arrived, and that we needed to come here, because neither of us could live any longer with keeping such a terrible secret from you, my lady."

"From me?" Meri asked, astonished, at the same time tightening her grip on Elliott's hand and grateful to feel him offer a reassuring squeeze in return.

"Oh, my lady!" Lara exclaimed and burst into tears, spurring Meri's heart to race wildly. "I am so sorry! So very, very sorry! I felt guilty every day, but Lord Sturgess had threatened me with my life. He had to know where I was, because he was sending money to support us, and I feared that if I deviated from his instructions he would surely do us both harm." She took a deep breath and attempted to control her sobbing. "I'm so very, very sorry."

Meri observed the depth of her emotion and the harshness of her fear. She had empathy for both. But this was not making sense. She considered all that Lara had said, then asked what seemed an obvious question, "What do you mean by . . . *us*? Who? Vera was still at the manor."

Lara took a deep breath to try to calm herself. Meri noticed the way that Vera put a hand on Lara's arm, as if to offer her strength and assurance. Lara said, "Brace yourself, my lady. The news I have will be difficult to hear." Meri's instinctive response was to take hold of Elliott's arm, and she was glad to feel him put his hand over hers. Following another strained, ragged breath, Lara blurted, "Your baby did not die, my lady. Your husband sent me away with him in the middle of the night. He told you that he had died. Only the doctor and one of the maids knew the truth, and they were threatened into secrecy as I was." She drew breath and repeated, "Your baby did not die."

"What?" was the only word Meri could get out of her mouth even while she felt herself beginning to tremble from the inside out. "What . . . are you saying?" It wasn't that she hadn't heard Lara; she simply couldn't comprehend it. "Why . . . would he . . . do such a thing?" The trembling now became evident in her voice and she felt Elliott's arm come around her shoulders. "I . . . I . . . don't understand."

Lara avoided the question and moved to the edge of her seat, turning more toward Meri as she eased back the blanket that was partially covering the baby's face. Meri gasped and leaned against Elliott as if she might melt onto the floor if he didn't keep her upright. She heard him say exactly what she was thinking. "He looks just like Crispin."

"Oh!" Meri practically howled the word before she curled around a tangible pain in her middle. She could barely breathe as the memory of that horrible night marched through her mind and she tried to find any clue that something so devious and horrible might have happened. She'd endured a terrible labor. When it was over, she'd heard the baby cry but she'd been completely exhausted and still throbbing with pain. She remembered asking the doctor if something was wrong with the baby, realizing it had been taken out of the room by the maid that had been assisting him. He'd only told her to rest, and he'd given her some medicine he'd said would help ease the pain.

The next thing she remembered was her husband at her bedside, telling her—without compassion or kindness—that their son had died. Meri had refused to believe it and had begged to see the baby and hold him, but Lord Sturgess had ridiculed her for wanting to do so. Somewhere during her days of recovering from childbirth and trying to accept this loss, she was told that a proper burial had taken place. She now wondered if an empty casket had been buried to make the ruse more convincing. Meri had visited the gravestone once she'd been strong enough to do so. It had said *Baby Sturgess* with only one date—that of his birth and his death.

Meri had grieved deeply for the loss of her baby, and it had been even more difficult since her husband would get angry if he saw any evidence that she'd been crying or upset, and there was absolutely no one in the household with whom she had been able to talk. She had written long letters to Annabel, who had sent much love and compassion in the letters she wrote back.

It was only after Lord Sturgess's untimely death that Meri had started to feel she could move on from the loss of her infant son, and she had brought her children here to make a new start. And now. Now! Now this woman was telling her an entirely plausible story that completely contradicted all she had been led to believe. Everything Lara had said held credibility simply because it sounded so very much like the Lord Sturgess Meri had known. And if she'd had any doubt whatsoever, it had been erased by the striking physical resemblance of this child to Crispin, and even to Elaine.

Although he was sleeping and bundled up, he looked about the right size to have been born when Meri had supposedly lost her child. But she couldn't believe it. She just couldn't get her mind to grasp this as truth.

While the present evidence swirled in her mind with memories that now didn't seem real, Meri lost all control of her emotion and she sobbed helplessly in Elliott's arms, barely aware of the women in the room—and the sleeping baby that had apparently come from her own womb. She could hear her own grief echoing through an otherwise silent room, as if everyone present was willing to allow her all the time she needed to try to accept what she had just learned.

Meri became distracted from her tears when she realized that Lara was kneeling on the floor beside her. She turned to look at the young woman and considered the steady stream of tears rolling down her cheeks. "I did my very best to care for him, my lady. I would ask myself every day what *you* would do for him, and I did everything I knew how to keep him safe and healthy. And right from the start I knew that one day I would find a way to get him to you."

Lara eased the baby toward Meri, almost as if she feared that Meri might reject the offering. Meri drew courage to look at her son's face, again struck with how he was a miniature version of Crispin. She could see his little shoulders moving with his breath as he slept in perfect oblivion of the drama surrounding his life. His cheeks were rosy and plump, and wisps of blond hair peeked out from beneath a pale-yellow bonnet.

"Oh," Meri murmured and gasped softly as Lara set the baby in her arms. She knew his birthday, but her brain felt too clouded to calculate how old he was. Six months? Seven? Gingerly she touched his face, almost surprised with the evidence that he was real. "He's not a ghost," Meri said, laughing softly but with fresh tears.

"No, my lady," Lara said. "He is real enough. You'll know it for certain when he wakes up." The young woman laughed softly. "He's got a healthy set of lungs and a great deal of energy."

"What do you call him?" Meri asked, unable to take her eyes off the baby.

"I've called him Miles; it was my father's name, and he was a good man. But he's your son. It is for you to give him his name."

"Miles is a fine name, Lara," Meri said, gently stroking the baby's face.

"Yes, I believe it is," Elliott said, startling Meri to the recollection that he was beside her. Glancing at him snapped her out of something akin to a trance, and a hundred questions burst into her mind. She turned to Lara, who was still kneeling on the floor. "Why would he do this, Lara?" she asked. "Vera?" she added, including the other young woman who had worked in that horrible house. "You both know that my husband was a cruel and wretched man. It was certainly not something he attempted to keep hidden beneath his own roof. But why would he do something so . . . horrid? I know he didn't care for children; he barely tolerated the others. But with a house so enormous, and so many servants to help care for them, why would one more child matter to him? Why would he concoct such a deceptive and heartless scheme?"

"It was me who cleaned the baby and took him to his father," Lara said, wringing her hands. "He had nothing at all to say, until . . ." Lara reached over the baby Meri was holding and folded back the blanket to reveal that one of his little feet was turned inward in a distorted, unnatural way. "Lord Sturgess got angry and declared that he would not have a son who was anything less than perfect."

"Oh, my sweet boy!" Meri said, touching the little foot. She looked at Lara, almost feeling panicked. "Does it cause him pain?"

"No, my lady," Lara said. "He's healthy and happy otherwise. And of course, he doesn't know any different. I spoke with a doctor in the town where I was living. He told me it's called clubfoot. He said that little Miles will have difficulty walking normally, but he's known of people with this malady to walk on their ankle or the side of their foot, and they otherwise lead a normal life."

"Then it's just a bit of a nuisance," Meri said with a little laugh.

"That's exactly what I thought," Lara said and moved back to her seat on the sofa. "He's crawling and does so very well. Learning to walk might be a bit tricky, but he'll do it in time. That's what the doctor said. I would think you'd want to consult your doctor here and see if he agrees."

"We'll send for him in the morning," Elliott said, touching the baby's foot. Then he touched Meri's chin and tilted her face towards him. "He's a beautiful boy, Meri. We'll give him a good life."

Meri nodded, unable to speak. She wouldn't have worried for a moment that Elliott might feel any other way, but they had just agreed to get married as soon as possible, and now another child—an imperfect child—had been added to the complications of her life. She could never tell him how grateful she was for his love that just seemed to grow and grow.

Miles began to wiggle in a way that indicated he was working toward waking up. Lara said, "I must warn you, my lady, he's in a bit of a stage where he's not wanting to be held by anyone but me. He used to love to be held by the ladies at church and by neighbors who came to visit. But he's become clingier. I've been assured babies go through such stages, although he might not take to you right away. You must know, however, that it only took him a couple of days to take to Vera. I suspect it won't take him long before he knows his true mother."

Meri nodded; it made perfect sense to her. She was still in shock over the very fact that this was happening. It would likely take her a few days to accept that he was truly her son. She said to Lara, "The two of you must stay . . . at least for a week or so. It's late. You both must be exhausted. We can work out details tomorrow."

Meri stood up and handed Miles back to Lara before he came fully awake. She didn't want to have him wake up and see a stranger and be startled. Lara said, "He was awake most of the day. I believe that once he's got a clean diaper and some milk he'll go right back to sleep. We were able to acquire some fresh goat's milk at our last stop, which he drinks from a bottle very well."

Meri just nodded, recalling how painful it had been when her mother's milk had come in following the supposed death of her baby. If she'd had any idea then that he'd been alive, drinking goat's milk from bottles, she would have surely lost her mind. Feeling numb and in shock, Meri watched as Miles came awake and began fussing at being in unfamiliar surroundings. But the way he sat up on Lara's lap of his own volition and looked around made it evident that he was indeed healthy and strong.

Meri felt suddenly tired, and she knew that Miles needed attention that she could not give him right now. She was grateful for the way that Elliott stood up and went into the hall, where Susan had been waiting. And Meri hoped the maid had overheard everything. She wanted and needed the household to know all about it. They had a new member of the family, and the baby's presence in the home was never going to be any source of mystery or speculation. Meri wanted them to know the truth; she wanted everyone to know what a monster her husband had been.

Meri heard Elliott asking Susan to see that Lara and Vera were taken to guest rooms and given all they needed, including food and fresh water.

"Of course," Susan said kindly and stepped into the room, turning her eyes to Lara. "There is a guest room with a crib. I assume that would be preferable."

"Oh, that would be lovely," Lara said as both she and Vera stood up, and Meri did the same.

"We'll talk in the morning," Meri said to Lara. "If either of you need anything, just ring and someone will come to help you."

"Thank you," both women said as they followed Susan out of the room.

When Meri was alone with Elliott, he stood to face her and asked with tenderness, "Are you all right?"

"No," Meri said and shook her head. She took hold of his arms with trembling hands and set her face against his chest. "I'm not all right." Now that there was only Elliott around, she let loose the full torrent of her shock and grief and horror. She sobbed in his arms for countless minutes while he just held her with the silent reassurance that even though she was not all right now, she would be with time. She had her baby back in her life. And even though she'd not known of his existence, she knew in her heart that having him back in her arms and in the loving circle of her family would surely help her heal. She had every reason to believe that everything was going to be all right.

Chapter Ten

BABY BROTHER

MERI RELUCTANTLY ALLOWED ELLIOTT TO guide her to her room. Her feet felt immensely heavier, making it difficult to lift them up each stair. But Elliott kept his arm firmly around her, supporting her with each step until they arrived at her door where they had no choice but to say good night. She didn't want to be alone, but knew that any other option was impossible. She wished then that they'd been married weeks ago so he could stay with her and help her work through the horrible shock consuming her, and the sheer elation at the center of it—both of which made her want to curl up in bed like a child and just cry and cry.

"I don't want to be alone," she whispered, clinging to Elliott as they procrastinated parting.

"And I don't want to leave you," he said and kissed her brow. "But you just need to try to get some rest." He took her shoulders and looked into her eyes. "I suspect that even by morning you will have adjusted more to what's happened. Although there's no need to rush yourself in accepting all of this. Just . . . take your time. And I'm here for you—no matter what."

"Except that until I marry you I have to spend my nights alone," she murmured.

"We will remedy that as quickly as possible," he said fervently.

Meri looked up at him, needing reassurance. "Does this mean . . . that nothing has changed between us?"

She saw his brow furrow. "Why would you ask me that?"

"Another child for you to take on?" she asked. "A child with obvious physical challenges?"

"Meri," he lowered his head to look directly into her eyes, "I love you. I am more than prepared to commit my life to your happiness and well-being. And I love every part of you, and that means every child that has come from you already feels naturally attached to my heart. If there's a dozen more I will feel the same."

Meri chuckled without humor. "I assure you there is no possibility of that." She touched his face. "I want to have more children, Elliott . . . with you."

"I certainly hope so," he said, "and I will love those children no more than I love Elaine and Crispin and Miles."

Hearing their names spoken together that way tugged at Meri's heart; she had *three* children. In her heart, she had never stopped loving the child she'd lost, and she'd never gone a day without thinking of him and wondering what life might be like if he had lived. She had kept such thoughts and feelings to herself, believing that nothing could change what had happened or bring him back. Never could she have imagined something like this happening. But it had, and she needed to allow her mind and her heart to catch up to this new reality.

As her mind drifted off into deep thought, she teetered slightly from the exhaustion consuming her. Elliott tightened his hold on her and insisted, "You need to go to bed. I will meet you in the morning as usual." He kissed her brow again. "Just try to get some rest."

"You too," she said before he kissed her quickly and hurried away, as if he knew that staying any longer would only prevent her from getting the rest she needed.

Meri got ready for bed in a slow methodical way, as if her body could barely be forced through its routines. She crawled between the covers and extinguished the lamp on the bedside table. A moment after her head relaxed onto the pillow, tears came. She wept all over again for the death of her baby and how deeply it had wounded her, and how hard she'd fought to keep that wound hidden. Her husband had not tolerated any visible evidence of her grieving, and he'd allowed her very little time to herself where she could shed her tears privately. Looking back, she felt increasingly furious with him, knowing what a horrible thing he'd done in sending her baby away and telling her that their child had died. She couldn't believe it!

Along with grieving over the child's death all over again, Meri cried for all these months she had not known of his existence, for all the precious experiences of infancy she had missed. She felt intensely jealous of Lara for being able to have those sweet moments that could never be replaced, but she felt equally grateful for Lara—who was obviously a kind and loving young woman—for taking good care of Miles and for making the effort and sacrifice to bring him back to his mother. She had clearly grown to care for Miles; she surely could have found the means to support herself and continue to raise him as her own.

Meri cried so hard she believed more than once that she might throw up. She managed to keep from doing so, and after a long while her tears dried, and the next thing she knew the room was growing light with the coming of a new day. As soon as Meri's mind caught up to the events of the previous evening, she hurried to freshen up and get dressed. Her baby was alive! And he was here! She didn't want to wait another minute to see him.

While Meri hurried toward the room where she knew Lara and Miles had spent the night, she recalled Lara's caution that it would take time for Miles to become accustomed to her, and she needed to allow their becoming acquainted to happen naturally. But oh, how she wanted to see him! Even if he wouldn't yet allow her to hold him, she wanted to be in the same room with him, certain that every minute she spent with him would aid her in healing from the trauma of what she had believed was his death.

Approaching the door to Lara's room, Meri had to check her enthusiasm and remember that she had to take this slowly, and she needed to be respectful of the tender relationship that Lara obviously shared with Miles. She wondered if the baby might still be asleep, and she should wait. Hesitating at the door, she couldn't imagine doing anything but pacing the hall until she could see her son. Not a minute later she heard him making typical baby noises and she knew he was awake. Just hearing his sweet little voice made her smile, and she knocked lightly at the door.

Lara opened the door just enough for Meri to see that she was still in her nightgown, and was holding little Miles on her hip.

"I was hoping it would be you," Lara said with a smile that made Meri feel more at ease. "He hasn't been awake long. I rang for a maid who is getting some warm milk from the kitchen. Come in."

"Thank you," Meri said. "I hope you're comfortable here . . . and Vera as well. Is she?"

"Her room is next door," Lara said. "We're both being well taken care of. Thank you."

"And did you sleep well?" Meri asked, feeling mildly awkward.

"Yes, thank you," Lara said. "Little Miles slept well; I think the journey wore him out. He's not fond of being in carriages, I think."

Lara sat down and motioned for Meri to do the same. Meri couldn't take her eyes off Miles, marveling again at the family resemblance. If not for it being so evident, she wondered if she would be able to believe this was her son. The baby gurgled more happy noises that made Meri laugh softly. Lara patted the little sofa where she sat and said, "Come and sit closer. Let him become accustomed to you."

Meri sat next to Lara, and Miles examined her with curiosity. As long as he remained on Lara's lap he didn't seem distressed at having a stranger nearby.

"He's always most happy right after he wakes up," Lara said.

"He's so beautiful," Meri said, a quiver in her voice.

"Are you all right, my lady?" Lara asked. Meri hesitated, wanting to be able to answer with a steady voice. Lara added, "I've been worried about you ever since Lord Sturgess sent me away with Miles. And when I realized Lord Sturgess was dead, and Vera and I made the decision to come and find you, I've been worried about how difficult this would be for you."

"I confess I cried many tears last night," Meri said, feeling completely comfortable with this woman. If nothing else, she was grateful that of all the servants in the Sturgess household, Lara had been chosen to take care of her son. "It's difficult to accept that he's alive when I've been grieving over his death for months. But . . . this is a miracle for me, Lara. Despite this stirring up some grief—and it's certainly made me all the angrier with my deceased husband—I cannot feel anything but grateful to have my son back."

The maid arrived with a bottle for the baby, and while Lara fed him, Meri gently stroked his little arms and legs—which didn't bother Miles in the least. After he'd been fed, Lara encouraged Meri to help her change and dress the baby. Again, it seemed that if Lara was there, he was fine with Meri's assistance. Although when Meri tried to hold him, he whimpered slightly and reached for Lara.

"He'll warm up to you quickly," Lara said. "You mustn't worry."

"I'm not worried," Meri said and was thrilled to watch over the baby while Lara got dressed and prepared herself for the day. Meri sat on the floor with Miles while he crawled around the room to explore it, caught up in his curiosity enough that he didn't notice Lara's absence. Meri was fascinated with his little deformed foot, which was clearly evident despite both his feet being covered with crocheted blue bootees. Miles was not impeded at all in crawling with speed and efficiency. She knew that walking would be a different matter altogether, but she didn't care at all about whatever challenges it might create. He would always be loved and supported by his family, and they would do everything possible to help Miles live as normal a life as possible.

"Let's get Vera and go have breakfast with the children," Meri said when Lara was ready to go. "I can't wait for Elaine and Crispin to meet their brother, and I do believe you will love Elaine and Crispin."

"I helped watch over them some in the past; perhaps they will remember me." Lara said the words with hope, and Meri wished they could have been this open and honest with each other before, instead of living in constant fear of Lord Sturgess's ridiculous household rules and harsh punishments. Meri knew that every one of the servants had lived in fear of losing their jobs, and employment in a wealthy household was not necessarily easy to come by. And Meri had lived in fear of many different forms of punishment. She reminded herself that everything was different now.

"Perhaps they will," Meri said with the same hope.

"What will you tell them?" Lara asked as she picked up the baby.

"The truth," Meri said. "I've seen the damage that can happen when secrets are kept within families. I won't allow it to happen with my children. They never liked their father, and I have no need or desire to try and honor his memory. Nothing less than the truth will do, even if it's difficult for them to understand."

"It's difficult for *me* to understand," Lara said, "and I've been trying to understand it since the day Miles was born."

"We will work on that together," Meri said and they went together to Vera's room to find her all dressed and putting on her shoes.

They walked together, mostly in silence, to the sitting room where Meri and Elliott always shared breakfast with the children. Meri opened the door and led the way in, immediately seeing that Elliott and the children were nearly finished with their breakfast—since she was late—but there were enough places set at the table and covered dishes of food to indicate that Mrs. Biddle knew there were guests in the house and they likely would come here for breakfast. Meri wondered how the servants might be perceiving the gossip that had surely spread since these visitors had arrived the previous evening. And more importantly, Meri wondered if her aunt and cousins had heard, and what they might be thinking.

"Good morning," Elliott said and stood, greeting Meri with a quick kiss. He told her quietly that Alice had gone to take care of some personal things, which he believed meant that she knew what was happening and wanted to allow them their privacy.

Elliott then nodded toward the other women and added, "Good morning, ladies. I hope you have been comfortable here."

"Oh, yes!" Vera said with enthusiasm while Lara said, "Very much so. Thank you."

The children's curious attention was drawn to their visitors, and especially the baby. Meri greeted Elaine and Crispin with a hug and a kiss before she looked at both of them and said, "This is Lara, and this is Vera, and the baby's name is Miles. I want to tell you something about Miles just as soon as we have all finished our breakfast. All right?" The children both nodded and they all sat around the table and began passing and serving food. Elaine and Crispin ate very little of what was left on their plates, given that they were clearly very curious about these women, and they could hardly take their eyes off Miles.

While they were eating, Meri asked the children, "Do you remember Lara and Vera? They helped take care of you sometimes in our old house."

"I remember," Elaine said. Looking at Vera she added, "You told us stories at bedtime. The other nannies never told us stories."

"Oh, I believe children should always have bedtime stories," Vera said.

After silently studying these newcomers for several minutes, Crispin said to Lara, "We did find a callepitter."

"What?" Elliott chuckled, but Lara smiled, clearly knowing what Crispin meant.

Lara said directly to Crispin, "We *did* find a *caterpillar.* Do you remember what we did with Mr. Caterpillar?"

"Mr. Callepitter did crawl on our arms and it tickled," Crispin said. "Then we did put him on a rosebush so he could find a safe place to change his clothes and become a butterfly."

"That's right," Lara said to him with a little laugh. "You have a very good memory, Master Crispin!"

Meri felt deeply warmed at the evidence before her that Elaine and Crispin had not always been with cold and harsh nannies. It was evident these two women had privately been kind and loving to the children, and they had done their best to work around the bizarre emotional detachment Lord Sturgess had expected—even demanded.

When they were all finished with breakfast, Meri told the children they needed to have an important conversation and they all moved to the sofas and comfortable chairs that were situated close together, making it ideal for such a tender and difficult revelation. As always, Meri appreciated the way that Elliott sat right next to her and took her hand, letting her know he was not only beside her physically, but he would support her in whatever difficulties might confront them throughout their lives.

"Elaine, Crispin," Meri began, her heart pounding. Could she even say it out loud? She'd been so preoccupied with her baby coming back to her, and how it was affecting *her,* that she hadn't really thought about how she would tell the children. She meant what she'd said to Lara, that she knew they needed to hear the truth. But actually saying it wasn't necessarily easy. She cleared her throat and just forced herself to at least start speaking. "I have something very important to tell you. It's strange and sad and wonderful all at the same time."

The children stared at her expectantly while she struggled to know what to say next, then Elaine startled everyone in the room by saying, "Miles looks just like Crispin." She looked at her brother and said in a motherly scolding tone, "Crispin, did you have a baby?"

Meri bit her lip to keep from laughing, aware of the other adults all trying to hold back their amusement. While Elaine's distorted assumption about such a thing was amusing, Elaine had asked the question with serious intention.

Meri hurried to explain, "No, Elaine, darling. Listen to me. People can't have babies until they are grown up. Someday Crispin will be a father, and you will be a mother, but you are both far too young for that to happen. However, you're right. Miles does look a great deal like Crispin, and he looks a little bit like you. The reason for that is . . . well . . . Miles is your brother."

Elaine gasped. Crispin furrowed his brow with confusion. And now that Meri had gotten past the most important point, she hurried to explain. She did not express any anger toward their deceased father, but she stated in a matter-of-fact way the children could understand that he had not been a kind man, and that he had also been very dishonest. Since their memories of their father were anything but pleasant, they had no trouble taking this in. But they were still obviously confused. Elaine expressed Meri's own astonishment when she asked, "Why, Mama? Why would he send away our brother and lie to us? Why did he want us to all be so sad and think that he had died?"

"I can't understand all of the reasons, sweetheart," Meri said. "He was very difficult to understand. But we think that the biggest reason is that your brother was born with a little problem. His foot is not the way it's supposed to be, and we think that perhaps your father didn't like that. I think he's a beautiful baby and he's going to grow up to be wonderful—just like the two of you—and a silly little thing like an imperfect foot doesn't matter a bit."

"Would you like to see?" Lara asked and pulled back the little blanket covering the baby's legs. She removed the little bootee as the children stood up and moved closer to investigate.

"That's not so bad," Elaine declared in her miniature adult tone. She touched the baby's foot gently, and Crispin followed her example. Miles got suddenly excited as it seemed he was quite taken with the children. Within just a few moments both Elaine and Crispin had figured out how to make sounds that caused Miles to smile and even giggle a little. They were all laughing, although Meri had tears mingled with her joy.

When Miles wanted to get down on the floor, Elliott suggested they all go to the playroom. Lara sat the baby in the middle of the floor before she looked around and said, "What a beautiful room!"

"It *is* lovely," Meri said. "I played here as a child, so the room has many wonderful memories."

The adults sat down to watch while Crispin and Elaine gathered some toys that might appeal to the baby, and the three of them played together beautifully. Miles was entranced by his brother and sister, and Elaine and Crispin both looked as if they'd never been so fascinated by anything in their entire lives as this adorable little human being, their lost brother who had now come home to them.

"I've imagined this moment," Lara said with a little sniffle. "I do believe I feel more at peace than I have since the night he was born."

Meri felt touched by Lara's comment and was considering how to respond when the door came open and Annabel rushed into the room in an unusually flustered state. "Is it true?" she asked breathlessly, her eyes seeking out Meri who stood to greet her. "Is it true?" she repeated, still out of breath, looking only at Meri, so focused on getting an answer to her question that she hadn't even noticed Elaine and Crispin's new playmate. "He's alive?" Annabel asked, her chin quivering.

"He is," Meri said and turned her eyes toward Miles, who was exploring a small toy horse with his mouth.

"Oh!" Annabel muttered and clapped a hand over her mouth, which barely held back her sobbing. Meri put an arm around her and guided her to the sofa. "It's a miracle!" she added once she'd recovered from the initial shock. "It is truly a miracle!"

"It is," Elliott agreed.

The adults all sat quietly for a long while, just watching the children play as if it were absolutely the most fascinating thing any of them had ever seen. Alice came to see if they needed anything, and she was thrilled to meet Lara and Vera—as if knowing their employment in caring for the children meant they had all come from the same small town or something. Meri invited Alice to sit and visit with them, and the young woman got tears in her eyes as she observed Elaine and Crispin with their new little brother.

Meri moved to the floor so she could be closer to her son, wanting so much to hold him but not wishing to do so before he'd become familiar with her. Miles was now happy to have Elaine hold him, and even Crispin, as long as the young boy got some help. But the baby was much more timid regarding the adults. Lara kept reassuring Meri, as if she feared Meri might be hurt by the baby not recognizing her as his mother. But she didn't feel hurt at all, and she told Lara so. She could feel nothing but grateful—if she didn't think about the atrocity committed by her husband, and how it had robbed her of all these months with her baby, not to mention all the grief she had experienced. Meri knew the grief would likely still surface, but for now she chose to just focus on having her children reunited.

When lunchtime came, the children were not interested in leaving their brother to go downstairs and eat with the family. Alice gladly volunteered to share lunch with the children and these two young women who had brought Miles home. Lara told Meri that Miles would be needing a nap soon anyway, and that she would bring him back to the playroom after he woke up. When Meri left the room with Elliott and their aunt, Alice and the newcomers were caught up in conversation, and Meri heard them all laugh.

Once in the hallway, Meri said to Annabel, "We'll be down soon."

Annabel nodded and moved on. Meri turned to Elliott and eased herself into his embrace.

"What is it?" he asked.

"I just . . . need a minute," she said. "The sisters will be full of questions, but . . . I feel so overwhelmed. I'm so filled with joy, Elliott, but . . ."

"But of course, there is sorrow as well," he said with compassion.

"Yes," she admitted. "And I think I'm still somewhat in shock."

"That's understandable," he said and held her more tightly. "Oh, but Meri," he added and drew back to look at her, "he's such a beautiful boy; so precious! And you don't ever have to worry about what other people might see as an imperfection. If he's never able to walk, I will carry him on my back until I'm too old, and then Crispin will do it. We will give him a good life—the best life."

Meri laughed with perfect delight. "After all that's happened," she admitted, "it's still difficult to comprehend how very good you are to me . . . and to my children."

"Our children," he corrected. "That monster you married was never a father to them, and he never would have been. I'm glad he's dead, Meri. I know I need to forgive him, and I'm working on it. But I'm glad he's dead."

"I'm glad too," she said, trying to maintain her composure, knowing the family would be waiting for them. "And we'll work on forgiveness together."

"Agreed," he said and held her hand as they went down the stairs and into the dining room.

As Meri had predicted, the sisters were full of questions and a great deal of excitement, although every one of them also expressed enormous astonishment and anger toward Lord Sturgess. Meri found their feelings validating and reassuring.

Even though the sisters were anxious to meet the baby, Annabel suggested they wait a day or two, so as not to overwhelm him when big changes were already underway. Meri appreciated her aunt's insight, and she decided that she would like to attempt a nap, since she felt thoroughly drained. She was glad when Elliott took her to the library and they each rested on separate sofas.

Meri fell asleep quickly and woke up when Elliott nudged her, saying, "You slept a long time, my love. Miles is upstairs waiting to have tea with his mother."

"Is he?" she asked, sitting up quickly and then needing a minute to come fully awake.

"I suspect he might be more interested in the biscuits," Elliott added and sat beside her. "Did you get some rest?"

"I did, yes. Apparently, I needed it."

"Apparently so," he said and kissed her before they went upstairs together. "I sent a message for the doctor," he added as they walked side by side, "and asked if he could come and examine Miles, but that it certainly was not urgent. He sent word back that he will come tomorrow morning."

"Oh, that will be good," Meri said. "Miles looks healthy, but it will be nice to know everything is all right. And perhaps the doctor can educate us more on the problem with Miles' foot."

"Perhaps he can," Elliot said just before they entered the playroom and found all three of the children on the floor having a wonderful time. Lara and Vera were watching over them, and it was evident a tea tray had just been brought up and left on a table surrounded by chairs, near the window.

"Alice went down to the kitchen to get some milk for the baby," Lara said.

"She's very kind," Vera added, "and it's evident she loves the children very much."

"Yes," Meri agreed. "She's been a great blessing."

Elliott invited the women to join him at the table for tea. Miles began to fuss and Lara sat him on her lap, where she put a tiny piece of cake into his mouth, which he apparently liked very much. She then put a plain biscuit in his hand, which he tried to bite with his two bottom teeth.

"See," Elliott said to Meri. "What did I tell you?"

Meri smiled at him, then focused her attention back on the baby, unable to stop watching him. He smiled up at her, which warmed her heart and made her laugh.

"It won't be long now," Lara said, "and we can leave him in your care."

"Oh, but . . ." Meri felt a little panicked by the way she'd put that, and she realized that she had just taken something for granted that needed to be voiced. "I was hoping the two of you would stay . . . indefinitely. If you want to." She turned to Elliott and said in an afterthought, "I'll pay for their salary from my own money; I have money."

"Why would you even think of such a thing?" Elliott asked her. He turned to Lara and Vera in a way that made it clear he wasn't going to continue a private conversation with Meri in front of anyone else. "You are both very welcome to stay. There is always plenty of work to be done, and you may consider this your home if that's what you want."

Lara and Vera both looked as if they could jump up and down with joy, but they were trying very hard to remain dignified. "Having the opportunity to work here in your home would be a great blessing," Lara said, "but I can assure you we did not come here expecting such an offer."

"Do you have family somewhere?" Elliott asked. "Or potential employment?" Their silence and the amazed glance they exchanged made the answer to his questions evident. "Then it's settled," he added.

"We will talk with the housekeeper," Meri said, "and with Alice, as well. I'm certain we can work out a schedule that is comfortable for all of us."

"Thank you so much," Vera said, looking as if she might cry.

"Yes," Lara added. "Thank you. I can't thank you enough."

"Nor me," Vera said. "I'm certain we would have been able to find work somewhere, because we both have a great deal of experience in various tasks, but . . ."

"But your home is so lovely," Lara added when Vera hesitated. "More than lovely, it's so very . . . loving."

"A stark contrast to the place from which we've all come," Meri said.

Alice came in with a bottle of warm milk for the baby and handed it to Lara. "The temperature is just right," Alice said. "At least that's what Mrs. Biddle told me."

"Join us," Meri said, motioning to an empty chair. "How would you feel about Lara and Vera staying on permanently?"

"Oh, can they?" Alice replied with immediate excitement.

"You must be honest with us," Lara said. "We would love to stay but we don't want to infringe on your routine with the children, or—"

"Oh, I *do* want you to stay!" Alice said.

Vera interjected, "I'm proficient at other tasks. You surely don't need three women to care for your children, especially when you've said that you are personally involved in their care."

"Oh," Alice sounded mildly distraught, "but I don't know a thing about babies." She turned to Meri and admitted, "I was afraid you'd be wanting me to help take care of little Miles, and I just wouldn't know what to do."

"Then that works out nicely," Meri said.

As they continued to converse over tea, it became evident that while Lara loved caring for babies and was very good at it, Vera's greatest love was teaching, and that she had once worked as a governess. It was decided that for the time being, Vera would start tutoring the children with some simple lessons—which was something Meri had been thinking she needed to arrange now that they'd gotten settled in and comfortable at Rosewell Abbey.

During the conversation, the subject of Meri's forthcoming marriage to Elliott came up quite naturally. Now that Meri had become more comfortable with Lara and Vera, it was nice to hear how genuinely thrilled they were on Meri's behalf. They both made comments on how much they had detested her deceased husband and that working in his household had been the worst experience of their lives.

"That gives us something in common," Meri said and changed the topic of conversation. She enjoyed discussing with these women their plans for a simple and quiet wedding at the church and a celebration afterward that would mostly be for the family and those who worked here, since they were much like family in many ways. Meri enjoyed these women's excitement over the upcoming event, but she enjoyed even more the seemingly permanent smile on Elliott's face as he just sat and listened, often glancing at her with a sparkle of love mingled with anticipation in his eyes.

That evening after supper, Lara encouraged Meri to try to hold Miles. "I'll stay where he can see me," Lara said, "but if you're the one to give him his bottle, he'll be fine with that I think."

Meri felt a little hesitant, especially when Miles seemed to resist coming into her arms. But as soon as the nipple of the bottle popped into his mouth, he relaxed on Meri's lap, with his head cradled in her arm. Meri cried silent tears as she fed her son, forcing away thoughts of how it should have been. She was determined to look only forward in every respect. She had believed her son was dead, but he was here in her arms, and they were all safe with a bright future ahead. Miles looked up at her and smiled, and Meri felt the past and the future fall away. In that moment everything was perfect, and she felt impossibly happy.

* * *

After Elaine and Crispin had been put to bed and Lara had gone to her room to put Miles down for the night, Elliott said to Meri, "May I talk to you? We've not had a moment alone all day."

"Of course," Meri said, feeling mildly nervous. He didn't sound upset, but perhaps concerned, and she wondered what might be so distressing. They went to Meri's sitting room where they each lit a couple of lamps to brighten the room before they sat down side by side on the sofa, although Elliott turned to look directly at Meri and took both her hands in his.

"What is it?" she asked, her concern growing.

"I need to ask you a question," he said. "I don't want you to feel offended or get upset. I just need to know."

"All right," she said, wondering if something about the drama that had recently been taking place had created doubt or worry in him that might have changed how he felt about their relationship. She felt decidedly nervous.

"Meri," he began, "I'm very glad you asked Lara and Vera to stay, because I would have if you hadn't. It's not only the right thing to do, considering all they sacrificed to bring Miles back to us, but it also *feels* right. They fit in well. They will be a pleasant addition to the household."

"I'm glad we're in agreement on that," she said. "I realize now I should have talked to you about it before I made the offer, but—"

"Meri, this is your home as much as it's mine. I agree it would be best if we consult each other regarding big decisions, but you have the right and privilege to oversee anything you feel strongly about regarding the children, the household; anything."

Meri felt a little disoriented, but she couldn't quite discern why. She knew Elliott respected her as his equal, and it was one of the things she loved most about him. She also knew that Rosewell Abbey was legally his, and it was expected that a man should oversee his household. She'd grown up seeing her Uncle Angus declaring his place as the man of the house, and she'd certainly seen it from her husband. Meri knew that Elliott was so much different than these men, but perhaps a part of her hadn't fully come to accept those differences.

Meri couldn't think of anything to say when she could hardly figure out how she was feeling. She was surprised when Elliott got to the point he had obviously been working toward. "Meri," he said, his voice kind but perhaps mildly frustrated, "why would you think you'd be expected to pay for their salary out of your own money? That's ludicrous!"

"I *do* have my own money," Meri said. "Surely you know that."

"I assumed," he said, "but I don't care. This is not about money. If men legally inherit property and are responsible for their families, then it is my right and privilege to care for you and the children."

"We're not married yet," Meri said.

"Close enough," he countered. "But let me make it impeccably clear, Meri, that I consider it an honor to care for you every bit as much as I do to care for our aunt and our cousins. The ridiculous fortune that came with this estate will not even notice giving up a fair salary for these two brave young women who made it possible for you to be reunited with your son."

Meri looked at the floor and muttered, "Thank you."

"You don't have to thank me, Meri. This does not sound at all like you. Help me understand."

Meri said nothing for more than a minute while a torrent of thoughts swirled in her mind. Then without hardly giving it a thought, she stood abruptly, saying, "I'll be right back." She picked up a lamp and hurried through the open door from her sitting room into her bedroom. Setting the lamp on the floor near her wardrobe, she opened it and felt her way to the farthest corner at the bottom, behind multiple pairs of shoes. She took hold of the valise she'd hidden the day they had returned to Rosewell Abbey and pulled it out, shaking the dust off it. She'd thought of it occasionally, certain there was surely a place its contents could be kept that would be more appropriate and safe. But she'd procrastinated doing anything about it. Now she felt it was important for her future husband to know about the contents of the valise, and perhaps he could help her know what was best to do with them.

Picking up the lamp and the valise, she returned to the sitting room where Elliott looked immediately curious over what she was carrying. She set the lamp down from where she'd taken it and said, "I assume there is a safe in the house; a place where our uncle kept valuables locked away."

"Yes," Elliott said with suspicion furrowing his brow.

"And I assume that since his death you have access to it."

"Yes, Meri. What are you trying to say?"

"This should all be best kept there rather than at the bottom of my wardrobe," she said, dumping the entire contents of the valise onto the carpet near Elliott's feet.

"Good heavens!" he muttered as the collection of expensive jewelry and an enormous amount of money fell into a heap. "It's a king's ransom!"

Meri sat down and hurried to explain to Elliott how she had begun putting away portions of her monthly allowance right from the beginning of her disastrous marriage, with the intention of someday being able to leave. She also told Elliott how her husband had spoiled her with expensive jewelry, as if it might somehow compensate for his bad behavior. "So, you see," she concluded. "I have my own money."

"And you certainly earned it!" Elliott declared, sounding mildly angry. More softly he added, "Must I repeat everything I just said?"

"No," she admitted with a long sigh. "But just as you are willing to share all you have with me, what I have is ours. I want you to put it someplace safe, and we'll know that it's there if we ever need it."

"Fair enough," he said, but his expression left her still feeling a distinct tension between them. Meri took a deep breath and forced herself to look at him, wondering if such moments would be common as she continued to be haunted by all that Lord Sturgess had done to her. That would certainly explain how disoriented she felt. "We lived in such preposterous lavishness," she said, "and so much went to waste. He gave me all this expensive jewelry, and my allowance was absurdly generous, but it was evident these were meant only to improve my appearance as his wife. He wanted me to be seen in town spending money, and when I went into public I was meant to look perfect. He had more money than ten frivolous men could spend in a lifetime, but if I requested something I felt would benefit me or the children, or even the household in some way, he ridiculed me and implied that he should not have to spend money on such things; he said more than once that I would have to acquire such extras from my own money. I only pointed out once that I was his wife and his responsibility, and I had no means of acquiring money. He beat me for what I said, and I never brought it up again."

Elliott listened while his expression went from shocked to angry to sad. He then took her into his arms and just held her, whispering near her ear, "Just to be clear, I *want* you to make any decision you like regarding our family and our home, and if you spend every last farthing, I would love you no less."

"You're very good to me," Meri said and meant it, but she wished she could shake off the deep rumbling inside of her that still felt disoriented and perhaps confused. She reminded herself that having Miles come back to her was no small thing and it would take time to adjust emotionally. But she knew that what she felt was more than that, even though she felt more than a little afraid to even acknowledge what it might be.

Suddenly fearing she might burst into tears or drift into shock that might render her immobile, Meri came to her feet and said, "I feel exhausted. I think I'd do well to go to bed. Will you . . . take care of this?" Meri motioned to the pile of wealth on the floor and the empty valise beside it.

"I will put it all in the safe tonight, and tomorrow I will give you the combination and show you how to open it so you can get to it whenever you want, because it's yours."

"Thank you," Meri said, feeling distinctly relieved to put her valuables into his capable and trustworthy hands. She'd given him her heart; trusting him with her money felt irrelevant—but in both cases, she couldn't deny her relief in not feeling alone. "I'll see you in the morning." Meri kissed him quickly and rushed out of the room, aware that she'd left Elliott confused over her hasty departure, and he would therefore be concerned. But until she figured out what was going on inside herself, she couldn't very well explain it to him. She just needed some time alone.

Chapter Eleven

THE STURGESS HEIR

AS SOON AS MERI GOT into bed, something akin to a volcanic eruption came from the deepest parts of her spirit, spilling into the open with such volatile emotion that she had to bury her face in the pillow to avoid the possibility of being overheard by those who slept in nearby rooms. While her mind replayed the many horrors and deceptions to which she'd been subjected, her heart and spirit seemed determined to expel the associated grief by any means possible. She could literally feel a great purging taking place in her body as her own sobbing frequently made it difficult to breathe.

Somewhere in the darkest part of the night, Meri finally felt released from all the pain she'd kept bottled up inside for so long. She huddled in the center of her bed, holding a pillow tightly against her, lost in a stream of thoughts that seemed to have a will of their own, declaring the need to be heard and purged from her along with the associated pain. Despite acute exhaustion in body and spirit, Meri just lay there, unable to sleep, blanketed in shock.

Her shock abruptly leapt into a need to be with Elliott and to be able to speak aloud everything that was swirling in her mind. She felt a great healing taking place inside, and she didn't want to halt its momentum. She desperately wanted to be free of the pain she'd been carrying around, and she knew that putting a voice to suffering allowed it to be set free. She'd seen it with her cousins, with Elliott, and especially with herself. And there was no one she trusted more than Elliott. He knew more about her life's experiences than anyone else, and he loved her without condition or reservation. She needed him, and she needed him now.

Meri put on a robe and slippers and carried a candle to guide her to Elliott's room at the opposite end of the huge house. She knocked lightly but got no response, which let her know he was probably asleep. After opening the door, she peered in carefully before she entered and set the candle on the bedside table.

"Elliott," she said as she nudged him.

"What?" he asked, startled, coming awake more quickly than she had expected.

"It's me," she said.

"I can see that." He leaned up on his elbow and forced his sleepy eyes to focus on her. "What's wrong? What are you doing here?"

"I'm sorry to wake you, but . . . I need to talk. Everything feels like it's bursting open inside of me." Her voice quivered. "And you're the only one who really understands, and . . . I just need to talk."

"It's all right," he said. "I'm glad you woke me. Talk to me."

"Not here," she said, knowing it wouldn't be appropriate. "Get dressed and meet me in the library."

Meri took up the candle and hurried out of the room, closing the door gently behind her. She went down to the library and paced the floor there for only a couple of minutes before Elliott arrived, adequately dressed but looking disheveled. He set down the candle he'd carried before he plopped onto one of the sofas and patted it. "Come and sit," he said. "Talk to me."

"I don't know where to start," she said and continued to pace.

"It doesn't matter where you start," he said. "Just talk to me." When she said nothing and kept pacing he added, "You're the one who woke me and said you needed to talk. Come sit down, Meri."

Meri sat by his side and grasped his hand, squeezing it tightly. It took her a few minutes to gather her thoughts enough to be able to start speaking. She began by talking about her courtship with Lord Sturgess, and her realization now of how purposely he had deceived her into believing he was a kind and thoughtful man. She told Elliott about the wedding, and how quickly afterward her husband's true nature had begun to show through his carefully practiced façade. Tears came as Meri told Elliott about some terrible things that had happened during the honeymoon, and her dread and horror in realizing how wretched everything was about the home where she would have to live and the people who resided there. Meri heard herself talking about events and incidents that she had never believed she would speak of aloud. There were some things she felt certain she should have been embarrassed to say to a man. But Elliott didn't seem at all embarrassed, and he reminded her that he would soon be her husband and she could tell him anything. He encouraged her to keep talking, and he offered perfect compassion for bouts of anger that made her get up and start pacing until she would wear herself out and need to sit down again.

When Meri couldn't think of anything else to say, she turned to look at Elliott, almost fearing that he would surely now change his mind about wanting to spend his life with her. But the love in his eyes shone as brilliantly as it always had. He wrapped her in his arms and thanked her for trusting him enough to share such difficult things, and he expressed once again his commitment to making her happy, caring for her in every way, and doing the same for her children.

Meri settled comfortably into his embrace with her head against his shoulder. She thought she should have been amazed or surprised that he could love her so perfectly despite how damaged she was by the life she'd lived. But when she really thought about it, she couldn't deny that she'd known he would love her regardless. He was just that kind of man. And she likely wouldn't have awakened him and forced him to sit through her tirade if she hadn't believed she could trust him to help her repair all the broken pieces of her heart.

Feeling as if she'd been purged of a terrible poison, Meri suddenly felt more at peace than she had in years. And with that peace came exhaustion. Not only was it the middle of the night and she'd not yet been asleep, but she felt as worn out from this monumental emotional purging as if she'd been running for hours. She didn't realize she'd fallen asleep against Elliott's shoulder until she woke up for only a moment when he eased her down onto the sofa, placing a pillow beneath her head. She was barely aware of him putting a blanket over her before she drifted back into sweet oblivion.

Meri awoke to daylight, disoriented by finding herself in the library until she recalled all that had happened in the night. She was surprised to see Elliott asleep on the other sofa, although as soon as she moved, he opened his eyes and she realized he was awake.

"Good morning, darling," he said with a smile, reassuring her once again with the evidence of love in his countenance.

"Did you get any sleep?" she asked, forcing herself to sit up.

"Enough," he said. "I just woke up a few minutes ago. I know *you* didn't get enough sleep."

"I'm fine," she said. "Perhaps I'll take a nap later."

"I love you, Meri," Elliott said after he sat up too.

"I am happier about that than I could ever say," Meri murmured with fervor. "After everything I told you last night . . ."

"It's in the past," he said, "and now you don't have to carry those burdens alone. If difficult memories ever surface, you know you can talk to me about it, and we'll get through it . . . together."

Meri smiled at Elliott, feeling strangely light and peaceful. Perhaps with time she would become accustomed to being free of the burdens of her past, and surely the passing of time would continue to put distance between the blessings of her present life and the nightmares of the past. It was easy for her to say, "I love you too, Elliott Rosewell. I think you'd do well to speak with the vicar and make your intentions known."

"What an excellent idea," Elliott said, his eyes sparkling. "As soon as the doctor has come and gone, I believe I will pay a visit to the vicar. We have a wedding to plan."

Elliott and Meri went upstairs together, then shared a long and tender kiss before they parted ways in the hall to go to their separate rooms before anyone realized they hadn't slept in their beds. Meri crawled into her bed and took advantage of the peacefulness of early morning to ponder the progress she had made and her gratitude for God's hand in her life. He had blessed her with many miracles that had made it possible for her to start her life over and make everything better for herself and her children. And most recently, He had brought Miles back into her life. She smiled to realize that the pain of believing she'd lost him was barely perceptible. Mostly she just felt gratitude, and she looked forward to the time she would spend with *all* her children today.

Meri got up and readied herself for the day, hoping to make some progress today with Miles. She wanted to feed him as she'd done the previous evening. She went to Lara's room, knocking very softly so she wouldn't wake the baby if he was still asleep. Lara immediately opened the door and smiled to see Meri.

"He's just waking up," Lara said. "Your timing is perfect. Come in."

"Thank you," Meri said and went straight to the crib, hoping Miles wouldn't be upset when he woke up to see her there. Having Lara at her side aided her confidence as she watched Miles wiggle himself into consciousness before he looked up at the two women and smiled. Meri instinctively did what she'd often done with her other children during such morning greetings. She tickled Miles and made a funny noise that caused him to giggle. They played their little game for a couple of minutes before Miles reached his arms toward Meri, which made both women laugh softly. As Meri picked Miles up, she realized that Lara was dabbing at her eyes.

"This must be difficult for you," Meri said, loving the feel of Miles in her arms but at the same time feeling compassion for how this must be affecting Lara. "I know you've grown to love him, and you've taken such good care of him all these months."

"These are tears of joy, my lady," Lara said. "As I said, I always knew he would come back to you one day. I *do* love him, and I'm so grateful that I'll be able to stay here and help care for him and be a part of his life, but I feel nothing beyond happiness to see the two of you reunited."

"Oh, Lara," Meri said, impulsively hugging her. "Dear, sweet Lara."

Miles protested at being sandwiched between the two women, which made them both laugh again, easing the tension of an emotional moment.

Miles didn't express any objection to having Meri change his diaper and dress him for the day. She also fed him his bottle and carried him to the sitting room, where Elliott and the children were already seated for breakfast.

"He seems to be doing fine," Lara said at the door. "I'm going downstairs to have breakfast with Vera and the other servants. Just ring if you need me."

"Thank you," Meri said, caught a little off guard at being left completely in charge of Miles. She imagined Lara shedding a few tears on her way to the kitchen, but as she'd said, she would always be a part of Miles's life.

"Good morning," Elliott said and rose to kiss Meri's cheek as if he'd not yet seen her today.

"Good morning," she replied, then said the same to the children. "It looks as if we are in charge of Miles now."

"We'll help take care of him, Mother," Elaine said maturely.

"He's our brother," Crispin said with pride.

"It seems that everything is under control," Elliott said with a chuckle as he helped Meri with her chair.

Miles was completely content during breakfast as long as Meri kept putting little bits of food into his mouth. After their meal, they all went to the playroom where Miles had already figured out the location of his favorite toys and how to crawl there and dump them on the floor. This made the children laugh as they sat down to play with him, entirely enthralled.

"Do you think the novelty will wear off?" Meri asked Elliott when he sat beside her on the sofa.

"Perhaps some," he said, "but I think they will always want to help watch out for him."

"Yes, I believe they will," Meri said and took his hand.

A short while later, Susan brought Dr. Sheddon to the playroom, as Elliott had instructed her to, and Alice came with her to take Elaine and Crispin out to the stables to visit the horses so the doctor could speak privately with Meri and Elliott.

Elliott greeted the doctor with a handshake after the maids and the children had left the room.

"Did I read your message correctly?" the doctor asked Elliott. "A baby believed dead has been returned to the family? And you want to be certain he's healthy?"

"That's right," Elliott said. "It's a strange and remarkable thing."

While Miles played contentedly on the floor, they all sat down and Elliott told the doctor the most important points of the story.

"Then he appears to be healthy except for the foot?" Dr. Sheddon asked.

"That's right," Meri said and rose to pick up Miles so the doctor could get a better look at him. While the baby sat on Meri's lap, Dr. Sheddon talked in a funny voice to Miles and made silly noises to keep his attention while he gently examined him thoroughly, including the malformed foot.

"Well, I agree with you," the doctor concluded. "He appears to be in excellent health. Clearly the woman caring for him has done a very good job."

"And what about his foot?" Meri asked. "What kind of problems might it cause when he gets old enough to walk?"

"Children are rather adaptable," Dr. Sheddon said. "I've seen people adjust to challenges far worse than this and lead lives that are fairly normal. And I've known more than one person with a club foot; they often learn to walk on the ankle or the side of the foot depending on how far the foot is twisted. However, I know of a cobbler about half a day's ride from here who makes special shoes for just such problems. I believe that with such a shoe, Miles can learn to walk without having any pain or injury to his ankle. When he starts standing up next to the furniture, I believe taking Miles to visit this man would be beneficial."

"Oh, that's wonderful news," Meri said.

"Indeed it is," Elliott added.

Meri thanked the doctor after he'd played with the baby for a few minutes, then Elliott left to escort the doctor out. Meri was surprised to realize this was the first time she'd been alone with her son. She held him close to her and closed her eyes, taking in the smell of the soap he'd been bathed in, the sound of his sweet little baby noises, and the feel of him wiggling on her lap. She had her son back; it was truly a miracle.

Miles wouldn't sit still on her lap for long, and she set him free so he could crawl across the floor, back to the toys with which he'd been enthralled before the doctor's visit. Meri admired what a beautiful boy he was, and she smiled to think that having special shoes made for him could help a great deal. It occurred to her that he might not ever be able to run fast or do certain things, but he would be able to walk, and he was otherwise strong and healthy. He would have a good life, and he was such a blessing to her and everyone else in the household.

During the next few weeks, Meri enjoyed every minute she spent with Miles, and she loved the way the other children and Elliott had taken so well to him—and he to them. It was almost as if he'd always been present. A crib was moved into Meri's room as she took over most of his care, although she was glad to have Lara take charge of him for part of each day, which gave Meri time to be with the rest of the family and to work on plans for the wedding. She also knew that Lara missed being the center of Miles's life, and it was surely good for both of them to have time together.

Lara and Vera quickly settled into the household, and they both declared more than once how much they liked their new home and working with—and for—such wonderful people. They both connected well with Alice in a way that made Meri realize Alice hadn't previously enjoyed any real friendships in the household. She was well liked by the staff and comfortable with them, but she'd not had much in common with those who were near her age. The three women worked out their schedules and responsibilities with the children on their own and with the guidance and approval of the housekeeper. They also each had other tasks for which they were responsible elsewhere in the house, which allowed Meri and Elliott to have their time with the children and helped the maids become better acquainted with other servants and to have a more balanced life at Rosewell Abbey.

Meri enjoyed the way her cousins and aunt each wanted to get to know Miles, and they doted on the baby in a way that clearly brought them all much happiness. Meri and Elliott agreed that they all seemed to slowly be doing better. Except for Charity, each of the sisters continued to speak openly about their ongoing progress—and their occasional setbacks. Confiding in the family had begun the healing process and had helped each of them feel more comfortable with each other, even if there had initially been some difficult feelings. Now, with some time and many more conversations, they were each recognizing more fully the things in their lives that were not healthy or that had caused them pain and unhappiness.

With the help of her sisters, Hope was doing well at weaning herself from reading all the time. And they were also eagerly following through on their promises to help engage her in other activities and in sharing open conversations about her reasons for wanting to avoid her own disappointments.

Comfort had stopped hiding food, and despite a few reversals, she was doing well at slowly adjusting to better eating habits. She was also being open with her sisters and mother, who were all helping her monitor the amount of food she ate. She had also spoken with the doctor, seeking his advice on things she could do to be healthier. Going on brisk walks for daily exercise was one of his suggestions, and every member of the family enjoyed an opportunity to accompany Comfort on her walks. If the weather was unfavorable, she had taken to walking the long halls of the house in order to follow the doctor's advice.

Joy had stopped secretly helping her sisters cover up bad habits in every way, and Faith had become somewhat of a leader to her sisters—

given that she was the eldest—but she'd also been through something traumatic enough to give her a great deal of compassion for their struggles.

Annabel was mindful every day of her daughters' moods and how she might help them continue to progress. They all knew that problems developed over the course of many years could not be alleviated in a matter of weeks, but they had all made marvelous progress, and they were committed to helping each other remain on the right paths.

Even though Charity had not yet shared her own personal struggles, she was extremely supportive of her sisters. Then a day came when—without warning—Charity declared over tea that she had stopped seeing the man with whom she'd fallen in love. And even though she knew that her feelings for him were inappropriate, she couldn't deny that she *had* grown to love him, and breaking off their relationship had been very difficult for her. But her sisters committed to helping Charity find distractions to help her heal, and she expressed her gratitude for being guided and supported in ending something that never could have made her happy—no matter how much she might have loved this man. Annabel helped Charity understand that no matter what feelings of attraction or fondness this man might have felt for her, if he was committed to a wife, then any actions toward a relationship he might share with another woman would have always been based in something hollow and selfish and deceitful, and Charity would have never found any kind of lasting happiness. It came as a relief to everyone to learn that Charity had never become intimately involved with this man beyond some passionate kissing; they had all just assumed otherwise. But Charity's strength in keeping the relationship from going into irreversible territory proved admirable, and it helped her now in believing she was strong enough to move on and heal.

While Elliott had been present for every family gathering where his cousins had talked openly about their challenges and discussed their progress, he had been endlessly supportive and encouraging, and was always eager to express his love for them. Meri could see evidence of how they had all grown closer through this season of healing, but she was surprised one day when Elliott admitted to the rest of the family that through much prayer and pondering of the situation concerning his own family, he had finally found peace over his brother's death and the subsequent disdain of his other family members. He was confident in declaring that it didn't matter what they might think of him; he had a clear conscience, and he was determined to move forward, knowing that despite his imperfections he had done the best he'd known how to do regarding his difficult biological family. It was the family he belonged to *now* that mattered. Meri felt deep relief on his behalf, and she also felt proud of him for the effort he'd put into arriving at this point—and she told him so at the first opportunity.

While evidence of all the healing that had taken place among the family meant a great deal to both Meri and Elliott, she knew they were both becoming far more preoccupied with their forthcoming wedding. Everyone in the house—family and staff alike—had been involved in the planning and preparations. Even though Meri and Elliott wanted a simple wedding, it seemed that everyone who cared about them wanted to be involved, and the celebration afterward at the house would surely be enjoyable for all who attended. Plans were being made that would make it possible for each member of the staff to not be so busy with helping that they couldn't get in on the fun.

The night before the wedding, after the children had all been put to bed, with the nannies nearby in case they needed anything, Meri went to the solarium and made herself comfortable, leaning back in a soft chair to look up at the glass ceiling, against which rain was falling. She wrapped herself more tightly in the heavy shawl she'd brought with her, knowing the rain would make this room cooler, but she loved to be here when it rained, and life had been so busy that she'd not come here at all for far too long. While Elliott was engaged in his regular weekly meeting with the overseer, Meri just enjoyed the quiet surrounding her other than for the sound of the rain pelting against the glass, which had a soothing effect. Elliott usually met earlier in the day with the overseer, but the man had sent word that he'd needed to help one of the tenant families do a repair on their roof, and an evening meeting would be better. Elliott had gone off for a few hours in the afternoon to help with the roof and had returned barely in time to get cleaned up for supper.

While the rain lulled Meri into a deeper relaxation, she considered the vast evidence of Elliott's goodness, his genuine concern and compassion toward his fellowmen, the way he took his responsibilities so seriously regarding this estate and caring for his aunt and cousins, and his sincere love for her children that had made them all quite naturally love him. And most of all, Meri thought about the continually mounting evidence of how deeply Elliott loved *her.* All the things she'd been afraid to tell him had only made him love her more and treat her with even more kindness and respect. She never would have believed that such a thing was possible, but she looked heavenward and silently thanked God for so many miracles in her life. She had too many blessings to count, but she was more than willing to give full credit to her Maker for freeing her from a life of pain and imprisonment, and now giving her a life filled with love and peace on every side.

Meri heard the door and turned her head without relinquishing her relaxed position. "Oh, hello," she said, seeing Elliott.

"Hello, my darling," he said and bent over to kiss her. He then scooted a chair right next to hers and sat down where he could hold one of her hands, while she kept hold of the shawl around her shoulders with the other. "How are you this evening?" he asked.

"I am very well, thank you," she said. "I've just been contemplating how very blessed we are."

"We are indeed," Elliott said, sliding down in his chair so that he too could gaze up at the rain hitting the glass ceiling.

"How did your meeting go?"

"As well as always," Elliott said. "Everything is in good hands. For all of Angus's challenges as a husband and father, he was sharp in business. Those who worked for him and now work for us have a great respect for him; they're honest and more than earn their salaries. It's not been too difficult a transition, given how well they do their jobs. I just have to make certain that everything keeps working as it should."

"I'm absolutely certain that Rosewell Abbey couldn't be in better hands," Meri said.

Elliott turned his head toward her. "I'm very grateful that we can call this place our home and never have to leave."

Meri looked at him and smiled. "I wholeheartedly agree, Mr. Rosewell."

"You are so beautiful . . . Mrs. Rosewell . . . almost."

"Almost," she said, smiling again.

"We're really getting married tomorrow," he stated, as if he had to remind himself that it was real.

"We really are," she said, "which means we ought to try to get some sleep."

"We can try," he said and chuckled. "I'm just glad that this is the last night of my life I have to sleep alone."

"I agree wholeheartedly," she said again.

Meri was surprised when Elliott stood abruptly and declared, "All right, I believe it's time for the bride and groom to keep some distance until they are married." He cleared his throat loudly and Meri let out a soft laugh. She knew he was implying that the intense attraction they felt was becoming more and more difficult to keep in check. But he had never been anything less than a perfect gentleman, which made her love and respect him even more. Again, as in all things, the contrast between his behavior and that of Lord Sturgess was astonishing. But Meri pushed all thoughts of her previous marriage away. Elliott was completely different; her life was completely different. Everything was just as it should be, and she felt nothing but happy.

Elliott bent over to kiss her; he smiled and kissed her again. "I'll see you in the morning, my dear."

"Good night, darling," she said and briefly touched his face before he left the solarium. Meri sat there a while longer, counting her blessings once again and anticipating the events of the next day with great joy.

* * *

The following morning the rain had ceased and the skies were blue with scattered, floating clouds that seemed lovely decor for a wedding. Meri saw Elliott at breakfast, but it was a hurried meal since Lara, Vera, and Alice each came to take one of the children as soon as they were done eating to help them get ready for the wedding. Elliott gave Meri a quick kiss and hurried out of the room, saying over his shoulder, "I will see you at the altar, my dear."

Meri laughed softly, then took in the silence of the room for only a minute before all five of her cousins rushed in, all partially ready for the wedding, wearing robes and dressing gowns over their underclothing, their hair in various stages of being styled for a special occasion. They escorted Meri to her room and sat her down in front of her mirror while they took turns helping style her hair just right along with assisting each other in doing the same. Amidst all the attention to curling, combing, and pinning hair into place, the sisters all chattered excitedly about today's grand event, and Meri felt warmed by their sincere happiness on behalf of her and Elliott. The camaraderie among them was comfortable and absent of any negativity; they had all come far, and for that too Meri was grateful.

With the assistance of her cousins and a little help from Annabel as well, Meri was all ready to go to the church right on time. She knew that Elliott had left the house already, taking Crispin with him, since he had been chosen to stand with Elliott at the altar and hold the ring. Vera, Lara, and the baby, along with Mrs. Biddle, were also riding with him. It would take two carriages to get Meri to the church—accompanied by Elaine, the sisters, and Annabel. They all had to squeeze themselves in tightly, but there was a great deal of giggling during the ride to the church.

Once they'd arrived and settled down enough to take this event seriously, Annabel embraced Meri and gave her a beaming smile before she left to take her place at the front of the church. Meri watched her wedding unfold as if she were dreaming. Through the veil over her face, everything assumed a dreamlike effect. Standing at the back of the church while Elaine walked up the aisle, scattering rose petals from a basket, Meri thought of the contrast to her first wedding, but she pushed that thought away only to have it replaced by memories of Lord Sturgess's funeral, and how she'd hidden her true feelings behind a black veil. Today she wore white, and there was no need to hide anything. Her happiness filled her completely, and she wanted the world to know.

Once Elaine got to the front of the church, she stood beside her brother—who was standing beside the groom, who looked breathtakingly handsome even through her veil and from a distance. Meri's heart quickened, and she felt very glad that the wait was over and she would now be his wife. She watched as the five sisters all walked up the aisle, each holding a little bouquet of mixed flowers and each wearing a dress of a different pastel color, making them look like a variety of mixed flowers.

As Meri walked up the aisle by herself, she thought for a moment of how Uncle Angus had walked with her when she'd married Lord Sturgess. Today she walked alone, but that seemed somehow fitting. She didn't need any man to give her away or to control her life in any way. She gladly and willingly was offering herself to Elliott, to be his equal in all things.

At the altar, Meri handed her bouquet of flowers to Elaine for safekeeping. She smiled at her children, who looked exceptionally adorable, especially with the pleased expressions on their faces. She quickly glanced to where Lara was sitting with Miles on her lap, surrounded by her friends and other servants from the household, all of whom looked happy. Meri then turned her full attention to the groom as she slipped her hand into his and felt him squeeze it.

The ceremony was perfect, and the vows that Meri exchanged with Elliott meant even more to her considering all she'd been through. She had no delusions regarding how bad a marriage could be when those vows were not honored, which made her deeply grateful for her personal appreciation of the sacredness of marriage vows, and her knowledge that Elliott would indeed honor her, care for her, and do everything in his power to make her happy. And she would do the same for him. This was how it should be, and nothing could make her happier.

Elliott laughed after he kissed her to seal their marriage, and he kept laughing spontaneously as they exited the church and returned with their family to the house to enjoy the food and music and dancing. It had all been so well planned and prepared that it all fell into place with very little effort from the staff, all of whom appeared to be enjoying themselves. Elliott brought Meri's attention to the fact that more than one of the sisters was spending a great deal of time on the dance floor, having drawn the attention of some eligible local men. One was the son of a tenant farmer on the estate; another ran a shop in town. Since Angus was no longer around to demand that his daughters not marry into a different social class, Meri couldn't help but wonder if her cousins might be less inhibited about enjoying themselves. She also wondered if the healing that had taken place in their lives made them feel more valuable within their own souls, and therefore perhaps not as standoffish as they might have been in the past.

"Maybe romance is brewing," Elliott whispered to Meri.

"Maybe," she said and looked up to see him smile. Romance was definitely brewing in her own life, she thought.

A few hours into the celebration, Meri noticed how everyone moved to the edges of the room and the center of the floor became empty. She was wondering why until Elliott took her hand, saying just after he'd kissed it, "Mrs. Rosewell, may I have this dance?"

"I thought you'd never ask," she said, smiling at him, which made him laugh again, as if he were so perfectly happy he just couldn't hold it inside.

While they danced to the lovely music being played by a hired string quartet, Meri gazed into Elliott's eyes and wondered if she'd ever felt so loved, so valuable, so beautiful. He truly had healed so many wounds her first husband had inflicted upon her, when she had believed for so long that such a thing wasn't possible. But Elliott had taught her that love could heal any wound, if it was companioned by trust, respect, and a willingness to allow those who loved you to help carry your burdens. Miracles had taken place in her life and in the lives of her family members, and Elliott had become the center of all that was good for Meri. In that moment, the future was nothing but bright and perfect.

When the celebrating finally all died down and the children had been put to bed, Meri took Elliott's hand and led him to her room—the room he would now share with her. She closed the door and urged him to kiss her, grateful beyond words that they would never have to part at bedtime again. By the way he drew her fully into his arms and kissed her again and again, she knew he felt the same.

* * *

Meri and Elliott had decided against going away for any kind of honeymoon, mostly because Miles was still just getting used to his new family—and for Meri to leave him now would likely create confusion for the child, and perhaps even some regression. And taking Miles with them would hardly contribute to a relaxing holiday. So, they decided to wait a few months until Miles would be more settled and comfortable. In the meantime, they were both glad to simply be sharing a room and to be able to go to sleep and wake up next to each other. Meri tried not to think of her previous marriage or make comparisons, but it often happened of its own volition. Marriage to Lord Sturgess had been a nightmare; being married to Elliott was bliss. How could she not compare?

With nannies aplenty to help care for the children, Meri and Elliott could spend a fair amount of time together alone while still showing up to be with the children according to their normal routine—for the most part—and for Meri it was a perfect honeymoon. She had the luxury of having Elliott as her husband while still being able to spend time with her children and the rest of the family.

Within a few weeks, life had settled back into its typical routine, and Meri could hardly imagine how it had been to *not* be married to Elliott. They'd already been spending their days together long before they were married, and to everyone else in the house, the routine was mostly as it had been prior to the marriage.

On a warm day following a few days of rain, Meri felt the urge to take Elaine and Crispin outside after lunch. The air held a hint that summer was easing toward autumn, and she looked forward to the beauty of these gardens as the leaves turned color and fell. For now, they were still lush and green, and she hoped that allowing the children to run around and expend some energy would encourage Crispin to take a nap. He'd not done so the last couple of days, and he'd been cranky during the evenings.

While Elliott met with the overseer in his office, Meri enjoyed setting out across the lawn with Elaine and Crispin. She believed it was important for her to spend some time alone with her children every day. They enjoyed playing with the nannies and being with the family, and they especially loved spending time with Elliott. But there were times when Meri just wanted them all to herself. With Miles already down for his afternoon nap, this was the perfect time to be with the older children.

Meri walked a short distance behind them as they ran toward the long rows of flowering plants and neatly groomed shrubberies so they could play hide-and-seek. Even though Meri couldn't see them, she could hear them frequently laughing—except when one of them was being quiet because they were hiding. But once found, they would both laugh and begin again, taking turns hiding. Meri took in the sound of their joy and smiled as she sat down on her favorite bench where the children would know where to find her. They knew not to go so far that they couldn't hear her voice when she called for them, and they sometimes played an echo game of repeating each other's words as they shouted across the garden, even though they weren't within sight.

Meri opened the novel she'd brought with her and began to read, all the while being keenly aware of Elaine's and Crispin's pleasant conversation and laughter nearby. The children each shouted at her now and again, wanting to hear her echo their words, as if they liked the reassurance that she was there every bit as much as Meri appreciated the evidence that they were close and safe and happy. It was a typical routine for a sunny day, and Meri enjoyed the serenity of the experience.

Meri's appreciation of the moment was shattered when she heard Elaine shriek as if she'd encountered a terrifying specter. All her feelings of safety and happiness shattered, forcing Meri's heart to beat painfully hard as she ran toward the sound of Elaine's continued shrieking, wondering what on earth could have happened. She ran down a short corridor of shrubbery and turned the corner, then stopped so abruptly that she almost toppled over. She could only think what a fool she'd been to believe that coming to Rosewell Abbey with her children had somehow guaranteed their safety. She recognized the two men holding Elaine and Crispin; they had worked in the stables of the household she had fled. They both looked more like street thugs than stable hands. And each of them was holding one of her children, a hand over their mouths to keep them quiet now that Elaine had screamed enough to get her mother's attention.

While Meri's mind worked frantically to try to decipher what this could possibly be about, she was most focused on the terror in her children's eyes. "It's all right," she assured them in a barely calm voice that expressed nothing of her rumbling fear. "Everything will be all right." Meri then looked back and forth at these two men and adjusted the tone of her voice to sound firm and strong—neither of which she felt. "What are you doing here? I don't know what you're hoping to gain by coming here and terrorizing my children, but I won't have it!"

"We got your attention, didn't we?" one of them snarled, showing stained teeth and a deep scar that wouldn't allow one side of his mouth to move when he spoke.

"So, you have my attention. Let the children go and tell me what you want."

"Oh, I'll tell you what I want," another man's voice came from somewhere she couldn't see, but it sounded so much like the voice of Lord Sturgess that her flesh and bones threatened to disintegrate into a formless mass of immovable terror. Given her absolute knowledge that Lord Sturgess was dead, she knew it could only be one man, whom she hated almost as much as she'd hated her husband. And the possibility of his present motives left her utterly terrified.

"And what is that?" Meri demanded, trying to sound brave.

Rowan Sturgess stepped out from behind a tall hedge, and a barrage of debilitating memories assaulted Meri. But she could not allow herself to be incapacitated now, not when the safety of her children was at stake.

"What are *you* doing here?" she demanded, proud of herself for the outrage in her tone.

"I have come to claim what is rightfully mine," Rowan said in the same demeaning and haughty tone that had been so common with Meri's husband. Oh, how it grated on her nerves and sparked terrible memories!

"I have nothing that is rightfully yours," Meri said. "I took what is mine with me when I left, and I have no intention of ever going back."

"Oh, that has become evident with the amount of time you've been gone," Rowan said, while Meri tried to remain keenly aware of his every move and at the same time keep an eye on her children, who were still being held tightly by these monstrous thugs. "The problem is that everything still legally belongs to you . . . or more accurately . . ." Rowan's visage took on a distinct evil that also reminded her of his brother; it was how he'd looked before he'd flown into rages that had generally led to her being beaten. But Meri fought to keep her instinctive terror from showing. She needed to be strong; stronger than she had ever been.

"What?" she demanded when he seemed to be purposely leaving her in suspense.

"More accurately, everything belongs to your son," Rowan concluded, almost spitting venom as he said it. "Do you honestly think that I would tolerate living indefinitely in my own home, knowing that it legally belonged to this little brat, whose worthless tramp of a mother weaseled her way into the family for the sake of her own gain?"

Meri snapped, "If that's what you believe, then you are as full of delusions as your deceased brother."

Without even the tiniest hint of warning, Rowan slapped Meri hard across the face, sending her to her knees from the shock of the sting and the way it made her head spin. Through the ringing in Meri's ears she could hear her children whimpering in fear, and she longed to assure them that everything would be all right. But in that moment, she wasn't sure that it would be.

Chapter Twelve

House of Evil

Meri gathered her strength and struggled to get back on her feet, even though she wavered slightly. "I don't want *anything* that you believe belongs to you! I don't want the house, or the estate, or the money. And I certainly don't want it for my son. As far as I see it, everything I left behind is cursed, and you are welcome to it. I'm never going back."

She thought of how Rowan would surely see it all into ruin with his drinking and gambling—unless the family solicitor and overseers could manage to keep him in check. But that was neither her problem nor her responsibility. She would do whatever it took to free herself from this family and to protect her children.

"Well," Rowan said, "I'm glad we see eye to eye on that. And once I have all of that in writing—legally binding and all that—you may have your son back."

"What?" Meri shrieked, unable to hold together any façade of courage in the face of such an implication. She didn't want her son in this man's care for even an hour.

"It's simple, you little tramp," Rowan snarled. "The heir of my father's estate will remain with me until *I* legally become the heir and until all that should be mine is rightfully in my possession."

He nodded toward the thugs holding Meri's children, one of whom released Elaine; she rushed to take hold of Meri, whimpering softly. But the man holding Crispin hurried away wiith the boy, disappearing behind the hedges.

Elaine screamed for her brother while Meri shouted, "No! You can't take him like this! You have no right! This is kidnapping!"

"Call it what you will," Rowan countered with an arrogance that made Meri wish she had the physical strength to do him great harm. "I see it as the means to get what is rightfully mine."

Meri resorted to petty begging. "Please don't take him. I'll do whatever you want me to do so that it's all legally yours. Just . . . please don't take my son."

"He'll not be harmed," Rowan said, as if that should make all this acceptable. "The sooner you get a solicitor to draw up the necessary documents and bring them to me, the sooner you will get him back." He turned to walk away, following closely on the heels of the men who had taken Crispin. Over his shoulder he added, "You know where to find us." He laughed maniacally and added, "It's hardly kidnapping when I'm just taking him home."

The moment Rowan was out of sight, Meri crouched down and said to Elaine, "Run, my darling. Run to the house and find Elliott. Run!"

Elaine did as she was told, and Meri lifted her skirts and ran in the direction these men had gone, frustrated by the twists and turns of the hedges and shrubbery that kept her from seeing them. By the time she came breathlessly out of the other side of the garden, she could see three horses galloping across a meadow toward a nearby road that led out of the valley. She ran frantically as fast as she could, her instinctive need to reach her son overpowering any reasoning that might tell her there was no way she could ever catch up with the horses that were growing smaller in the distance. She finally collapsed in the meadow as the horses turned a bend in the road that led through the woods, and she could no longer see them.

Meri screamed her son's name, as if that might somehow bring him back to her simply by the sheer will of her maternal desperation. When the futility of the situation fully settled in, she wrapped her arms around herself and wailed in a way she hadn't done since she'd been told that her baby had died. Somewhere on the outer edge of her ability to process thoughts, she couldn't help but consider the irony that Miles had finally come back to her, and now Crispin had been taken away. She grasped on to the hope of knowing that she had the means to get him back, but just the thought of how terrified her little boy was in this moment—and how traumatized he would surely be from all of this—made it impossible for her to do anything but sit in the meadow, too weak to move and too much in shock to think clearly.

Meri screamed when Elliott appeared beside her and dropped to his knees. She hadn't heard him coming due to the intensity of her shock, but she was grateful beyond words to see him there. She doubted she could have ever made her way back to the house on her own.

"They took him," she murmured, taking hold of Elliott as if he could save her from drowning. "They took my boy."

"Elaine told me," he muttered, holding her against him where she wept uncontrollably, amazed that so many tears could be inside of her. "We'll get him back, Meri. Everything will be all right."

When Meri had calmed down, Elliott took her shoulders into his hands and looked at her directly. "Tell me what they said, Meri. Elaine could only tell me that until you give them the house and the money they won't give Crispin back. What did she mean? Tell me everything."

Meri repeated what had happened and exactly what Rowan had said, ending with a firm resolve. "We have to get him back, Elliott. We have to do whatever it takes."

"Yes, we'll do whatever it takes," he said with controlled fury. "There is nothing more important than getting him back safely. Do you hear me?"

Meri nodded, inexpressibly grateful to have him in her life—now more than ever.

"Come along," he said, helping her to her feet. "We need to meet with Mr. Browby immediately and be on our way. I doubt either one of us will be able to sleep until we get him back."

Meri silently agreed and leaned into Elliott as they walked back toward the house, grateful for his strength and determination that kept her upright and in one piece. She would have done whatever it took to get Crispin back, and somehow, she would have managed. But she was glad that she wasn't in this alone.

* * *

Back at the house it only took a matter of minutes to be assured that Elaine was with Alice and was being cared for and distracted, and that Annabel had already sent a detailed message to Mr. Browby since she'd been able to get enough information out of Elaine to understand what likely had to be done. Annabel guided Meri to a sofa where they sat close, and she wrapped Meri in a motherly embrace, offering reassurances that this would be quickly solved and that Crispin would be back in her care in no time at all. But all Meri could think about was her terrified son in the company of these horrible men, not understanding what was happening and not knowing what to expect. She knew better than to think that Rowan or his thugs would have enough sensitivity or kindness to offer a frightened child any kind of reassurance that he would soon be reunited with his mother. Meri thought of how long it had taken her and the children to travel here in the spring, and as of this moment Crispin was getting farther and farther away from her. It would surely take time to get the appropriate documents for such a significant transaction to take place, and then it would take days of travel to get to that terrible place, where Meri had sworn she would never return.

Suddenly overcome by the need to be ready to travel, Meri leaped to her feet and declared, "I need to pack some things. We must be ready to go at a moment's notice."

"Of course," Elliott said, following her out of the room.

In the bedroom, Elliott sat down and leaned his forearms on his thighs as if he couldn't move, while Meri vehemently tossed essential items and some spare clothing into a satchel.

"I should have expected this," she said, muttering the thoughts that were pounding their way to the forefront of her mind. "I should have known better than to believe that my leaving simply implied that I didn't want anything of what Crispin might officially inherit. If I'd taken care of this legally a long time ago, then—"

"You cannot blame yourself for this, Meri," Elliott insisted.

"Then who am I to blame?" she shouted and threw the satchel against the wall, scattering its contents on the floor.

Elliott stood and abruptly crossed the room to take hold of her shoulders. "You did *nothing* wrong, Meri. *Nothing*! Do you hear me? That louse of a man you married deceived you and treated you like trash because he was a deplorable person. And his brother is clearly the same. Any reasonable person would have come to talk to you about this, or would have written you, or would have sent information through a solicitor. Any reasonable person does not immediately resort to kidnapping a child to get what he wants. It's as if he believes he must throw some kind of adult tantrum and incite terror in you in order to surround himself with drama. This is not rational; it makes no sense."

Meri sighed and leaned against her husband. "How well you have just described the entire family and what it was like to live among them in that *evil* house—which is exactly why I should have expected this."

"Whatever may or may not have been done in the past doesn't matter, Meri. Right now, we just have to get Crispin back as quickly as possible. And we will! Do you hear me?"

Meri nodded and was once again pulled from her distress by the urgency of the situation. She bent down to put her things back into the satchel. Elliott helped her until she said, "I can do this. You need to pack your own things, because I cannot go back to that house without you."

"And do you think that I would even consider letting you go back there without me?"

"No," she admitted. "I just . . . I'm just—"

"It's all right. You don't have to explain."

As soon as Elliott had quickly packed a bag of his own, he went to speak to those who worked in the stables and the carriage house to make certain they could be ready to leave as soon as the solicitor had the documents in order.

While Elliott was gone, Meri went to the playroom where Elaine was sitting with Alice, both of them in tears. Meri sat down on the other side of Elaine and told them both in simple terms why this was happening and of their plan to solve the problem quickly and get Crispin back. Meri assured her daughter and the nanny that Crispin would be safe, and this would all be over very soon. Alice was quick to put on a bright countenance while she told Elaine about all the fun things they would do, and Alice promised to stay with Elaine every minute until her mother and Elliott came back with Crispin.

Meri thanked Alice for her kindness and perception, and once again reassured Elaine that everything would be all right. Meri kept to herself her own concerns about Crispin being terrified and traumatized. She truly didn't believe that Rowan would hurt his nephew, but he certainly wouldn't be kind. Rowan resented Crispin's existence and was using him as leverage to get what he wanted. But even as black-hearted as he was, Rowan surely had to know that if he harmed Crispin in any way he would face consequences with the law. Meri considered the reality that he could be arrested for kidnapping—but that was an issue she had no desire to pursue. She just wanted her son back.

After reassuring the frightened Elaine once again that all would be well, Meri left her daughter in Alice's care until they returned—whenever that might be—although she wasn't even certain yet if they would be able to leave that day. Every hour that passed felt impossibly painful, and she prayed that Mr. Browby would be efficient and compassionate.

Meri went to see Miles and explained to Lara what was happening. She was horrified and visibly upset, and the first words out of her mouth were, "Do you think this has anything to do with Miles?"

"No, I'm certain it doesn't," Meri said. "Everyone believes he's dead, and we'll keep it that way. I know Miles will be well cared for while we go and get Crispin back."

"Godspeed, my lady," Lara said, and Meri impulsively hugged her.

"Thank you," Meri said and hurried downstairs to see if the solicitor might have magically arrived in the short amount of time since a message had been sent for him. She went to the parlor hoping to find her aunt, but only the sisters were there, all weeping and in various states of panic. Their mother had obviously informed them of what had happened. They each expressed their compassion and concern, but they were so upset that Meri had to help reassure *them* that everything would be all right, even if the ever-tightening knot in her stomach attempted to convince her otherwise.

After a fair attempt at calming her cousins down, Meri went to find Annabel, concluding that if she were waiting for the solicitor she might do so in the drawing room. Meri was relieved to find her there, although the way she was pacing and wringing her hands did nothing to help calm Meri's nerves. Still, she sat down, answering the weakness in her limbs that seemed to be a symptom of the shock she was experiencing, knowing that her son had been kidnapped by a man who was clearly every bit as selfish and cruel as his brother—and Meri knew just how horrible it was to be subjected to such cruelty. A continual circle of prayer went around and around in her mind; her only spark of comfort was the hope that God would protect her son and keep Rowan from resorting to any kind of harm toward Crispin to achieve his evil designs.

"Mr. Browby is a good man," Annabel said.

"What?" Meri asked, startled from her own thoughts.

"The solicitor—Mr. Browby. Elliott's met him . . . done some work with him regarding the estate . . . but I don't believe you've met him."

"No . . . I haven't," Meri said.

"He's a good man. The message I sent expressed the urgency of the situation. I'm certain he'll do everything he can to help us." Annabel continued to pace. "I just hope he's not occupied with something that can't be interrupted."

"I hope so too," Meri said, knowing that until they were in the carriage and on their way, she would continue to feel completely helpless.

"Oh, Meri," Annabel said and finally sat down next to her, "I just can't believe this is happening. I simply *cannot* comprehend what a horrible family these people are. It breaks my heart that you had to live with them all those years, and now . . . now . . ."

"It will be all right," Meri said, now reassuring her aunt even though it was Meri's son in peril. But at least she could feel grateful that she had family members who cared enough to be so upset by this.

"I wish you didn't have to go back there," Annabel said, taking hold of Meri's hand with both of hers. "That alone must feel so difficult for you."

Meri gratefully acknowledged Annabel's compassion and allowed it to soothe her, if only a little. It was easy to say, "I feel as if I must walk into the bowels of hell to rescue my son. The memories alone are so horrific, but the thought of having to face Rowan . . . and perhaps his mother . . . just makes me ill. They're truly the most haughty, unkind people I have ever encountered, and I had wrongly believed I would never have to see them again."

"What's happening is a terrible thing, Meri," Annabel said, sounding stronger now and lending her strength to Meri, "but you are a brave, remarkable woman . . . and I know you would do *anything* to ensure the safety and well-being of your children. You will give Rowan what he wants, you will face whatever it takes to get Crispin back, and you can walk away from there with the absolute knowledge of your own integrity and strength. And you *never* have to go back."

Meri took in Annabel's words, and fresh tears tingled in her eyes. She nodded and squeezed her aunt's hand before they were both startled by a firm, repeated banging of the knocker on the front door.

"Oh, that must be him," Annabel said, shooting to her feet even though they both knew Susan would answer the door and bring any visitor to the drawing room.

Meri remained sitting, still overcome with a strange weakness. Susan guided Mr. Browby into the room and introduced him, but he didn't have a chance to speak before Elliott came breathlessly through a different door and announced, "The carriage and drivers can be ready to go with ten minutes' warning."

"Then tell them to get it ready," Mr. Browby declared with confidence. He was younger than Meri had expected—about Elliott's age, she guessed. His dark blond hair was balding on top, and his features were thin and angular. But he had a kindness about his countenance that immediately left Meri comfortable and confident in having his assistance. The solicitor continued, "I've spoken with my wife and my partner, and everything is arranged for me to go with you. I can work on drafting the documents as we travel, and I believe it would be beneficial to have me there to help represent you legally . . . if you agree."

"Yes!" Elliott said. "Yes, of course. Thank you!"

In less than twenty minutes the carriage was rolling away from Rosewell Abbey, while a group of family and servants waved them off. Meri sat close to Elliott, grateful to feel his arm around her shoulders, and to be able to lean against him. His strength sustained her in every way.

Mr. Browby asked them many questions and used a pancil to make notes that were not very neatly written due to the unexpected bumps of the carriage. But their travel plans included staying one night at an inn so they would not arrive disheveled and unprepared. Meri wanted to feel confident in facing these people she detested so deeply, and Mr. Browby needed time to prepare the document in a professional manner. He talked about exactly what it would say and explained every term to them, writing the document out in a rough form that he would be able to copy down quickly once he had a table on which to write with pen and ink.

Meri was grateful beyond words to have Mr. Browby accompanying them. His knowledge and confidence helped soothe her as much as it boosted her own confidence. The carriage ride seemed to take forever, even though the weather was fair and they made good time, stopping only briefly when it was absolutely necessary. They ate as they traveled and rested as much as they could. But Meri could hardly relax when her mind swirled with chaotic thoughts of her son and the fear he was surely experiencing, intermixed with so many horrible memories that made her dread of returning to that house of evil literally sickening.

After traveling more than twenty-four hours with only brief stops—the two drivers taking turns so the other could rest in order to stay alert—Meri finally drifted to sleep with her head against Elliott's shoulder. She fell asleep in daylight and awoke to darkness with no idea how long she'd been sleeping. She felt achy and tense from a combination of her anxiety and the endless hours spent on the uncomfortable carriage seats. But she felt more rested and was grateful for that; she didn't want to face Rowan or his mother feeling too tired to think clearly. She wondered then if her demeaning and intimidating mother-in-law knew about Rowan's evil deed—kidnapping her child to ensure his own inheritance to the entire estate. Perhaps she didn't. For all of the woman's lack of kindness and tendency to overt criticism, Meri wondered if she would approve of such methods. But then, Meri felt relatively certain that this woman had known her son was physically abusing Meri, and she'd said or done nothing about that.

Did the elder Mrs. Sturgess truly believe that her sons were above reproach and entitled to do whatever they pleased, no matter how unethical or unkind—or illegal—it might be? Meri concluded that this was likely the case. She couldn't comprehend such attitudes, but she'd spent years living under the same roof as these people, and in all that time she'd never been able to figure out why they behaved the way they did. There was no point in trying to figure it out now. She just wanted to be legally free of any connection to them, and above all else she wanted her son back in her arms, safe and sound, where he would know he was loved and cared for. Meri felt inexplicably grateful that her children would not have to be raised in such an ungodly environment.

After many more hours of traveling, they arrived late evening at an inn that was about seven hours from the estate Meri had gone to years earlier as a bride, naive and completely unaware that she had been sentencing herself to a hellish existence, as if she had married the devil himself. The room they were given was small but clean, and Meri hurried to change into a nightgown for the first time since the night before Crispin had been taken. She crawled between the covers and listened as Elliott locked the door and sat on the edge of the bed to pull off his boots. He let out an exhausted sigh before he extinguished the lamp and snuggled close to her.

"Are you all right?" he asked.

Meri didn't want to answer the question. Instead she asked, "Are Mr. Browby and—"

"The drivers and Mr. Browby are all settled in their rooms. Mr. Browby said it won't take him long to put everything in order, and we can all get some decent sleep."

"Decent sleep feels impossible," Meri said.

"I know," he whispered and kissed her brow. "I'm so sorry this happened, Meri, but it's nearly over, and I swear to you that nothing like this will ever happen again."

Meri heard a tremor in his voice and pressed the side of her hand to his face. "Are *you* all right? You do so well at making certain everything is taken care of—especially me—and I'm ashamed to admit that I've been so self-absorbed that I've hardly thought of how *you* are doing."

"You've been thinking about your son, as you should be. You have nothing to be ashamed of."

"But he's *our* son. I know how much you love him."

"I *do* love him, Meri. And I'm trying very hard to keep my anger in check. I don't know if I've ever felt so angry in my life. Well," he added, "yes, I have. I felt this angry when I found out the truth about how your husband abused you, and now his brother has done *this.*" Elliott cleared his throat as if it might somehow expel the anger growing inside him. "I find myself imagining how I could beat him to a pulp . . . and I see him turning into that monster you married . . . and I fear I won't be able to stop . . . and I'll kill him."

"But you wouldn't," Meri said gently, hoping to soothe him. "It's not in your nature to do such a thing."

Elliott let out a scoffing laugh. "I'm not sure I know *what* is in my nature anymore, Meri. If Crispin has been hurt even a little, I will—"

"Shhh," Meri said and put her fingers over his lips, grateful for the distraction of needing to help Elliott see reason. "We are going to give them what they want, and we're not going to stir up any trouble that could make things worse. We are going to leave with our son, and we will put all of this behind us—together."

His exhale was long and slow, as if he were trying again to release his anger, then he inhaled deeply as if to take in Meri's calming words. "It's a good thing you're here to keep me from doing something stupid."

"I understand, Elliott. I've felt the same kind of anger toward Lord Sturgess . . . so many times. And I would imagine myself retaliating with equal brutality—or worse. I wanted to see him on the floor, writhing in pain, begging for mercy. But I knew there was nothing I could do that wouldn't come back on me with further punishment. And even more than that, I always knew in my heart that God knows the truth. I don't know why this family is so cold and cruel; I can't begin to understand it. But God knows, and it will be for Him to judge them when Judgment Day comes. The only thing that really mattered was for me to know that I could face God with a clear conscience. He knew my suffering, and I believe He will see everything right in the end—even though the end doesn't happen in this life, and therefore more often than not, things appear to be so unfair.

"But God knows my heart, Elliott," seh continued, "and He knows yours. We will not lower ourselves to their kind of behavior. We will behave like Christians even though it's difficult, because we know it's the only right way to handle this or any other difficult situation. And we must trust that God will watch over our little Crispin, and that He will help all of us heal and find peace with this over time. That isn't only *all* we can do, it's the very *best* we can do."

Elliott was so silent that Meri wondered if he'd fallen asleep. He finally sighed again and murmured, "Listen to you. Even when I know you're terrified and feeling as if you'll crumble into pieces, the truth comes out." He gently ran his hand over her face and into her hair. "You are a remarkable woman, Meri, and I am so blessed to share my life with you."

"It is I who am blessed," she said before sighing heavily herself. "But, oh! I will be so glad when it's this time tomorrow, and we have our little Crispin back. My poor, sweet baby," she added and began to cry, and once she'd started she couldn't stop. She hadn't been able to cry, or even speak very freely of her emotions, what with Mr. Browby and one of the drivers in the carriage. But now that she was alone with Elliott, all her fear and worry came flooding out. Elliott held her while she cried, and she realized that he'd become very good at doing so.

Meri didn't think she could sleep, but the next thing she knew, Elliott was nudging her awake, and she squinted against the sunlight flooding through the window. She could see that her husband was dressed as he put one knee on the bed and bent over to kiss her. "They're bringing breakfast up to our room; it should be here in a few minutes. As soon as we eat, we need to go. Now that we're this close, I don't want to waste a minute in getting Crispin back."

"Amen to that," Meri said through a yawn.

"Meri," he said, his tone especially serious.

She looked up at him, her eyes now more adjusted to the light. "What is it?" she asked.

"I love you," he said. "This could be a very difficult day. I know that going back there is not going to be easy for you, but I want you to remember that what you experienced there is not your life anymore. Your life is with me and our children back at Rosewell Abbey, with our eccentric aunt and our slightly crazy cousins." He chuckled softly, then his expression became even more sober. "Don't forget it for a moment, Meri. I love you, and we are going to have a very, very, very good life together. Do you hear me?"

"Yes," she said, more grateful than she could say for his insight. It *would* be a difficult day, and she surely did need reminding that the past was behind her and the future was bright. Once they had Crispin back, she would leave and never look back.

"You are not the woman they think you are," Elliott continued. "You're not a product of the way they treated you, Meri. You are good and kind and loving. And I love you. I just didn't want you to forget."

"I love you, too," she said. "Thank you."

He kissed her quickly and moved away. "Hurry and get dressed. I want to get this over with."

"Amen," she said again.

* * *

The final stretch of the journey was as devoid of conversation as the previous days had been, but to Meri the silence felt increasingly strained with the dread of what they might face. She'd refused to even allow herself to think that Rowan might do harm to Crispin—more because she couldn't even bear the thought, rather than believing that Rowan wasn't capable of hurting a child. Mr. Browby had told her more than once that Rowan Sturgess could be in a great deal of trouble simply for kidnapping a child—and he had to know that; he surely wouldn't hurt the child and put himself at even greater risk of being in trouble with the law.

Meri appreciated Mr. Browby's insights and kindness, and she was glad to know that he was a stern and confident man who intended to tell

Rowan exactly how much trouble he could be in if he didn't cooperate fully. Still, Meri dreaded going back to that house and seeing the people who lived there, and her stomach knotted more tightly with every passing mile. She felt so literally sick more than once that she was prepared to have the carriage stop so she could throw up by the side of the road. But somehow, she'd managed to keep her nausea from overcoming her, and even more miraculous was the fact that she was able to remain calm when she wanted to be hysterical and fly into a frenzy.

Meri attributed this almost illogical peace to God answering her continual prayers that Crispin would be safe and that she would be able to handle the situation with her dignity intact. The other main contributor to the calm she felt was having Elliott at her side, which she considered a miracle, a blessing from God that she never could have believed possible not so many months ago.

When the passing scenery became familiar to Meri, the smoldering in her stomach became too much to bear and she *did* ask for the carriage to stop. She got out too quickly for anyone to help her and rushed to a cluster of wild shrubbery where she heaved for long minutes after her stomach was completely empty. As soon as the heaving stopped, she became aware of Elliott's hand on her back and wondered how long he'd been there.

"It should not be a requirement for a husband to watch his wife retching."

"I may well get even someday," he said. "It is one of those things humans do." More gently he asked, "Are you all right?"

"I will be," she said. "Better that I throw up here than in the house."

"Maybe," he said as if he thought the latter would somehow be fitting.

"At least I don't feel nauseous anymore," Meri said, and Elliott escorted her back to the carriage.

"Everything will be fine," Mr. Browby said with firm conviction as soon as the carriage was moving again. "I will make sure of it."

"Thank you," Meri said. "I hope it doesn't take long, and that we can be in and out of there quickly."

"I hope so too," Elliott said.

When the house came into view, Meri felt mildly nauseous again, but at least she knew her stomach was empty. Elliott leaned over her to look out the window at the menacing structure and said, "It looks like a mausoleum."

"Or a prison," Meri said. "It's as if even those who had the house built—generations back—didn't want it to actually be pleasing to look at." She craned her neck to look up at the gray stone towers at the corners of the mansion. "I often thought that the house itself could drain all the blue out of the sky."

"I think I agree with you," Mr. Browby said, also taking a good long look at the house before they went around a curve in the road, making it impossible to see the house until a few minutes later when the carriage came to a stop at the main entrance.

"Here we go," Elliott said, taking a deep breath as he took hold of Meri's hand.

"Let's get this over with as quickly as possible," Mr. Browby said.

"Amen," Meri added.

They all stepped out of the carriage and Mr. Browby knocked at the door. Meri appreciated the way the men who had traveled with them from Rosewell Abbey, taking turns driving the carriage, stood behind and to the sides of Elliott and Meri, as if they might lay down their lives for the sake of this endeavor.

Meri's heart beat quickly as they waited then it began to pound once the door was opened and she recognized a sour-faced butler. Mr. Browby handed the butler his card, saying sternly, "I'm here to see Rowan Sturgess. He *will* want to see us."

The butler looked past Mr. Browby and recognized Meri, which made his brow furrow. He scrutinized the man standing next to Meri and his scowl deepened. He looked again at Mr. Browby and said, "I'm not certain Mr. Sturgess is available."

"If he is *not* available, then we shall be going directly to the local constable to have the man arrested for kidnapping."

Meri was astonished by how quickly it became evident that the butler knew to what Mr. Browby referred. Did the entire household know that the master of the house had illegally taken his nephew? They'd likely have to; a child in the house couldn't go unnoticed, could he? Meri thought of all the times she had been beaten by her husband within these walls and how the servants had to have surely known—yet they had simply done their jobs and looked the other way. She felt nauseous again, but Elliott squeezed her hand in a way that helped her breathe more deeply, calming the smoldering in her stomach, if only a little.

The butler motioned for them to enter and led them to a drawing room that was all too familiar to Meri. It was still decorated in drab colors—just like the rest of the house—and Meri felt a chill rush over her shoulders, even though the room felt too warm. They were left to wait far too long. Meri couldn't bring herself to sit down, as if simply coming into physical contact with anything in this house might again contaminate her with an illness from which she'd been trying to heal for months. She chose to look out the window that showcased a vast lawn and the distant woods. It was a boring view, but far better than anything she could see looking in the other direction.

Elliott paced the room slowly and methodically, and Meri hoped that his anger would remain in check. No matter what might happen, she knew that anger would only makes things worse; it's as if these people derived strength from anger, and she was determined to not allow them to take anything more from her. She only wanted her son back.

Mr. Browby appeared to be completely calm as he sat with one knee crossed over the other, holding in his hand the documents she and Rowan both needed to sign in the presence of each other.

The door finally opened and Mr. Browby came to his feet at the same moment Elliott stopped pacing. Meri glanced over her shoulder only long enough to see that it was Rowan. Then she turned back to the view out the window, which helped her retain her composure. Mr. Browby had told them to let him do the talking, and they had agreed that it would be in their best interest if no one in the Sturgess family knew that she had remarried so quickly. Elliott was here as her cousin, a male relative who had accompanied her on the journey for the sake of propriety.

"Mr. Sturgess," Browby said as Rowan closed the door.

"Lord Sturgess," Rowan said.

Browby held up the papers in his hand and spoke in a coldly snide tone that seemed out of character for him; however, it seemed entirely appropriate to communicate with a man like Rowan Sturgess in a way that would get his attention. "Not until you sign these papers," Browby said. "Everything is in order. You are welcome to read it through if you like. Once you and your sister-in-law sign, and we . . ." he motioned to Elliott, ". . . sign as witnesses, the entirety of the estate will be transferred from young Master Crispin to you."

"And who are you?" Rowan demanded, looking at Elliott.

"Elliott Rosewell—Meri's cousin."

Rowan seemed to be sizing Elliott up before he turned to Browby and snatched the papers from him. "Let me see that," Rowan said and huffed into a large chair where he began to read.

"As you can see, it's fairly simple," Browby said. "There are two identical copies of everything. Once you both sign, a copy will remain in the possession of each of you to prevent further disputes."

When it seemed that Rowan was taking forever, Meri said without looking at him, "Where is my son? I want to know that he's all right."

"He's fine," Rowan said as if her concern was ludicrous. "He's been having a glorious time."

Meri recalled how cold and unfeeling most of the staff were in this house, and she wondered what Rowan's definition of *having a glorious time* might be. She finally turned to look at him. "I want Crispin here with me before I sign the papers. Send for him. Now."

Rowan looked at her in a way that reminded her so much of her deceased husband that the temptation to throw up again here and now became difficult to suppress.

"My brother told me you were a feisty and wicked tramp," Rowan said, "but until now I don't think I believed him."

"Keep your vile thoughts to yourself," Elliott said, "and send for the child."

"I'm still reading," Rowan said in a haughty tone to Elliott, but Meri noticed that Rowan *was* intimidated by him, even if he did well at covering it.

"You should know, *Mr.* Sturgess," Browby said, "that your sister-in-law is doing you an enormous favor to not report to the police the fact that you kidnapped her son. And you would do well to cooperate."

"A man does what a man must do," Rowan said, and Meri cringed. She couldn't count the times she'd heard her husband say that.

"All you had to do was ask," Meri said, keeping her back turned. "I would have gladly given you everything you wanted if you'd just asked. I assumed that when I left it would be yours anyway. There was no need for you to bring Crispin into it and cause all this drama."

Meri feared some kind of cruel retaliation from Rowan, but Elliott said, "You can read while the child is sent for." Meri saw movement from the corner of her eye and turned to see Elliott reaching for the bell rope. "Or here," he said and pulled it, which was considered offensive to do in someone else's home. "Let me take care of it since you look so comfortable." Elliott's sarcasm was evident to Meri, but she couldn't help being pleased with the way he talked down to Rowan. How grateful she was to have him here with her!

Chapter Thirteen

STARS AND WISHES

THE SOUR-FACED BUTLER ENTERED THE ROOM, and Elliott said to Rowan, "Tell him. If you want us to sign the papers, tell him."

"Bring the boy," Rowan said with an arrogant wave of his hand before he returned to his reading.

The butler left the room, apparently aware of what was happening. Meri was startled to recognize an appalling shock inside of her that had once been a nearly constant state of mind.

The room remained eerily still while Rowan read, except for the occasional turning of a page. Meri wanted to run away from here as fast and as far as she could—back to Northumberland, back to home and safety and peace. But not without her son! Her impatience was making it difficult to not start shouting, but she bit her tongue and kept her focus on the trees in the distance. At least Rowan's mother hadn't shown herself; she prayed that the old woman would remain hidden until they were able to leave.

"Everything appears to be in order," Rowan said in a tone that indicated there would be no problem. Then he immediately asked, "Can you assure me that it's exactly as it states here? She gets nothing? Crispin gets nothing?"

"Nothing," Mr. Browby said. "She only wants to sign the papers, get her son, and we'll be on our way."

"Fine," Meri heard Rowan say and she knew without looking that he'd stood up. "Let's sign these and get it over with."

"Not until my son is here in the room," Meri said without turning from the view out the window. "You'll get nothing from me until I know he is unharmed."

"He's fine," Rowan drawled with a little laugh as if she had no reason whatsoever not to trust him.

"Then there will be no problem," Meri said, keeping her back turned to Rowan. She was counting on Elliott to keep an eye on Rowan, and she knew from a quick glance that he was, which meant that she didn't have to.

The silence grew thick, and Meri could almost feel Elliott's anger in synchronization with her own. At the sound of the door opening, Meri turned, her heart jumping with anticipation. She dropped to her knees and lost all concern for her dignity when Crispin saw her and ran into her arms. She wept as she held him close, kissing his face and hair, checking to see if he was all right.

"Are you hurt?" she asked.

"No," he whispered as if he didn't want to be heard, "just a little scared. They said you would come and get me, and I knew you wouldn't leave me. But I don't like it here. Can we go now?"

"In just a few minutes," Meri said. "I need to sign some papers, and then we can go."

Elliott was there to lift Crispin into his arms with a hearty laugh and Crispin wrapped his arms tightly around Elliott's neck.

Mr. Browby put a pen into Meri's hand; everything was set out on a table, ready for her to sign. She signed her name as Grace Meriwether Sturgess in all the places where Browby pointed, then she watched while Rowan and Mr. Browby both signed their names. Elliott was motioned forward to sign as a second witness, and he managed to do so without setting Crispin down.

"That should do it," Mr. Browby said, handing Rowan one set of documents and gathering up the other set to take with them.

"One more thing," Meri said and turned to face Rowan. Now that she had her son back and the evil transaction had taken place, she would regret walking away without doing what she'd wanted to do ever since she'd seen him holding her son back at Rosewell Abbey. With no preamble or warning, she slapped him hard across the face. A second later, Rowan lifted his hand to strike her in return, but Elliott grabbed his arm, managing to do so while holding Crispin, although he quickly shifted the boy into Meri's arms so that he would have no impediment that might prevent him from remaining in control of the situation. With

Crispin in her arms, Meri hurried toward the door, with Mr. Browby staying close by her side. Just as he reached for the doorknob to open the door, Rowan snarled at Meri, "I don't know how you can live with yourself. You may have fooled the rest of them, but I know you killed him."

Meri sensed more than heard Mr. Browby's and Elliott's surprise over this accusation. Thankfully, Crispin didn't seem to be paying any attention to anything other than holding tightly to his mother. She turned slowly and looked at her husband's brother, saying with a fortitude that she did not feel, "You have no idea what happened that night, any more than anyone else. But his death left you exactly where you always wanted to be, *Lord* Sturgess. If any fingers are to be pointed, I'd think *you* of all people had the most to gain. I pray to God I never see you or this wretched place ever again."

She walked out of the room and then out of the house, grateful for Mr. Browby opening doors for her and remaining close by. She could hear Elliott following behind her and no other footsteps, but she still felt relieved when they were all inside the carriage in less than a minute, leaving all of this behind.

Meri found comfort in the movement of the carriage wheels beneath them and was grateful for the distance it was putting between them and the house that had once been a prison for her and her children. Beyond that, she was only aware of her sweet little Crispin in her arms. She held him on her lap and wept silently, glad that he couldn't see her face. She didn't want her own emotion to upset him, but her gratitude at having him back was difficult to hold back. Elliott's arms were tightly around them, and Meri leaned her head against his shoulder while she kept a tight hold on her son.

As soon as Meri could compose herself enough to speak, she began asking Crispin careful questions about his experience of the last few days. He cried here and there as he told them how frightened he'd been and how much he did not like his Uncle Rowan or the *bad men* who had taken him away. And he didn't like the house where they used to live, and he didn't like the *mean ladies* who had been taking care of him. But it was evident he had been kept safe and well fed, even though he was still wearing the same clothes and he hadn't had a bath since he'd been taken from his home. However, he'd never been allowed to go outside or exert any energy at all, so he hadn't had the opportunity to get dirty or sweaty.

After Crispin had talked almost incessantly for nearly an hour, he got drowsy and fell asleep on Meri's lap, although she carefully shifted him into Elliott's strong arms, given that Crispin was a growing boy and not as small as he used to be.

Once Meri knew that Crispin was sound asleep, she said to Mr. Browby, "How can we ever thank you enough? You knew exactly what to do . . . and made it so much easier. I can't imagine how upset I might have become if you hadn't been there to speak for me."

"I echo that sentiment, Mr. Browby," Elliott said. "You kept me calm when I doubt I would have been otherwise. You've far surpassed earning your fee for handling this on our behalf. I know it can't have been easy to leave your family and other business dealings on such short notice. Just know how very grateful we are."

"I'm truly glad I could help," Browby said. "I chose this profession so that I could aid the cause of justice—more specifically, so I could help good people handle difficult situations. It's turned out to mostly consist of composing documents and offering reassurances to people that their affairs are in order. I must say that it was rather a pleasure to stand up to such a cretin and put him in his place." Mr. Browby smirked very subtly. "All for a good cause." He nodded toward Crispin. "I'm just glad it all turned out well."

"As we all are," Elliott said and looked down at Crispin, sleeping in his arms.

They took the journey home with almost as much haste as the journey to retrieve Crispin. They spent one night at an inn where they could bathe and get a good night's sleep in a bed, but other than that they stayed on the road, switching drivers when necessary, wanting only to get home as quickly as possible. Meri not only wanted distance between her old life and Rosewell Abbey, she wanted to be home and safe and have everything go back to normal.

When they finally arrived at the Abbey—exhausted, aching, and disheveled—it took only a couple of minutes for the entire family, along with the nannies who brought the children, to swarm around Crispin as if he were a hero returning from war. Crispin laughed as he soaked up all the attention, and Meri could have swooned from the depth of relief she felt to see him back among his family and doing so well.

While Crispin was being questioned by the sisters about his adventures, Meri and Elliott both greeted Elaine with tight hugs. "Oh,

I missed you so much, my darling!" Meri said, kneeling to hold her daughter in her arms.

"I missed you too, Mama," Elaine said and Meri relished the way her daughter didn't seem to want to let go. Meri had no greater treasure than her children, and the man who loved them as much as she did. When Elaine finally let go, Elliott picked her up and turned her around in circles while he hugged her, making her giggle, which made everyone laugh.

While Elaine and Crispin enjoyed their reunion, Meri gravitated toward Lara, who had Miles in her arms. Meri feared that in her absence he would have regressed to being uncomfortable with her, but the baby held out his arms toward Meri and made happy gurgling noises.

"He's missed you," Lara said with a big smile, as if the baby's happiness in being with his mother gave her great satisfaction.

Once the excitement had settled somewhat, Meri took Crispin upstairs to help him bathe and get into clean pajamas. Meri and Elliott then shared a quiet supper with the children and put them to bed according to their well-established routine before Rowan had so callously snatched Crispin from his home. But it was over now, and all was well. Meri's relief was indescribable.

As soon as the children were asleep, Meri enjoyed a relaxing hot bath while Elliott took care of some minor business with the overseer. While she soaked in gardenia-scented water, she imagined washing away the taint of the Sturgess family and that horrible, cold house where they lived. When Elliott returned, Meri was sitting up in bed, feeling clean and warm and extremely glad to be home. She was putting scented cream on her hands when Elliott sat on the edge of the bed beside her and took over the job of rubbing the cream gently into her skin, silently studying her palms, her fingers, and the backs of her hands as he massaged them with great care.

"You are so very good to me," she said.

"You're a good woman, Meri," he said, still looking at her hand as he paid special attention to the wedding ring she wore. "You deserve to be treated like a queen."

"You've *always* treated me like a queen."

"And you have made me the happiest man in the world," he said, leaning over to kiss her. He was silent a long moment before he looked into her eyes and asked, "Will you tell me how he died, Meri?"

Meri suddenly heard her heart pounding in her own ears. She had wondered if he would ask her about what Rowan had said, but with all the exhaustion of traveling and the excitement of returning home, she'd honestly forgotten.

While she was struggling to find the words to answer his question—or a reasonable way to avoid it—he added, "You told me it was an accidental shooting. Why would his brother have any reason to believe you were responsible?"

Meri avoided Elliott's gaze and said, "Everyone in that family seemed to have a perverse need to make me the scapegoat for anything and everything that went wrong."

"There are clearly a great many problems in the family; I'm not disputing that. And the way they treated you has been nothing short of deplorable. But Meri," his voice softened, "that's not what I asked you." Still, Meri couldn't answer, and she couldn't look at him. She heard Elliott sigh before he went on. "We made a commitment to each other, Meri, to not have any secrets between us. I've always sensed there was something about his death that you weren't telling me. I assumed that your emotions regarding the incident were confusing. But there's something else; something you're not telling me."

Meri tried to fill her lungs with air, but it was as unsuccessful as her attempts to will her heart to slow down and her stomach to stop smoldering. She had to tell him the truth and get it over with, but the words wouldn't form in her mouth. Instead she murmured her deepest fear, "And what if the whole truth changes the way you feel about me . . . the way you see me?"

"Oh, Meri! You should know me better than that. *Nothing* could change the way I feel about you. Nothing!"

Meri took that as a challenge, which helped push the words up and out of her throat. She turned toward Elliott and just said it. "Rowan was right. I killed him." Now that she'd said it, she found it easier to lean toward Elliott and say more vehemently, "I killed him, Elliott, and I was so relieved to know he was dead; there was not a grain of remorse inside of me. What kind of person does that make me? How can you—who are such a good and loving man—love a woman who would do such a thing? Who would feel that way about another human being?"

Meri was surprised by how calm Elliott had remained. "Now, don't you feel better to have finally told me?"

Meri examined his demeanor and declared breathlessly, "You knew?"

"I suspected," he admitted. "But I don't know the details, and I think you need to tell me—if only so you're not holding it all inside any longer."

Meri could hardly breathe as Elliott's reference to *the details* brought the memories of that night rushing into her mind along with all the fear and horror she'd felt, although the reality that was likely most difficult to confront was the very fact that she *couldn't* remember all the details. There were flashes of memory that leapt into her mind at unexpected moments, and she had become remarkably efficient at pushing them away, unable to cope with even wondering if what she believed about that horrible event might be true. She had been determined to *never* speak of it—not even to Elliott. But he had figured it out—at least as much as he could, given what little he knew. There was no hiding from the truth any longer, even though the possible consequences were nothing less than terrifying. Despite Elliott's kindness and the ongoing evidence of the unconditional nature of his love, she wondered if they could both live with the knowledge that she'd done something so unspeakably horrible.

"Talk to me, Meri," he urged gently. "Tell me what happened."

Meri fought not to break down and cry, which had been such a common response when the difficulties of her past had come back to haunt her. Both Elliott and Annabel had reassured her repeatedly that the things she'd endured were by no means small or insignificant, and that the release of such emotion was surely better than holding it all inside. But right now, Meri felt too numb to cry. She just resigned herself to giving Elliott the information he deserved to know, and she prayed that—being the just and honest man he was—he wouldn't believe she should turn herself in to the police so that he could raise the children while she faced the consequences of committing a heinous crime.

Meri took hold of the numbness inside her and detached herself emotionally from the facts, certain that was the only way she could tell him what had happened and keep from crumbling. "He loved his collection of pistols," Meri began, not looking at Elliott. "He had them beautifully displayed in his study, and no one other than him was allowed to touch them. But he would show them off to guests whenever possible, and to him each one was unique and special. They all just looked like pistols to me. I think I resented the way he could have so much devotion and affection for inanimate objects and treat his wife and children so badly."

Meri sighed and tried to gather the words in her mind, still unable to look at her husband. Finding it difficult to fill her lungs with air she took a deep breath, but it didn't work and she had to take another. She felt Elliott's hand on her shoulder as he sensed her difficulty and offered silent assurance. She finally managed to go on. "More than a handful of times he had pointed a gun at me or held one to my head." She heard Elliott gasp but tried to ignore anything but her determination to now get this over with. "I didn't know whether they were loaded, but the things he said convinced me that he could kill me and get away with it. If not for the children, I would have preferred dying. But they needed me and I couldn't leave them."

Meri felt suddenly agitated and pulled her knees up to her chest, wrapping her arms around them and turning her face further away from Elliott. "One evening, very late, I had already gone to bed, but he came into the bedroom, angry about some ridiculous thing one of the servants had said to him that he'd distorted and blown out of proportion, making himself believe that I was manipulating the servants against him. The very idea was so absurd; they were all so frightened of him they wouldn't even interact with me at all." Meri shifted again, leaning her weight more fully against the headboard. "He dragged me down to his study, which generally meant he wanted to get hold of one of his pistols to feel more powerful . . . to demonstrate that he could kill me if he wanted to." Meri heard a quiver in her own voice, but she still felt enfolded in numbness. "I remember that he had the pistol pressed to the side of my head, and I was kneeling on the floor while he stood over me, taunting me more than he ever had, and I truly believed that he'd convinced himself he wanted me dead, and that he *could* get away with killing me. I heard the pistol cock when he pulled the hammer back, and I thought I was going to die. Then something snapped inside me and I reached up and grabbed the pistol and pushed it away."

Meri held more tightly to her knees, curling herself around them, hearing her own breathing become shallow as the numbness threatened to dissipate. "I remember hearing the shot, but it's like a quick flash that exploded in my mind, independent of anything before or after. I remember seeing him on the floor and realizing he was dead. And I remember rushing out of the room—silently. I was terrified, knowing that his family would send me to the gallows if given half the chance and my children would be left in that horrible house without anyone there to love them. I hurried up the stairs in the darkness and reached the top before I heard any noise to indicate that the sound of the shot had gotten the attention of some of the servants."

Meri sighed and hurried to finish, grateful to realize her horrible story was almost over. "Somehow I managed to think clearly at that point and act quickly. I believe it was nothing more or less than an instinct for survival—for myself and my children. Even then I remember thinking that I didn't know if I had killed him purposely or if it was an accident, because there were moments I remembered, and others that were completely blank in my mind. But I knew that either way, the family would destroy me for it if they had the tiniest suspicion I'd had anything to do with it. It took me only a minute to throw my nightgown into the fire, knowing there was blood on it. I changed into a clean one, cleaned my face and hands with a damp rag and threw that in the fire too. I waited just long enough to make certain they had burned. Thankfully, there had been a significant fire, so they were consumed quickly. I put on a robe and hurried back downstairs, pretending to investigate the sound of the shot."

She sighed deeply. "That's all I know. Rowan and his mother were hysterical with shock, and the servants were clearly upset. The police were sent for. An investigation was conducted, with the conclusion being that it was an accidental shooting. A part of me believed that was accurate, but another part of me has wondered . . . if something inside of me responded to all the times I'd wished him dead, and I pulled the trigger when I had the chance. I have no idea why Rowan would think I'm responsible, other than the general mindset of the family that everything bad that happened was somehow my fault."

Meri felt the relief of having finally said all of that to Elliott, and she finally found the nerve to turn and look at her husband, fearing what his response might be. The perfect love he'd shown for her up to this point had been miraculous in her view, but she'd just confessed to something horrible, and she wondered how he might feel about the possibility that she had murdered her first husband.

Meri saw nothing obviously different in his expression, but he didn't speak. She asked the question that had haunted her for many months,

"Should I go to the police? Should I have done so long ago? Perhaps the honest thing to do is confess my crime rather than hiding it."

"Meri," Elliott said and scooped her into his arms. "Oh, my sweet Meri," he murmured close to her ear before he eased back enough to look her in the eye. "Listen to me, my darling. The matter was settled by the police a long time ago, and you're right—an accidental shooting is an accurate conclusion. It was an *accident,* Meri. An accident! And you carrying around so much guilt all this time has been completely wasted."

"But I—"

Elliott put his fingers over her lips. "Listen to me, darling. It was self-defense. Do you understand what that means . . . in legal terms?" She shook her head, since he was still preventing her from speaking. "When a person has a valid reason to believe that her life is being threatened, it is perfectly reasonable and legal to protect herself. He was threatening your life, Meri. Whatever might have happened in the moments you don't remember was obviously some kind of struggle with the pistol. But I absolutely know that for all your difficult feelings toward him—and the fact that his behavior was so utterly deplorable—you would not have killed him purposely. I just know it."

"How can you possibly know that?" she snapped. "I *hated* him! I wanted him dead! I was inexplicably relieved over his death!"

"And those are all completely normal feelings considering that he had hurt you so much, and you were living in constant fear. Your feelings are human, Meri; they're the natural response that any human being living in fear would feel. But I know you, Meri. You have a good heart, and I know—because I know you so well—that nothing is more important to you than being able to face God with a clear conscience. You live your life in a way that naturally expresses your deepest beliefs; that caring for others and being a kind and good person are what matter most, because it's who you are, and because your relationship with God matters to you. A person who naturally thinks and feels that way would *not* purposely take a life. It was an accident; it was self-defense. If you don't believe me, then we can speak with Mr. Browby about it. But in my opinion, the entire matter should be put to rest and left in the past, and you need to stop feeling guilty for something that was *not* your fault. Do you hear me?"

Meri couldn't respond for many long moments as Elliott's words swirled around in her brain, attempting to battle with what she had believed for so long. But the battle was quickly over when she couldn't deny the truth and logic of what he was saying. Meri finally nodded, and with her admittance that she agreed with him . . . that she could let go of all this unnecessary guilt . . . the tears flooded out of her unheeded and without warning. With great practice and proficiency, Elliott held Meri while she expelled another layer of the pain she'd been holding inside, bringing her ever closer to a place of peace and healing.

Meri awoke to the room filled with sunlight and realized she'd cried herself to sleep. For many minutes, she pondered her conversation with Elliott before she'd fallen apart in his arms—again—and she felt a lightness in her spirit that she realized she'd not felt since she'd married Lord Sturgess. Now there truly were no more secrets between her and Elliott, and she was deeply relieved to let go of the burden of trying to carry all she'd been trying to hide. She recognized her own measure of hypocrisy in having been so insistent with everyone else in the family that they not hold secrets inside, while she had been harboring the biggest one of all. No one else in the family needed to know about this, but Elliott was her husband, her best friend, her partner in all things, and she'd been wrong to try to keep this from him.

Breathing in the palpable relief surrounding her, Meri turned over to find Elliott awake and leaning his head in his hand, watching her.

"How long have you been awake?" she asked, loving the life she shared with him and the simple fact that she could wake up every morning to find him there beside her.

"A few minutes longer than you," he said. "Are you all right?"

"I think I am incredibly all right," she said and touched his face, "as long as you can forgive me for not telling you. I should have trusted you with this . . . a long time ago."

"I understand why it was so difficult," Elliott said. "I think your life with the Sturgess family made you afraid of a great many things that weren't necessarily rational—because they are not rational people." He kissed her. "But now *all* of that is in the past, and we are going to leave it there."

"Agreed," she said. "Although—"

"Although what?" he asked, sounding mildly concerned.

"I think I *would* like to speak with Mr. Browby. Do you think that doing so could cause any unnecessary problems?"

"In his profession, he is legally bound to keep anything you say in confidence. If you want to speak to him—if it will help you put all of this to rest—then I think you should. I'll send for him to come at his earliest convenience."

"I think that would be good," Meri said. She liked and trusted Mr. Browby, and he had been present when Rowan had hurled his accusations of murder. Meri would feel better to be able to explain the situation, as opposed to always wondering how he might have perceived what had been said.

Their morning routine with the children went well despite some mild bickering between Elaine and Crispin and Miles being a little fussy due to a couple of new teeth trying to break through. But even in these minor challenges of dealing with the children, Meri found great joy in having Elliott as her partner and in observing the tender way he helped care for the children with so much love.

Shortly after lunch, Mr. Browby arrived. Elliott and Meri met with him in the study with the door closed.

"How might I help you?" he asked, making himself comfortable and offering a smile.

Meri was grateful for the way Elliott began by saying they wanted to clarify some things about the accusations Rowan Sturgess had made regarding his brother's death. At Meri's request, Elliott told Mr. Browby the story as Meri had told it to him. He concluded by asking the solicitor's honest opinion—given his understanding of the law—of how Lord Sturgess had died and of Meri's involvement.

Mr. Browby stated firmly and without hesitation his belief that it was self-defense, and he wholeheartedly agreed with Elliott's belief that the matter had already been legally settled and that Meri should stop feeling any guilt over what had happened. Mr. Browby had seen firsthand how deplorably Rowan Sturgess had behaved, and he offered Meri sincere compassion upon hearing how difficult her marriage to Rowan's brother had been.

After Mr. Browby left, Meri was overcome with such a deep relief that she could only sit on the sofa in the parlor and gaze toward the window, attempting to catch up to the luxury of being free of such a great burden. Elliott found her there after he'd seen Mr. Browby off. They talked for a few minutes before he said, "It's a beautiful day outside, Meri—especially warm for autumn. I think we should have Mrs. Biddle pack up the makings of our afternoon tea into a couple of hampers and we should all go out into the garden and make a picnic of it. What do you say?"

"I think it's a marvelous idea," Meri said and went to speak with Mrs. Biddle and assist her in packing the hampers while Elliott went to inform Annabel and the sisters that they were going *out* for tea, and they should come downstairs shortly, prepared to enjoy an outdoor excursion.

Tea in the garden proved to be delightful. Meri leaned back on her hands on one of the blankets they'd spread out on the lawn and took in the lighthearted chattering taking place among her aunt and cousins and the typical way Elliott was playing with the children, provoking them into much laughter. Meri felt content to just observe the evidence of happiness and love among these people who comprised her family. She contrasted her tumultuous past with the peace and contentment of the present—which was surely an indication of the future. She knew their future would never be without challenges, for challenges were the very nature of life. But she also knew that these people with whom she shared a home had proven they could face challenges and rise above them by helping each other and by putting their love and concern for each other above all else.

"Are you all right?" she heard Elliott ask, startling her out of her reverie.

"Oh, I'm more than all right, Mr. Rosewell," she said, making him smile. "I was just soaking in all the happiness."

Elliott's smile grew before he made a point of kissing her while no one else was aware, then he returned to playing with the children.

The following day, Elliott told Elaine and Crispin they were going on an adventure late that evening, and that they needed to take a good nap so they would be rested. The children were more excited than Christmas Eve over what this adventure might entail, but miraculously they did both fall asleep in the afternoon. Elliott wouldn't tell Meri what his plans were, but she suspected.

After supper, instead of preparing for bed, they left Miles in Lara's care and Elliott led the way out of the house, carrying a blanket and a hamper. The children were full of questions when he walked away from the gardens, but he told them only that it would be somewhat of a long walk and they needed to be patient. Neither Elaine nor Crispin complained about the significant hike, even though it was mostly uphill.

When they arrived at the intended destination, Elliott stopped at the familiar grassy spot at the crest of the hill that Meri had come to love so dearly. She and Elliott hadn't been here very often, given that their lives had been busy with caring for the children—among other things. But she believed coming here too frequently might lessen the magic.

"Look," Elliott said to the children, pointing toward Rosewell Abbey. "There's our home." There were lights glowing in some of the windows and lanterns burning near the doors.

"It's like a castle!" Elaine declared.

"It's very beautiful," Meri said. "Do you know what makes it most beautiful of all?" she asked. The children didn't answer and she gave them a hint. "Think for just a minute about the house where we used to live, and then think about this house where we now live. What do you think makes *this* house more beautiful?"

"It's happy!" Crispin declared.

"It *is* happy," Meri said. "Do you know why it's happy?" she asked.

"Because we all love each other," Elaine stated in a way that made it evident she'd been paying attention to Meri when she'd previously talked of such things with her children.

"That's exactly right," Meri said and turned in the other direction. "Now look this way."

The children turned to see the lights of the village in the opposite direction. They both expressed their appreciation of that view as well until Elliott urged them to lie back on the blanket he'd spread on the grass. The children both gasped as they were confronted with a clear view of the starlit sky, with no moon to diminish the light of the stars.

"When your mother and I were young," Elliott said, "we used to come here to look at the stars, and we talked and talked. I figured it was time the two of you came to this special place. Sometimes we saw a falling star and made a wish."

"Did your wish come true?" Elaine asked, very seriously.

Elliott chuckled, and Meri felt him take hold of her hand. "Not only did my wish come true, little miss, but many more wishes I never could have imagined also came true."

"Like what?" Crispin asked.

"Like you," Elliott said. "You and your sister and your brother are more than I could have ever wished for."

All was silent for a long moment until Elaine said, "I've never seen a falling star, but I wished a million times to have a father like you."

"I wished it too!" Crispin declared.

"I wished it too," Meri added. "And do you know a different word for *wish*?" When the children didn't respond, she said, "Sometimes a *wish* and a *prayer* are much the same thing, and when our wishes come true it's evidence that God has answered our prayers, and He has blessed us very much."

"We are indeed very blessed," Elliott said, squeezing Meri's hand.

Minutes of silence passed while they all just looked up at the stars, and even Crispin was remarkably still until he asked, "Is there any food in that hamper? Staying up past my bedtime has made me hungry."

"Yes, I brought some food," Elliott said with a chuckle. "I knew you'd be hungry after such a long walk."

They sat together on the blanket, sharing a snack and talking about stars and wishes and blessings. While the children were looking skyward, oblivious to anything going on around them, Elliott leaned over and kissed Meri in a way that expressed how deeply he loved her. And she loved him too. With him, her every wish had come true.

About the Author

Anita Stansfield has more than fifty published books and is the recipient of many awards, including two Lifetime Achievement Awards. Her books go far beyond being enjoyable, memorable stories. Anita resonates particularly well with a broad range of devoted readers because of her sensitive and insightful examination of contemporary issues that are faced by many of those readers, even when her venue is a historical romance. Readers come away from her compelling stories equipped with new ideas about how to enrich their own lives, regardless of their circumstances.

Anita was born and raised in Provo, Utah. She is the mother of five and has a growing number of grandchildren. She also writes for the general trade market under the name Elizabeth D. Michaels.

For more information and a complete list of her publications, go to anitastansfield.blogspot.com or anitastansfield.com, where you can sign up to receive email updates. You can also follow her on Facebook and Twitter.